Jon Templeton

The Romance of Robert Burns

A Pastoral of the Present and Drama of Days Lang Syne

Jon Templeton

The Romance of Robert Burns
A Pastoral of the Present and Drama of Days Lang Syne

ISBN/EAN: 9783337049805

Printed in Europe, USA, Canada, Australia, Japan

Cover: Foto ©Andreas Hilbeck / pixelio.de

More available books at **www.hansebooks.com**

THE ROMANCE

OF

ROBERT BURNS.

A PASTORAL OF THE PRESENT

AND

DRAMA OF DAYS LANG SYNE.

O, Caledonia! stern and wild,
Meet muse for a poetic child;
Land of brown heath and shaggy wood
Land of the Mountain and the flood,
Land of my Sires! what mortal hand
Can e'er untie the filial band
That knits me to thy rugged strand?
SCOTT'S *Lay of the Last Minstrel.*

NEW YORK:
WRIGHT & COMPANY,
PUBLISHERS.

TO

ANDREW CARNEGIE,

THAT KING OF SCOTS IN THE UNITED STATES,

whose enterprise and energy have given honorable employment to so many thousands of his fellow men; whose encouragement of industry has done so much to better the condi:ion of the worthy poor; whose libraries and liberal institutions, founded in the Cities of Great Britain and America, have so largely aided in the cause of a higher and a better education; whose words, written and spoken, have always been for the benefit of mankind; whose life of usefulness, integrity and generosity has been an inspiration and example,

THIS WORK IS DEDICATED,

WITH SINCERE RESPECT AND HONEST ADMIRATION.

AMERICAN ROMANCE.

A FICTION, fable—call it what you will—herein
becomes a fact!

We wise Americans periodically sit down and
figuratively "bay the moon with howling" for
An American Romance! This done, we wag our
heads and wait and watch, and, when the victim our lament has lured, comes from his lair,
we read his tag and note the ear-marks of the
"Common Cry," and if he's of the mongrel breed
that feeds on scraps and refuse stuff—the realistic carrion which so many crave whose tastes
are high—or broods on second-hand and thread-
bare things, we greet him with a recognizing
sniff and let him pass—but if he's of the Royal
Lion's blood and has ideal dreams of something
lying still beyond our sight, and in temerity at-
tempts to overleap the barrier by which we
hedge him in, why then let loose the pack. We
dog him down and seize and rend and tear until
there is not left the wherewithal to tell the tale!

This, sad to say, is not American romance,
but simple, sober, solemn fact.

Within a month Great Britain, in acknowl-edgment of worth, has knighted three illus-trious men—a poet, a player and a novelist—and France has added one to her "immortal" list—a writer of romance. Germany exalts and favors all her men of mark, and Spain, despite her poverty, still finds some way to honor those whose words have honored her.

What we have done within a century of years, the literary world well knows, and all must feel, except the lucky few who live by other means or dwell within the narrow circle of success.

Our Muse American is a Commercial Muse! Her duty is to count the cash. She opens a full "set of books"—not one. Beneath her rule Shelley and Keats had measured tape and Byron kept a clothing store. Beyond the realms of trade she never strays, and woe to those who do not follow in her steps, or, if they needs must write, deal only in realities which make the commonplace more common still. On those who would aspire to higher thought she frowns and cries "Forbear!" Doomed is the wretch who dares to leave the beaten track, to travel on an unknown path, to touch on grounds tabooed, or cross the boundary line of the con-ventional, or deal in interdicted things, or put a happy thought into a worker's mind, or cause a pleasant dream to ease his troubled sleep, or raise another joy within the human heart! These are the deadly sins which, in this modern world, we lash with ribald jests and scourge with whips of scorn. Say not, this is not true; it's more—it's verity confirmed.

Our parks are filled with monuments to foreign men—commemorating genius, which, to honor here does honor to ourselves! But those whose work of hand and brain helped make our country great, now, for the most part, sleep in humble graves, unmarked, unhonored, or unknown.

This is more sorry fact and shameful history. No wonder we must call in vain for men of pure poetic thought, or resurrect the dead to find a writer of romance.

We crush the seed, then ask that it shall spring!

We kill the spirit, then demand the song!

In vain. The overbroken horse becomes a common hack; and man—his spirit gone—is but a soulless slave!

What then?—why simply this:

What is encouraged thrives here and elsewhere alike. What man has done in other lands, mankind may do in this. If there is only one in every million Heaven-born give him a chance to live. He's but a poor minority—what should we fear? By nature self-endowed, he asks no school, no bounty of the city or the State, no public and no private charity. He goes his way and does no man a harm; his song is all of love and hope; his words are all of peace; his deeds are always kind; he gives to charity when it is his to give; he feeds and clothes himself, and what he lacks, the Ravens bring him in the dead of night when no man sees or knows—and when he dies, be sure some loving, gentle hands will bear him to his rest.

O Nation great, be great in this—encourage what's your own! An Argosy—if we would have, fitted to sail on any sea—loaded with gifts divine and bearing wealth from unknown shores—trim, then, the sails and bring them up from the dead level of the equatorial line, out of the doldrums and the trade-winds where they float, and steer for higher latitudes in fancy's course and broader longitudes of thought, and they shall bring us countless treasures back—rebuilding Rome and Athens in this Western World!

BOOK I

A Pastoral of Present Days.

ROMANCE OF ROBERT BURNS.

BOOK I.

A PASTORAL OF PRESENT DAYS.

I.

LOOKING down from Scotland Hill, over the farms of Rockland, across the intervening miles of roads and fields, beyond the valley of Montmoor, the eastern view is bounded by a range of purple peaks which mark the Hudson's course and give the name of Highlands to the heights on either side.

At Haverstraw, against the distant sky, appears the towering Torne, and farther south, and shading Rockland Lake, a strange formation shows towards the west—the figure of an Indian sleeping on the hills—a mountain and a monument reared by the hands of Nature when she labored here, and left a silent witness of her mighty deeds.

Over this range of hills, on summer nights, the moon appears, lifting her lanthorn slowly as she comes and showing all the splendors of the sylvan scenes for fifty miles around.

On such a night and viewing such a scene an old Scotch farmer sat within the shelter of his porch, and looked from off the western hill, straight towards the east, and saw the slowly rising moon, and watched it eagerly until the globe of yellow light, pushed up by unseen hands, stood out in all its glory, silent and alone. It lighted up the old man's face and marked the lines of care and age; the pallor in his faded cheek, the silver in his hair; his wasted form; his worn-out hands—a being of the past—a light about to fade; but in his eyes the living fire— the undimmed joy of other days.

"Oh, wife, gude wife!" he cried. "The moon! The moon!"

"Yes, Duncan." The poor old woman answered him—as if in fear of some fatality— "Well—well!"

"The moon is up, at last, gudewife! The moon! Through long dark nights I've waited till the storm should clear—through fever and through cold I've waited till she's come!"

"Yes—yes—be patient—well!"

"The moon! the moon! It is the same I've looked on near a hundred years—but ne'er will look on more."

"Duncan!"

"It is the same we saw in Scotland when we two were bairns. Dinna ye mind the happy days we wandered by the Doon and she the only witness of our love?"

"I mind it well—oh, Duncan, rest."

"Aye! I maun be contented now. She smiles upon us yet as once she did—she'll smile upon our children when we're gone to dust!"

"Yes, Duncan dear, and now come in."

"No. Bid the young ones come to *me*—here in the moonlight—let us part. I'll no die happy till they've said good-bye! But hark! His step and hers. Are love and death so close together?—Donald!"

"Father!"

"Mother!"

"Hush! Dear ones—he would speak to you!"

And now there knelt beside the father's chair a sturdy, dark-haired boy, and with him was the bright-eyed girl he loved. Behind the three, the mother wept.

"Children"—the old man said—"how sweet the time of youth and love. Be ye so loving always. Yonder moon is called inconstant, but she's not. Shadows may come and shadows go; but still behind them is her blessed smile— like my good wife's has always been to me.

Be patient in dark hours—the light will come——"

"Father!"

"But I maun leave ye now. My day is done and in the evening's light I pass away."

"Nay, husband dear, don't speak it."

"Seek not to stay me. 'Twill not be for long. Ye'll all come after—only live right here."

"Father! We will! we will!"

"Gudewife, bring me the books—the same we brought frae Scotland when we came—the only ones. Though old and worn, read and respect them still."

"We will! we will!"

"The Bible for the lass—the Burns, my boy, for you. Respect the good in each—the bad let go."

"Father, we promise you."

"That's well. There's good and bad in everything—in books and acts, in plants and flowers. The rose is lovely, yet it has a thorn; the thistle beautiful, but you must never touch. These lessons read in memory of me—and dinna all forget me when I'm gone!"

"Oh, father! never! never! Our blessing on the hands that worked for us, the head that sorrows bowed in our behalf!"

"Gudewife, draw near—here—hand-in-hand

for days lang-syne, and for the days to come!"

"Yes, father! Hand and heart and soul!"

"So—good-bye—good-bye—good-bye—to ye all! Live here—and keep the old place as it is. The woods and trees—the meadows and the pastures—and the cattle—and the fowls. Don't let them miss me when I'm gone!"

"We will remember—oh, father!—father!"

"So, good-bye. The moonlight smiles and lights for me the way. I mind the lines I used to speak—they're not by Burns, but Lowe—ye ken them well. There are some others something like in 'Kenilworth,' but not by Scott—in which the moon is called the 'regent o' th' sky'—See! see! she's mounting higher. Now—she's looking down on Indian Hill—and now she smiles on me, a sad farewell! Yes—yes—I mind me well:

> " 'The moon had climbed the highest hill
>   That rises o'er the source of Dee,
> And from its eastern summit shed
>   Her silver light on tower and tree.' "

"Father!"

"Hush!—there's something more—I can't remember it—but so it ends—as—my last—

words to you—yes—yes—an' then—ye'll—then ye'll——

"'Weep no more for me.'"

And starting up, he fixed his staring eyes full on the shining moon and fell back dead within his loved ones' arms.

.   .   .   .

And now a lapse of many years—some bright and quickly passed, and others long, hard wrought and sorrowful; but these kind silence views in charity and comes on tiptoe, with her finger on her lip, and beckons them away, and so they go—their griefs untold—all buried there in that small space of sacred ground where rest the dead beside the village church.

THE HILLS OF ROCKLAND.

II.

Come now to present days and the same rural scene—the landscape brighter than it was before; the bushy fields cleared up and sown with scented grass and blue-green rye; the pastures spotted by the daisy and the buttercup, and stone walls green with blossoming grape, woodbine and bitter-sweet; the woods grown taller, and the scattered pines with longer branches swaying in the wind, and over all the slopes, far as the eye can reach, ten thousand blossoming trees, scattering their spices on the warm May winds, and showering the green mantle of the fields with flecks of pink and white —a gaudy covering — outrivaling the honeysuckle's beauty and the dogwood's whiter bloom.

Within the wood, and up and down the lanes, on every fence, just as of old, field-sparrows twitter and the bluebird gives his changing note; the quail calls to his mate, the robins sing, all things revive and speak of happiness. Nature, rejoicing, lingers here and smiles on man, her friend, and daily comes to that same little house upon the hill to see the woodbine and clematis clinging lovingly about the porch where, in the bygone years, the old man sat, and where the good wife and the lovers held him in their arms that moonlight night on which he died.

And now these living blossoming things in Nature seem like the mortals did to him who passed away, and twine their arms about the ruins of the house, to wrap and fold it in a kind embrace, returning thanks for all the shelter and protection it has given them. The pansies and forget-me-nots look up in gratitude, and all the garden flowers nod in the wind and send the fragrance of their wasted lives in at the open door. The primrose and sweetbrier cling to the pillars which uplift the roof, and tall half-wild red roses, climbing the lower shutters, which they half conceal, reach up their hands and spread the crimson blossoms in the open windows of the old north room where the young couple sleep. In the soft air the branches sway and creak till the song-sparrow, nesting beneath their leaves, gets up and sings. The bob-white calls aloud, and from the woods which border on the newly planted corn, a thousand crows cry "caw!"

The sun shows red and gold above the notch on Indian Hill—another day has dawned on the Elysian fields—as erst it did in Eden—if mankind but knew.

"Diccon, get up, and to the barn. I'll make the fire and 'Dusky Joan shall keel the pot.' " So calls the master of the house. "Come, Barbara! The old clock says it's half-past five, and father's watch says six."

"Yes, Donald," answered Barbara, speaking down the stairs. "Let' Joan help Diccon with the cows and I'll do all the rest."

So, aiding one another, they begin the day; and so with many days gone by, and which have passed in peace—for this new master of the little farm, this mistress of his humble house, are the same loving ones who, on that moonlight night, knelt by the old man's chair and promised him to keep the homestead place and live respecting what was good in life—rejecting what was not. Honored and blessed, so far they had lived, doing their duty to the uttermost, and helping others while they labored for themselves. And middle life was creeping on; but still they were content. The wear and tear of daily work was in his sun-burned face, and in his hardened hands, and in his hair a tinge of frost; but in his heart was cheerfulness, and in his eye intelligence and kindness, courage for any fate, all clear as day.

And Barbara was everything that could be asked of woman—industrious, thoughtful, gentle, good, loving and faithful where she'd set her heart, and womanly in all that makes a woman loved.

The good wife—nearly ninety now, but still as cheerful as in younger days—was with them yet. To sit and knit and read and talk of all the follies of the present days and tell some tale old as herself, or to repeat some schoolgirl speech, or try with her cracked voice to turn a wornout tune, was her employment or expression of content, and well she carried it; for spite of an impatient bigotry and pride, she had those sterling qualities of mind and heart which never can grow old.

So master and mistress, mother, man and girl made up this simple home—save when a traveler benighted lost his way—or when some friendly visitor came from a distant place, or some acquaintance from the city called, or lingered over Sunday at the house. And to all others—idlers, tramps or lazy boys, and so-called huntsmen who tore down rods of wall to seize a rabbit which was miles away; or dug the meadows full of holes to catch a chipmunk

which sat chuckling on a limb above their heads
—the good dog, with more intelligence than
theirs, gave warning with a bark and said
"move on."

But now the spare-room held a visitor—a
mighty man and one, in brief, who knew all
things—except himself. A man who feasted on
the day's events, as detailed in the daily press,
until, in fancy, he was something more than
mortal "I" and used the plural "we" to awe
the millions of his fellowmen—a crank and a
reformer of the latest date, and with the necessary forwardness to make his mission thrive.

For reasons only known to Providence, Fate
set this subject down on Scotland Hill. He
knew the country always proved a fertile field
in which the inspired fool could plant his crop
of isms, leaving to time and better men the
task of tending them until the harvest came and
yielded his reward.

First he essayed the village school, and gave
a long harangue—telling his gaping listeners
when and what and how to teach and who
should teach it when 'twas taught. And then
he boldly entered the Seceder's Church and told
them all the newer kinds of sins—sins that
these innocent people never dreamed of—never
knew before—how, like the dock, the daisy and

wild-carrot in the meadows, and thistle seeds and scallions of the pasture lands, these things were spreading far and wide, and every family —like the farmsteads they possessed—was in a daily danger of these pestilential blights on their prosperity and peace.

He did not know what other men might do, but "for ourselves," he said, "we should proceed at once to seize these monsters by the throat and dash them down and trample them beneath our feet!"

As he spoke this he acted it, and grasped a section of the invisible air, and choking out what little life it had, he threw it to the floor and sprang upon it with his feet, and with a smile of triumph held it down. This performance—more than was promised, by the way, roused up his one confederate to say "Amen!" This was enough. Before the sound of this sole exclamation had died out the easy convert found himself on a committee, self-appointed by the Columbus who discovered all this sin, to visit, with him, every house and introduce reform.

Hence the spare-room at our friend's place was occupied—for courtesy and hospitality, never lacking in that little home, had made him welcome there, and Donald Stuart, knocking on the door, said in his kindliest manner:

"Breakfast is ready, friend."

And good Columbus Cant was nothing loath, but prompt on call, and answered the usual morning question with the usual reply:

"Yes, yes, we've slept well—and sleeping well has given us an appetite. In fact the work we have in hand has given us both appetite and inspiration."

He rolled his eyes a little as he spoke, which gave his long and churn-like face a curiously unsteady look; but this was counterbalanced by a broad and beaming smile as he accepted all the good things passed his way. To do him justice there was something satisfying in his look; besides, his manner was magnetic and his words could charm.

"There—there," he said. "Now, good friends, don't mind us; and brother Stuart, you go to your work, for you cannot neglect your fields, nor can we ours—so go. We'll stay and talk to the good lady of the house; 'for man and wife are one,' you know—eh? Yes. Ha! ha!"

"But you will stay to dinner with us, will you not?"

"We-e-l—let me see—we-el—yes; 'always room for one more,' you know—eh? Yes. Ha! ha!"

The novelty and unique wit of these remarks made Donald loath to part with so original a mind—however, with a promise of another double-feast at dinner time, he went; but what he thought, was hidden by good manners in his breast.

That the Pretender's visit was prolonged from dinner until supper time, and then another night, and then another day, and then a week, might be a matter of surprise to those who do not know how really good a man can be who gives his soul to a good cause, and, knowing his own value, takes his pay as he performs.

Donald said nothing, but thought much, and more than usual when, on coming home at night, weary and worn from labor in the fields, covered with dirt and dust, sunburned and overwrought, he had to listen to a homily from one who had passed the heated day in quiet and in shade, or swung himself to sleep in the broad hammock underneath the trees.

"You farmers don't know how to work," the visitor exclaimed. "You lack intelligence. Before we go—if we find time—we'll show you certain papers and the books you ought to read. You don't plow deep enough—nor fertilize enough, nor use good seed. Remember the parable of the sower, he——"

"Yes—yes," broke in Donald, impatiently, forgetting his restraint. "He sowed! And, though he wasted seed on stony ground, and though the thorns choked some—yet some sprang up and yielded fifty and one hundred fold! God bless the man who plows! The man who sows! The man who works! As well as men who talk!"

"Donald!—why, what do you mean?" questioned his mother and his wife.

"Oh, nothing! nothing!" said the visitor, to whom the sharp retort was merely pleasantry. "He doesn't understand; but after supper he can read our books. Awakening is what he needs. His methods and his logic are all wrong."

"Say that my manners are at fault, and I'll agree," said Donald, rising as he spoke. "Welcome or not, you are our guest, and never underneath this roof has a stranger been treated otherwise than with kindness and civility." Saying this, he started in, and as he did so, his dog came up, and standing at his side, looked back towards his visitor and growled.

III.

THAT night the troubled Donald had resolved to talk with Barbara. Often, of late, he had wished to speak about this stranger whom they sheltered; but just as often he had paused, fearing he might let fall some hasty word, or in some way imply a doubt of her, or her good taste at least, in seeming to encourage one who but a fortnight back was quite unknown to all, and who was half a stranger still.

And often since this strange man came, a guest unbidden, by him at least unwelcomed—whose presence was protested even by the dog—he had wondered why it was that he remained. Was it his mother's liking for the man who could talk Bible with her by the hour, while neither seemed to tire? Or was it Barbara's overhospitable way that made the stranger think he should remain, and caused him to assume so confident a tone? What could it be? Surely no man, unless encouraged in some point, unusual, unknown, would so prolong his stay.

The more he thought of this the more it puzzled him; and now, at any cost, he'd speak to Barbara. She never had withheld her con-fidence—he knew she never would, and he must speak or doubt would grow to a suspicion that Barbara, whom he had always loved, had found another's talk more pleasant to her ear, if not another face more favored than his own.

Then too, he missed their happy nights, when sitting by the kitchen fire, after the old mother had gone off to bed, and when no others save themselves were up—when the good dog kept watch outside, and puss and kittens played upon the floor—and when the wind went moaning round the house, and cricket chirped beside the ruddy hearth—when by the lamp-light Barbara read the best books that their scanty means could buy—and when on Saturday nights, the labors of the week all done and all was housed and put away—the horses in their beds of straw, the cattle underneath the warm dry shed, and Luath in his cozy kennel by the door; when he had read from Barbara's book and she from his, and the old father's gifts were priceless still and loved and honored for the good they had done and for his sake who made their memory dear.

How many nights like these had passed—how

many ended with a kind "good-night" to father's picture on the wall. How many a time within the shaded light, these two had knelt and asked a blessing on the dear old house that sheltered all from ill. And now—with these recurring thoughts—he sat and mused, and then at last he spoke.

"Barbara, if I may trespass on your time which now I know is taken up with hospitality, pray tell me, if you will, what books are these?"

"Those, Donald dear, the ones our guest has sent you—why?"

"Oh, nothing. They're appropriate. I lack intelligence and stand in need of reformation. But, Barbara, the first I seek from you—the last I'll ask from him."

"Donald! What do you mean?"

"Barbara, you know me well—and till these two weeks gone I've thought that I knew you. Tell me if I have been mistaken?"

"Donald!"

"Forgive me, but I think I have, or something strange of late has come between us!"

"What do you mean?"

"This—your confidence is turned away, and when I come home nights from labor in the fields, I find no welcome as I used. You look at me, not kindly, but reproachfully, as if

ashamed to see the honest sweat upon my sun-
burned face, the homely patches on my working clothes, the marks of honest labor on my
hands. Is not this so?"

"It is, but not for reasons that you give. It
is because I love you, Donald!"

"Barbara!"

"It is because I see you here, who might be
honored among men, wearing your life away
without a single gain and with a future showing
no relief and offering no reward."

"Beware, dear Barbara! The poisonous weed
of discontent—if once we taste it—grows in
time to be necessity, and kills at last! This
stranger's talk has led to this."

"It has revived what I myself have often
thought, but never dared to tell you."

"And that——?"

"That in the city yonder we could find
some useful occupation which would build
us up—not keep us down forever with the
slaves!"

"Hush, Barbara. Imagination all. Have
you forgot my father's dying wish? The lessons in the books he gave us? Dear wife, go
bring them now, and doubt not we shall find, in
one or both, some story of content."

"Yes, Donald dear; but I forget. Your

mother took the Bible with her when she went upstairs, and Burns I cannot find."

"It's in the stranger's room."

"It was; but now it's gone. Joan told me of it first, and we both looked three days ago. It doesn't matter though. He says it's very common, out of date, and low and vulgar as the writer was—that poetry is dead, that only facts and news are useful now; that there's a war on fiction and on verse; that Shakespeare, Scott, Byron and Burns, Longfellow, Irving, Poe and such like men must go—and modern moralists will rise and take their place!"

"Rise! Rise!" cried Donald, who had listened in amazement to this revelation of suspected things. "Rise! They have need to rise! A resurrection would not raise them high enough to take the place of any one you've named!"

"Donald!"

"Don't mind me, lass," said Donald kindly, as he walked about the room. "It's not your fault; but now I see—the cry is up! the war is on! No wonder my poor book is gone—no wonder!"

"I'm sorry that I told you now," said Barbara in distress.

"I'm glad you did. You should have done so

sooner. I should have known what animal we lodged within the house, whose place was in the barn. The dog knew at the start we should have set him on."

"But, Donald—patience. Is there not some truth in what he says? Some wrong—some error—and some evil in these things?"

"There is. There's right and wrong in all this world and everything which it contains. Gardens have weeds; the purest diamond has a flaw; there's not a field I till but labor must subdue. The best of books has in it errors scattered far and wide, but its sublimities are there, like mountains capped with snow above the level wastes. The surface of the earth is hardly habitable, save where mankind has wrought and toiled for years and years, and I believe man's mission here is but to make it some day worthy of a God-like race!"

"Donald!"

"That's my belief. And every century's improvement shows it's true. For that I daily do my part—knowing it is a duty which should be performed for Him who placed me here!"

"Dear Donald—will you listen?"

"Not to such arguments as his. They are as much too plausible as he's too good. What does he here? We were content and happy till he came, and now all's wrong—and even she I've always loved sees faults in everything I do, and wrong in everything I prize!"

"No, Donald. Do not turn away. See here, I put my arms about your neck, and look into your honest face, and say I love you more than all the world; and only because it is so, do I wish to see you have a higher place in life and higher thoughts, if any such there be."

"God bless you, Barbara, but let us not be self-deceived nor take a stranger's word before the best of books, for these are best of words by best of men, and no mere would-be wise man has a right to cry them down."

"But, Donald, this man says it is the world in arms against the erring few. A crusade for the right, no matter who may fall."

"Then let those fail and fall who most deserve to do so, Barbara. Right will survive when all crusades and those who lead them on are low in dust! As for this canting stranger, let him go his way. Our house was blessed before he came. I do not want an evil spell to settle on it now."

"Nor I, dear Donald, only I had thought—as we lived here alone—away from all the greater world—there might be something we had missed —something we had not learned—something to better both our lives, and other lives as well, which, may be, we had left undone!"

"Nay, Barbara, it was a loving, kindly thought, and I'll not chide you for it. I've often noticed how good women try to help the world—as angels fallen—knowing what we've lost—would lead us back to Heaven!"

"If I deserved that thought I'd cherish it. But, Donald, dear, ours is a very lowly, earthly lot, and, save our books and all the fancies in your fertile brain, it sometimes seems discouraging."

"Barbara, unwittingly, you have confessed; our books, my fancies have made light to you —as God in mercy knows they have to me—the burthens and the troubles of this world! Then let the bigot say whate'er he will; let strangers come and strangers go; let canting hypocrites or true crusaders fight these follies down—we'll not desert them any more than we'd desert a friend who stood unshaken in our hour of need."

"I cannot argue with you, Donald dear; nor shall I longer try to do so. What you say always seems the best that can be said, and may be you are right, for you have read and studied much, and thought and talked on subjects only dear to honest-hearted men who understand. But grant me one request."

"Name—and I grant it, Barbara."

"It's only this: To-morrow night this man makes his report. The meeting's at the yellow schoolhouse, as you know, and all the neighborhood is asked to come—ourselves among the rest. Forget all prejudice and let us go—hear what is said, and then decide—you to conclude with me there may be higher, better things in life—or I, with you, believe as Shakspeare says:

> "'Poor and content is rich and rich enough;
> But riches endless are as poor as winter
> To him who ever fears he shall be poor!'"

"Barbara, come here, and let me kiss the honest lips that spoke those honest words!— And he's to be replaced! What incandescent light, shining from out a vacuum, shall shame great Shakspeare's sun? What puerile popinjay, with senseless twaddle of the times, shall step into Longfellow's shoes? What moralist, with an affected modesty, shall in the foulest terms urge on the rest? But, Barbara, as you have said, we'll wait until to-morrow night. Meantime, no more. God bless you! Go to bed. I want to sit and think awhile, alone."

"Bless you, Donald. So, good-night! Don't let what I have said make you unhappy. My thought was but to lighten care, and not increase it for you, dear."

"I know—I know—don't say another word. Burns says it all in the old book:

> " 'It's no' in titles nor in rank—
> It's no' in wealth like Lunnon bank
> To purchase peace and rest,
>
> .　　　.　　　.　　　.　　　.　　　.　　　.
>
> If happiness have not her seat
> And centre in the breast!'

Good-night!"
"Good-night!"

IV.

THE schoolhouse waited for Columbus Cant, as evidently it had waited for him when he was a boy. The night had come. His auditors expectantly listened for his bold "Ahem!" and watched for his approach. The final day of grace had passed. The sinners shivered in their seats. The hour of judgment was at hand.

Strange as it may seem, the coming of this solitary warrior on the field had captured all the camp. Audacity had conquered, and by its very boldness won respect. The call to meet the conqueror was as imperious as Cæsar might have issued to a race of slaves, commanding them to pay their homage and their tribute at a certain hour. Further than this, these simple people—overawed by what appeared the greatness and the goodness of their judge—were ready to confess to sins which he suggested, but which they, in worthy ignorance, had never seen or known.

The day so big with fate was one to be remembered. "To-morrow," he had said, "we'll hear what you've to say," and children on this day had waked before the sun and asked their mothers: "Is it to-morrow now?" and had been answered: "Yes—to-day's to-morrow—now keep still." And well they might. Mothers cried "Fie!" to every little fault, and said "I'll tell the man!" Old women whispered and gave knowing nods in lieu of silly speech. Old men looked puzzled, but forbore to smile, and others laughed the matter off—while some, appropriately shocked at such unseemly levity, held up their hands. The village humorist was even sadder than his wont. The cogitating dog wandered about and hung his head with a disgusted and a guilty look, and many times sat down and closed his eyes, as if to shut out some unpleasant sight. Nature seemed hushed. A Sodom and Gomorrah haze hung o'er the landscape like a cloud. The strain on all the day was great. Night only brought relief. The guiltless penitents, with *mea culpa* on their lips, were ready to confess to every crime in all the calendars of past and present time.

But, hark! His voice! Committee of himself and one walked down the aisle and mounting to the teacher's place, turned on his smile as he'd turn up a lamp, and so surveyed the subjects of his will. The smile died out. He donned his frown, that all might see he set his gentleness aside, and stood for duty which he must perform.

This understood, Jove-like he launched his thunderbolt and smote in the good cause.

"Beware the lightning stroke!" he cried so suddenly, that many dodged, and following his swift gesture, as he pointed to the roof, expected the impending crash! "Not now!" he said, "not yet; but it will come to drive you forth and cast you down! O, race of vipers! Henceforth you shall crawl and hide you in the dust. For doom is yours. Your sins have found you out, and your iniquities cry even unto Heaven!—Your lands shall pass away, and your inheritance be set at naught! And ignorance shall still be yours—and poverty shall curse you all your days! Behold in us the spies sent out by Israel to tell your downfall to a coming race! Lo! hear the list of your enormities!"

Then followed in detail the unknown crimes, which took a good half-hour to tell, and which had such high sounding and imposing names that some felt glad that they were guilty of them. "The money changers in the Temple," were especially elate, and chuckled in their usual country style. And "women who

thought more of home and husbands than in
'tending meetings for reform," seemed rather
proud to own it.   But there was one offence too
great for words to counteract.   "On that," cried
Cant, "we march with weapons in our hands.
An army of Davids, we charge upon Uriah!   I
mean—Goliath! Goliath—yes—ha! ha! Though
he walk forth a giant in his strength as well as
in his sin, a single stone shall bring him down
—and then—ha! ha! we'll seize him by the
throat and tread him underneath our heel!"
And here again, the seizing and the stamping
process was renewed—this time with variations
—for he grasped an unoffending book and tore it
into fragments which he scattered on the floor.
"So perish all our enemies!" he cried—"All fancies and all fictions of the brain!   All poetry—
frivolities and all romance.   Yea, everything, in
fact, but fact itself.   Let those who would be
happy read the Pentateuch!—or Saints of latter
days—or save your worthless souls by this my
Sermon upon Sin—protect yourselves at once!
Procure it while you still have time.   Let our
committee rise and pass about and bid the erring and repentant buy!"   (The committee rose
and did as was decreed.)   "Now, money
changers, ply your trade in a good cause, if you
would be forgiven; for, look you—all your idols

are cast down—our Juggernaut annihilates and none was spared! From simple Shakspeare down to driveling Irving all are gone! Why even in the house where I have made my short sojourn, I was insulted by the soulless Burns! But I destroyed the book, as he who wrote it was destroyed, and now both burn in everlasting fire! In flames unquenchable! In——"

In what he did not say—he got no further. No peroration—no doxology closed this too clear a scheme. A man sprang from a seat beside the door—the money changers gave him room, but the committeeman was overturned, buried beneath his books—women who honored homes and husbands all stood up! A single man retreated—and that so-called soul—too small to be perceptible—was sheltered in the carcass of Columbus Cant!

Before the eye of Donald Stuart he shrank back amazed and trembling in the farthest corner he could find; but Donald never paused nor looked toward his foe, nor said a word—he merely raised the centre window and he dropped his dear guest out—an unexpected exodus—no more—and then he shut the window down so softly, easily, that the slight jar it made was as a pin fall or a breath—and then he turned and faced his friends!

Shouts had been heard on Scotland Hill; but never such as rose in wild approval of the scene. It was a blending of the best that blood of Scotsmen and Americans could do—with women's voices like the shrill scream of the pipes, swelling and rising with a higher note than all the rest, and falling back to rise and rise again!

It was the war cry heard at Bannockburn, repeated in our later days and for a love as loyal and a cause as true!

V.

In the far distance, faintly heard, at intervals, the booming of the British guns, announced relief to Lucknow. Here it was the steady roar.

The silence of the last two weeks had found a voice and now resolved to try it to its last resource. Restraint was at an end. The exit of the enemy in such a sudden, unexpected way was magical. The disappearance of the one and bringing forth another in his place was something more—so startling the effect. Add to this a double joy—relief that one who held them bound was gone—delight that one who set them free had come—and then a joy supreme at sight of Donald Stuart's honest face.

Say no more there is no love and sympathy in man—that all is coldly selfish in this world—and every one is for himself alone.

"Speech! speech!" they cried; but many minutes passed before he could be heard, and when he was, the frenzied crowd gave him his texts and furnished inspiration for his theme.

"The man! the man!" "The book—the book!" "Our friends—our only friends!"

"Burns!—Robert Burns!" "Our ignorance and poverty!" Old men—their voices gone—used only gestures now, and women pressed towards the front and smiled through tears of joy. Donald alone was calm. In his familiar, friendly style he talked to them as he had often done; but those who knew him best saw something was suppressed—asperities rang in his voice—and smouldering passion showed itself at times — for words came from his lips as touched by flame, straight from a heart on fire.

"I should not say a word at such an hour," he said, "for what is personal to me may well be answered in a better way and at a fitter time; but we are friends upon these hills—the living and the dead the same—and while there's manhood left we'll stand by one another."

"Aye! aye! We will—we will!" they cried.

"And suffer our inflictions as they come, this last among the rest."

"No, never! no!"

"Yes. Some say our punishments are measured by our sins, and now you all may judge how grievous our offence."

"We do—ha! ha! We do! But tell us, Don, what sin have we committed that we should suffer this?"

"That book you were compelled to buy?

Why, none. It's one of those intended to re-place the trifling works of all our poets and philosophers by teaching us instead the newest kinds of sins. Your pardon that on this I speak my mind, but words will out when men must use them in a just defence, and here we stand between an open insult and our homes!"

"Hear! Hear!"

"The war is on. The Shakspeare-Bacon con-troversy proved how bold is the design. Begun in secret, it has grown an open foe. Its forces are sent out to 'skirr the country round' until our firesides are no longer safe. The invader's hand has seized our household gods and set a brazen idol in their place. The stroke of the iconoclast has shattered all it touched and now would break the very images of thought itself. Fictions and fancies—poems and philosophies must perish all. The honored dead are tram-pled on—the living laughed to scorn. The monuments which love has reared above de-parted greatness have been undermined and totter to their fall.

"For, sooth to say, this is an age of plain utili-ties in which the vulgar rules and shallow things hold sway. Nothing is sacred now. Sin is a jest, and wornout sayings masquerade as wit. The coarse, the common and the homely are in vogue. Nothing has worth beyond its vital use. Polish is vulgar save upon a shoe; and even facts, to be believed, must be distinctly plain.

"Daily we hear the worldly homilies. Discard all fancies. Only read the news. The beautiful don't pay. All art is dead and inspiration is a dream! The world, just as it is, is what we want, and what it might or may be is a theme which common sense cares nothing to discuss! Ah, well a day! Then to that realm called commonplace let those depart who will, and take along their everyday realities. Leave me in all my poverty, I pray, with only thoughts of things which make a brighter world! The beautiful in everything—the inspiration and the dream—a sound of music and a sight of art—a word of love—the last faint echo of a poet's voice, sounding from out the past! These seeming useless things, which never pay, but which are riches greater than a Plutus boasts to him who knows their value to the world.

"Look you, my friends, our homes are founded on a favored spot. From yonder Highlands down the long Blue Ridge, along the Hudson and the Delaware, throughout the Empire city and the Empire State we wander over famous scenes which Cooper, Irving, Bryant, Drake and Edgar Poe, and later giants like to these, have made a classic ground. Across the river yonder, on the western slope which ends in Sleepy Hollow, and within a stone's throw of the ancient church, is a neglected grave. About it and above it and on every hand are monuments to millionaires and those who fought for wealth and lived their little lives of selfishness and commonplace. But no one stops to ask their names or read their epitaphs—while at the grave of Irving men take off their hats and women kneel in homage and respect.

"What shall prevail against a tribute like to this?"

"Nothing! Never! never!"

"Nothing shall—for look ye, friends, a man's work is the man himself—nay more—his better self, his worth, his intellect, his heart, his soul! I take a book, as I would take a stranger in my house, and prove it by its worth. Is it unworthy—then it goes; but once a friend, it is a friend forever! Such was Robert Burns!"

These four words, coming from a heart o'ercharged, and uttered with an emphasis of reverence and love, renewed the wildness of the scene just passed. The fire relighted shone in every eye. Shouts came anew from every friendly voice. Women and men arose and waved their hands, and well it was no foe was in their reach, or those Scotch Grays of Waterloo had given their inspiring cry and trampled them to dust!

VI.

WHEN silence was restored, urged on by all, Donald resumed.

"My friends, we're simply country folks and ignorant and poor, therefore the little that we prize possesses double value.

"To me my father's gift was more than what it seemed. It was a souvenir as honored as himself, and one of the few things he brought from his old home. Upon its leaves his name was marked, with comments and erasures in his hand, till not an unclean word or thoughtless line was left to mar its worth.

"You knew my father well, and know it was his custom, as old age unfitted him for any work, to go about the lanes and fields and pull up every weed and useless plant that scattered its foul seeds about the farm. So had he done with this, for every one to read; for, as he said: 'Faults should be remedied, no matter where they're found. Nothing is sacred that is wrong. No error ever was inspired or ever will be—nor can we teach pure thoughts with impure words.

No matter what the ground, the seed you sow will bring you harvest of its kind. Then welcome good, wherever it is found, and let the evil go.'

"I mention this, not to bemoan my loss, but that you all may know how honest was my father's way compared to this crusade. Father! your gift is in my heart and only He who gave me life can take it from me. As for the other, let it go, an offering and a sacrifice for good, in memory of you.

"One hundred years ago, in Dumfries, Scotland, died the poet Burns—his last days, passed in dire distress and hopeless poverty, were sorrowing penitential days for all the errors of his early life.

"Within his grave was buried all reproach for the light lapses he had made. The gentle, loving, feeling heart was laid at rest. The grass that covered him was wet with sympathetic tears, and over him was reared a glorious monument in memory of the loved and lost. From Aberdeen to Ayr—aye, and in many a distant land these sad memorials stand as witnesses and record still the greatness of the inspired bard—but all in vain! For in these late degenerate days come the self-righteous tribes—the rigid, scant religious ones denounced by Burns

—the offspring of the Holy Willies of the past, with curse on lip and stone in hand to war upon the helpless dead. Envy, jealousy and hate are theirs—and for encouragement the bigots and the pharisees plead and uphold their cause.

"But let them come—the 'common cry of curs,' an unknown clan of little souls who shame their own obscurity.

"In this defence let those assist who will. Let lukewarm friends stand neutral or retire; cowards retreat, or cravens hide. My answer is no plea for mercy or restraint; nor protest, nor a favor asked; but my defiance uttered here— my gauntlet at the foeman's foot, my weapons in my hand!

> And be this labor an expression of my love,
> This service give I here with all my heart,
> This stand I take for auld lang syne!

Scotia, dear land of romance and of song, I owe thee much. From thy wild scenes my good forefathers came, bequeathing me the iron will of every clan that scouts the sun and storm on Caledonian hills, and with it the true love of country which all Scotsmen own; but to the poor man's bard I owe far more, and if the day could ever come when bigotry could banish Scott or Burns, and leave but cant and realism

in their stead, I never more should care to visit
thee—to tread thy shores or see the glory and
the glamour in thy name!

"Ask not, my friends, why I am with the
weak against the strong; the wrong against
the right; the one against the many—I am not.
That which seems strong and right and hedged
by many friends, is only fraud in thin disguise.
Hypocrisy in the good churchman's borrowed
clothes, and all the might they boast is but the
coward host whose cause unstable, shifts and
vanishes, or changes with the fashion of the
hour. Against all these one honest man's a
giant, and inborn nobleness of thought is better
than a world of their miscalled morality. Join
then with me for what we honor and for those
we love."

"Aye! aye! through life—through life!"

"Your hands—that's well—who will not stand
for right must ever suffer wrong. Who will not
fight for honor is a coward slave."

"Right! right! But then our ignorance and
poverty."

"Wonder no more, since you have heard me
speak, that ignorance should dare to lift its
voice. God bless the little schoolhouse where
we stand and yonder convent with its cross and
bell. With these to aid, let's make life better

as the days go by and teach our boys and girls,
as best we can afford, to make them good and
useful in the world; and, whatsoever else they
lack, let them but learn the lessons taught by
honor and by love and they will never more be
ignorant or poor.

"O, charity and kindness, gentleness and
truth, thou modest teachers in the school of
life, let thy sweet virtues but adorn their minds
and none will see the sunburn on the honest
face or heed the homespun of their poor attire.

"And poverty—well, what of that? I hail it
as an old-time friend. I've walked with it, and
talked with it, and asked it to forbear me many
a time; but still it clings and lodges in the attic
of my house, and many times comes down like
famine to the board and shares our scanty meal.
It steps into my leaky shoes and wears them
out in cold and sleet, and wraps its shivering
form in my greatcoat until the elbows gape and
shine. It sits on watch while I am working in
the fields, but never raises hand to help. It
takes my only coin with a remorseless smile—
but suffer as I must, and turn the matter as I
may, I still believe that poverty's my friend.
This much I know: the world owes more to
want than wealth. All progess comes from our
necessities. Nature has said to man: 'This

world is yours; but there are certain things you need. Go, work, and you'll receive them.' Poverty produces—wealth consumes. Poverty is strength—wealth is weakness. Poverty is a giant—wealth a sickly slave. The hardened hands of toil upraised the Pyramids and builded Babylon and Nineveh. Poverty created the seven wonders of the world. Poverty of resource made necessary all the great inventions of the age. The poverty of thought—our inability to know what lies beyond—has kept us cheerful here. Poverty—the non-possession of the things for which we yearn—has given us the poets and philosophers. Poverty gave us Ferguson, who, lying on his shepherd's plaid at night, with strings and beads mapped out the constellations in the heavens. The engine and the telescope—the needle pointing out the pathways of the seas—the loom and printing press and all that makes the comfort and the glory of the world sprang from necessity alone. 'Tis poverty that digs the diamond from the deepest mine and makes it shine in crowns of queens and emperors. The silks and velvets in the robes of royalty are woven by the hands of poverty, and sorrow sews the ermine as she sits and weeps. Poverty builds palaces, and wretchedness uplifts the monoliths to fallen kings.

"In poverty and tears have been wrought out the noblest thoughts that animate the hearts of men. The sweetest melodies have sprung from discords in the human breast.

" 'Sweet are the uses of adversity,' Shakspeare says, and so say all who know and feel —yet poverty—poor poverty! outcast, despised, how many do thee wrong! Thy friends are few —thy votaries none. All shun thee, all despise thee; and thy first offspring—wealth, well dressed and proud—knows not his parent, but denies thee as he passes by. Thy home, alas! is in the open street, thy covering charity; and so you sit and ask for alms, this label on your breast: '*That man alone is rich, who uses wealth which Heaven has given him, to aid his fellow man; but he who grasps his millions with a greedy hand, and hoards wealth only for himself, that man alone is poor.*'

"And now don't ask that I shall say another word, or my disjointed speech will be as poor as poverty itself. Take much for granted which I need not tell, and this believe that while I live, in all that's right I'm with you heart and hand—and when I'm dead I hope I still may come, and like 'the spirit of the Gregarach walk' with those I love 'mid these familiar scenes!'"

Bowing, he stepped upon the floor to meet a welcome shout and grasp an hundred outstretched hands.

Like some great knight—whose quarrel just had won the day might stand—so now stood he. Men welcomed him with loud acclaim and women offered him their thanks. A crowd of girls encircled him; but bonnie Barbara put them all aside and placed her loving arms about his neck, and looking up into his smiling face, she kissed him then and there.

VII.

CONGRATULATIONS at an end, a little old bald-headed man, mounted upon a chair, stood in a corner of the room and vainly tried to speak. His voice, or what was left of it, came forth at intervals in feeble pipes like those which beggar-women constantly turn out, in grunts and squeaks, from imitation organs on the street; and still he made the motions as a windmill might, and swung his arms, and stamped his foot, and turned red in the face, and struck an attitude, till presently all eyes were on him.

"Father Lindsay! Father Lindsay!" they all cried; "a speech! a speech!" And Father Lindsay, like the great chief Tamanend, was borne along by all the warriors of the tribe, and fairly lifted over seats and ladies' heads, and spite of his gesticulating kicks, was placed upon the platform, where he stood, the council's hope and pride.

"Hurrah for Father Lindsay!" Father Lindsay bowed return, and then a matchless piece of oratory swayed the helpless crowd.

Sign language did it all. He never spoke a word. A lot of motions, postures, stamps and nods made up his whole discourse. Yet he was earnestess itself,and emphasized each whispered point in such a way that laughter, shouts and bravos sounded on all sides. At every pause came cries of "Good! Good!" "Bravo! Bravo!" "Hear!" Then, after a long meter of gesticulated words, some one would cry: "Second the motion!" Then, as he struck the desk, they'd all cry "Carried!" and repeat the whack until it rang again.

"Hurrah for Father Lindsay!" Father Lindsay rose to the occasion now. He stood up on the teacher's desk and made his points in such a way that every resolution ended with a bang; and not until the desk gave way was Father Lindsay carried off.

"Hurrah for Father Lindsay!"

Sandy Ramsey took his place. He was a tall and raw-boned Scot, with leery eye, which twinkled with delight and looked as full of mischief as a wildcat's on a summer night.

"An' now!" he said, "we've carried everything, includin' the last speaker to his seat, I'll just make bold to move that all the resolutions we've just heard be sent—exactly as gude Father Lindsay spoke—to that same saintly spy o' Eesrael that our gude frien' Don dropped out o' yonder windy there."

"No—no," exclaimed the crowd.

"Yes! yes! It's our appreeceation—a sort o' blonk endorsement, don't ye ken? Here, Handy-Capper—you committeeman!" he called to that unfortunate—who during all this time had been preparing for departure, gathering up his traps and searching for his sacred books.

"Here, you! spy No. 2. Tak a' yer bukes an' keep the siller ye ha' got—an' here's a dollar more if ye'll no show yer long sour face in this veeceenity again. There, this blank paper just taps off yer load—now go—and stay. Haud on! I'd help to carry that; but ye'll soon find the other spy awaitin' ye ootside. Ye should be goin' wi' a pole upon the shoulders of ye two, and, hangin' down between, a bunch o' grapes—that's the old Bible pecter—but ye're too airly in the season here. Our grapes are green—an' yer two faces would turn milk and honey sour upon the way—and onyway we don't believe the gude Creator ever made one lot o' children to be blessed and ithers to be dommed, because auld Eesreal was sa' unco gude—and thenk ye were too long a-comin' anyway, and wasted time for forty years a-playin' in the Welderness —and makin' golden serpents an' the like—

till we ha' got a little Canaan here, an' now ye want us folks to gie it up; but you two manna-eatin', sarpent-makin' tramps, gae back an' tell the rest that we don't budge a fute except to kick ye oot—now go."

Upon such gentle invitation the silent and the saintly stranger went, a goodly servant in a worthless cause.

The eyes which followed him now turned to meet a more familiar face. The schoolmaster was in his place and patching up his desk.

"I wish," he said, "the men who came to mend our morals would stop their tinkering at unknown trades and take to mending desks; but, Father Lindsay, it is all your fault. You'll stay in after school for this, and I will give you something to take home and think of over night. Here, order now! We've had 'hurrahs' enough to last a month. Boys, get on your own side. Girls to your place. I've got a lesson that I want to put before you all, for I confess I've learned one here to-night myself. We all know now what friendship is, and what forbearance means, and if our better natures speak, we'd add, forgiveness too."

"Right! Right! Hear! Hear!"

"I move, then, that before we go we thank good Master Stuart for his manly words, and

Sandy for his Sunday-school discourse, and Father Lindsay, too, for all he said—and more he didn't say."

"Carried." "Good!" "Hurrah for Father Lindsay!"

"Furthermore, I think, if we consider the result, we can afford to offer thanks to him who has abused our hospitality and laid his impious hands upon the things we loved and prized."

"No—never—no!"

"Yes! For his act has made us one; has taught us self-respect, and roused us up and joined our hands in honor of our homes."

"Good! Good!"

"What say ye then if Saturday night we all meet here and plan to turn this evil into good, and welcome every honest friend they've tried to take away?"

"Good! Good!" "We'll all be here!"

"Then school is out to-night. Let us go home, and keep our lessons in our minds; and in our hearts a fixed resolve that right shall ever rule our humble homes and every fireside while it's free, shall claim the world's respect!"

At this even Father Lindsay found a little voice to aid the final and approving shout.

The shock was over—Scotland Hill stood firm.

Like children going home from school these

honest people talked and lingered on the way; and where they parted at some lane or path, or at the corners where departing roads led off into the darkness, there "good-night!" in differing voice was heard—and calling back and shaking hands again, with promises to "come over to our house and spend the day"—and then a distant call or merry laugh—and, finally, the voices dying out, and in the distance, barking dogs, and one by one the sudden lights—like will-o'wisps—as windows were lit up; and then the darkening as they passed, and then at last each party in the stillness of their lonely house, then silence over all.

O peaceful country scenes—what can compare, in all the glare and glory of the world with these sweet times of rest? What can replace the stilly nights, the slowly waking morn, the short siesta, or the *dolce far niente* of a lazy afternoon when summer holds her sway.

VIII.

Donald and Barbara, on arriving home, went up the path and opened the back gate. Luath had followed them so quietly they did not even know he'd been away from home; but now they called him in and patted him upon his shaggy head and asked him what the matter was—for strange to say he sniffed the air and whined and then ran to the road and back again, his nose upon the ground. Meantime a light shone from the window of the summer kitchen, causing Barbara to start.

"Donald," she asked, "what light is that? We left the house quite dark and closed the doors."

"Oh, nothing," Donald answered. "Mother must be up. Go in this way. I'll go and see."

And, as he spoke, he entered the back door and went into the room to find the light turned up—but no one there. Only a letter left for him beneath the lamp. He sank into a chair and opened it and read.

Barbara, meanwhile, had passed into the

front room by the porch, to find the door wide open and the night wind blowing in. She lighted a small taper match and held it up—nobody there—but as she turned to close the door, a hand grasped hers—the light went out—and her sharp cry was answered by a cautioning——

"Hush!" and then a hurried speech which told her everything. "No noise. I come to say good-bye, and tell you all. I love you. Loved you from the first. For that I lingered here. For that I brave all now. You know that this is true. I have no time to tell you more. Say only you believe—that you some day will leave this cur and come to me. Here is my card and my address. Keep it and write. One kiss, and now good-bye."

Her answer was one word—her husband's name—as she rushed out upon the open porch and struggled to be free. But Donald heard no cry. He only saw the letters dance before his eyes, and read these words:

"A curse upon you! You have spoiled my scheme. But my revenge shall strike where most you love! This is the wound I leave within your heart—and so good-bye!"

Two strokes upon the window which he

faced, and he looked out to see the paws of Luath on the pane, and his great anxious eyes look in. Then the dog barked and ran away a moment and returned, repeating the same action as before, and Donald bounded to the door. Luath had said as loud as canine words could speak: "My mistress—come with me!" and one loud cry of Barbara answered him! "The Jibbonainosay was up" in Donald Stuart's heart. An instant and he faced the foe—to him in this dark hour, Wenonga Cant! He used no words--he drew no weapon—left no mark or cross upon his victim's breast, but in his hands of iron he grasped him by the throat, and cast him to the earth, and trampled him beneath his feet—the dread *Lex talionis* which he had been taught, with all forbearance and forgivenness cast aside.

He dragged him to the fence—he raised him up and threw him over in the road—while Barbara looked on and Luath fairly cried for joy.

Curses and groans, and noise of fast departing feet—kept up till they were lost beyond the hill, where Luath, following, sat and barked— ended the schedule of Columbus Cant.

Barbara came out where Donald stood and held him in her arms, and leaned her head upon his breast; but neither said a word, and presently the dog came back—turning, and barking at each turn-and then at last he came inside, and following his master and his mistress to the porch he lay down quietly and placed his head upon his paws before their feet.

"Good Heavens! What's the matter here?" asked the old mother,in a half crying voice, as she came down the stairs, wrapped in a shawl, and peeped out of the door.

"Oh, nothing—mother—nothing!"

"Nothing? Why I thought the house was falling down. · I never heard such noise in all my life. What was the dog barking at?"

"He barked at nothing, too."

"Huh! Just like that dog. He'll bark at nothing all night long; but if a robber comes to rob the house, I'll warrant you he will be sound asleep."

"Yes, mother, yes. There, go to sleep yourself. It's getting late."

"Well, I'll go back. I do hope there won't be any more ado for nothing, anyway. You'll wake our guest."

"No, mother, he has gone."

"Well, well, he's gone. That's good! Well, thank Heaven, he didn't hear the noise. Did he leave any word? What did he say?"

"Damnation!"

"What?"

"Damnation!"

"Oh, and all for nothing. Well, maybe you two know everything, and all that I'm to know is—nothing! Well, good-night. Go to bed. Nothing—eh? Well, I never saw such times—I never—" and so she talked till she was back again upstairs.

Now in the silence of the night, with no one near, and only faithful Luath lying at their feet, Donald and Barbara sat alone.

So strong the bond 'twixt man and wife that, where they love, they can divine each other's thoughts—can almost see the mysteries of the mind, and read each other's faces in the dark. So Barbara, as she leaned on Donald's breast, knew all his troubled thought. Its silence told her more than words and forced her lips to frame an answer which should break the spell.

"Donald," she said, "you are silent—yet I know a thousand words are working some distrust within your generous mind. Oh, Donald, speak to me."

"Well, Barbara."

"Only my name—and coupled with a sigh. What is the matter, Donald?"

"Nothing, Barbara."

"Yes, but there is. You cannot put me off with such a word. There is some worry in your heart; and now, when I've to bless you most for your protecting arm, it only clasps me with a cold embrace and shows your confidence and love are gone."

"Forgive me, Barbara; but I cannot help but feel—and he said right—a sting is in my heart."

"Not a distrust of me?"

"No, Barbara, no—and yet why is it that I feel it here? Tell me if you have ever led that man to think he could address you with dishonest words. You, my dear wife, of all the world the one most trusted and beloved?"

"Donald, I need not answer no. When you are calm enough to think, your trusting heart will answer fully in my stead and tell you all your confidence and love have never been misplaced."

"Barbara."

"Oh, husband, if I've had a thought it was to do you good, and in some way repay you for the honest love you've ever shown to me. I told you this last night, and I repeat it now—despite of all that's chanced since then—despite of what you think or all the world may say—my heart is yours alone."

"No more, dear Barbara, no more. I take

you at your word as I have done these long
years past. No witness shall be called 'twixt
you and me, for when I can no longer trust I
shall no longer love or longer wish to live."

"Donald!"

"Remember long ago—the night we both
knelt here beside my dying father's chair—the
moon came up and looked upon the scene, con-
firming father's loving words: 'Be faithful in
dark hours. The light will come.' And see,
she's rising over Indian Hill as bright and constant as in vanished days, and chaste and beautiful withal; but not more lovely, loving, faithful than my Barbara is whose home is in my
heart."

Clasped in each other's arms they seemed
again the youthful pair of other years. Their
hearts were just the same and all about them
took the color of the past and led them back
through the long lane of yesterdays to that
sweet halcyon time of love no mortal e'er forgets.

Oh, happy is that man whose honest faithful
wife can with him so retrace the journey of
eventful years and find no shadows on the road
they are ashamed to pass, or haunted houses
at the end they dare not enter in! And blessed
the wife who, for the love and trust she gave.

has found a guide who leads her fearless
through the world—whose word is honored in
the haunts of men—whose name with women is
a title of respect—who wears no weapon, bears
no shield; but who—no matter what his poverty or state—stands a true gentleman in every
place—*sans peur et sans reproche.*

IX.

WHEN Donald closed the house that night he said "good-night" to Luath at the door and called him his "good friend." The dog responded with a whine in which affection was as clear as such sounds could convey. Then he put out his paw and wagged his tail and licked his master's hand.

"My good old dog," said Donald, patting him upon the head, "go to your kennel now. No one will bother us again. And see—the wind is shifting to the east and clouds are gathering around the moon. To-morrow it will rain. Well, as I can't work in the fields, I'll make you a new house. Good-night, my faithful fellow. You're better than the man you followed down the road. He plundered my poor home by day—you guard it in the night. While he deceived, he seemed a friend and looked me in the face and smiled —a thing no decent dog was ever known to do; but, Luath, justice recognizes right and always spurns the wrong. The man is in the street — you in your house. He has the world's contempt—you its respect. Good-night."

As Donald had foreseen, the morning opened cold and brought a northeast storm; but bright fires made it cheery in the house, and the restraint was gone which, for a fortnight back, had weighed upon it worse than gloom. Diccon and Joan went singing to their work and Barbara was like a girl released from school, enjoying the first holiday; and good old mother Stuart sang a dozen tunes, each one beginning on a wornout note and ending in a droning sound in concert with the kettle on the fire. At length the call of breakfast shut her off; but finding Donald did not hurry from the barn, she went to the back door and let her voice out in a prolonged yell—a "B-r-e-a-k-f-a-a-a-a-st!" in a quavering cadenza, good and strong, which brought an answering "whoop," then she was happy and came in again and sung her little ditty by the fire.

"Barbara," she said, while she was waiting for another tune, "did I get up last night and come downstairs?"

"Why, yes, of course. Don't you remember how you talked to us?"

"Yes, I remember that. I asked you something, but I couldn't understand what it was you said.   Who was it fell downstairs?"

"Why, nobody, of course."

"Well, then, who was it made that noise?"

"Nobody—yes—that is—nobody, too."

"Oh, I didn't know.   Maybe I'd better sing:

> " 'From Greenland's icy mountains
> To India's coral sands——' "

"That's beautiful, mother," cried Donald, coming in.   "What song is that?"

"Oh, nothing."

"I mean who wrote it, mother?"

"Nobody.   You see I make up my songs, just as you do your stories, as I go along.

> " 'The wicked flee when none pursue—
> I am bound for the land of Canaan!
> If you get there before I do
> Just tell them I am coming too,
> For I'm bound for the land of Canaan!' "

As she finished this the knowing look she gave set Barbara and Donald in a roar; but the old lady never cracked a smile.

"I'd be ashamed if I were you," she said, "disturbing people in the night by throwing visitors over the outside fence into the road. I hope you didn't break the palings off."

"Who told you that?"

"Oh, nobody, of course. I saw that in my dreams."

"What else, mother?"

"Nothing. Only this I say—the money I gave that fellow for the heathen reached the right hands for the first time.

> "'The heathen in his blindness
> Bows down to stocks and stone!'

Well, well—no wonder he knew everything from Genesis to Malachi. Why, he knew nothing else. Well—show me a thief and I'll show you a liar—that is true if he was not. Don Stuart, you ought to be ashamed to touch that little six-foot man. Why didn't you call me? Give him some coffee, Barbara—hot. He don't deserve to have a single thing—except the best the house affords. Oh, laugh! I'd laugh myself; but there's a certain kind of humor that's so bad we can't tell which is best, to laugh or cry."

"Laugh, mother, laugh," said Donald, with delight. "When women smile within the house men never heed the stormy world without. This is our happy day."

And so their merry talk beguiled the time till, breakfast over, Luath had a feast. Then Donald took him to the shop and made a kennel for him with a gothic roof, a sliding door, and at the back, a window; this, not only for the light, and sun and air, but that—as Donald said—"some time a friendly face may look in there and warn you of mischance, as last night you warned me."

It was the middle of the afternoon before the task was done; then Donald and the dog went out, despite the rain and dripping grass, to make their usual survey of the farm.

"The night will be quite cold," said Donald, as he took his coat. "I'm glad the storm continues and the wind still holds and makes the wet trees shiver in the blast, for should it clear to-night the frost would come, and do more mischief in an hour than all a summer's work could mend. Come, Luath, come. First up in the back fields, then down the woods and then below the road, and when we come back home we'll bring the cows along. Diccon, put dry straw underneath the shed, and some in this new kennel for the dog, and take it when you go down to the house. We'll bring the cattle up. Come, Luath, come."

And so the friends went out together in the rain, across the open fields. The man with merry calls and bits of song—the dog, with such poor voice as nature gave, responding from the gladness of his heart.

Within the house both Barbara and Mother Stuart found enough to do—and as for questions —the old lady, who had learned the art, now found her opportunity and plied her trade. Suffice to say the little that she didn't know about the troubles of the night before, was like a dictionary to her now, with every word pronounced and properly explained.

When satisfied that she had got it all, she said no more, but took her knitting and sat down and carolled some more songs:

> "'Arise! Arise! my soul, arise!
> Sha-ake off your guilty fears!'"

And then these scraps she'd interline with a soliloquy.

"Wonder they didn't break the fence," and then repeat, in song, the few last words:

> "'Sh-a-a-ke off your guilty fears!'"

"I'll thank that dog, when he comes home, if it's the last thing I ever do in my life."

> "'A-rise—arise—my soul, arise!'

"Wanted to kiss her—huh!—no wonder he went over the fence quick—

"'And like a coward fell.'"

She always went to bed at dusk; but days in May are long and she had time before the cow-bells and the barking dog broke off her song to run down, like the clock upon the mantelpiece, and then wind up again.

"Come, now," said Barbara. "Donald has returned. Let's have our supper before dark to-night. What do you say?"

"Well—just a cup of tea for me; but give that dog a rouser. Luath! Here!" she called, opening the back door. "Here, good old dog. I treated you just like a cur last night; but now I take it back. I meant the other man."

"No matter, mother," Barbara said. "We know now who to trust. Here's his new kennel Donald made, and here is Don himself. Come in, you good old darling, you—and take off your wet coat. I'll hang your hat up. There's the rain water in that pail. There's castile soap, and a dry towel's on the rack—and the best supper that we ever had is waiting on the fire."

"Thanks, Barbara, for thought of me. I'm glad that every thing is housed; for as the Macbeth murderer says: 'It will be rain to-night.'"

"Words full of meaning and appropriate,"

said Barbara. "But I have four more apt and eloquent."

"And they?"

"Come in to supper, sir."

Never is day too dark for cheerful hearts, or those who make best use of present joys. And never, never is our fate so hard but pleasant words can make all bright again.

That night brought back the good old time. The peaceful house—the mother gone to bed; Joan's chattering talk, and Diccon's hesitating telling of his love, as he sat in the corner by the kitchen stove, and watched his rustic sweetheart do her work; the pattering rain; the noise of waterspouts, and dripping eaves; the distant murmurs of the brook beneath the bridge; the fitful gusts of soughing winds, and moaning of the bending pines; the chippering swallow in the chimney top, and the faint cry of mice inside the wall; the purring of the dozing cat; the cricket's feeble "ait"; the ticking clock; the murmuring of the fire and—as the night advanced—the crowing cock, and then the hush that followed it till answer came far down the road—and then the barking of a distant dog; but Luath's quiet said to all within: "Peace is upon this house. Go on and whisper all your tales of love—and good friends sitting by the open fire, pull down the curtain that no eye intrudes, or passers in the night behold you happy in each other's arms; or nature in her strife come to disturb your dreams."

X.

THE call to meet on the appointed night was not forgotten. The cause which made it was alive and every day intensified. A clarion note was sounding in the air. A simple lantern borne along the road by some belated messenger, who had gone out to talk the matter over with a friend, was portent of the coming storm. It was the "emblem of sepulchral yew"—the blazing cross and signal Malise bore across the Scottish hills. It called him coward and it "doomed him woe," who failed to join the strife!

Time, never halting, never slow, soon went the round till Saturday was reached. This hurried by. The noon-mark scarcely showed ere it was gone. A few hours and it seemed the sun went down. Already afternoon had closed the windows of departing day. The shadows lengthened as they crept along. Dusk came, close followed by the deeper gloom—then Night —dark empress over half the world—stalked forth and sat down quietly upon her ebon throne. Her robe was velvet of the raven's hue, and the embroidery was jet. Her cestus and her girdle gleamed like eyes of fire. A starry diamond shone upon her breast, as Venus shines through rifts of cloud. Her black veil, spread across the heavens, was spangled with unnumbered stars, and the great Moonstone centered in her diadem, with countless brilliants circling it about.

Such was the radiant beauty of the queenly night.

How great the business of this little world—how all engrossing are the passions of mankind or else how insignificant, alas! great Nature's works must be that man so seldom turns his eyes upon the glories of such scenes as these.

But in the schoolhouse now, the men and women of the hamlet met, that which might change some portion of the world, or work out happiness and good for one or many of the human race, was in the passing hour, to be discussed. So simple are the ways, so seeming poor the instruments which, in the hands of Providence, are made to shape the fortunes of mankind.

Lo, the reviled, but patient Nazarene—
An outcast and a wanderer in Palestine!
To-day the master of the world's morality!
Whose words sublime have swayed the sons of men—
Whose deeds and death proclaimed a living God!

The goodly company was early on the scene, and there was no delay. The master who dismissed the meeting of the former night was in his place and opened the proceedings now. He rose and spoke:

"This meeting, called at my suggestion, Tuesday last, I call to order at this time. You know its object and will name the one who will preside; but first a word—let us begin where we left off and finish what we left undone."

"I'm thenkin' ye're jest right," said Sandy Ramsey, striding out upon the floor; "when workin' in the fields, we cut the swath where we have left the scythe—and take the corn row where we dropped the hoe, an' so there's naethin' skepped."

"Right—Sandy's right!" said several who sat gaping in his face, and Sandy smiled and raised his voice:

"Now, Mr. Overseer, or whatsoe'er ye are— the unfeeneshed beesness of the ither night was Father Lindsay's speech, and I've been lyin' wake o' nights a-thenkin' what it was—and maybe if we put him on the table there he'll be a human phonegraph—and if we oil his gudgeons an' adjoost his crank his ceelender will turn, an' out of every little groove he'll grind the words o' that same speech that's stored inside."

There was a roar at this and everybody cried out:

"Father Lindsay! Father Lindsay!" and carried him triumphantly to the stand—and there he stood without a smile—and presently began to imitate the turning of a crank, and moved his lips, as everybody bent their ears to listen—and sure enough—a splur—and—blur—and blup and blang—and then the following in a phoney screech, which made the listeners almost drown the piping voice by laughing out of place. This was one speech not "cut and dried"; but rather one preserved:

"Hu-hu-hu-rah! Hu-hu-rah! for the man—who—threw the other man out of the window! Good!"

And here a flourish and the gesture No. 1, and all cried "Good it is!" "Second the motion!" "Good!"

"And hu-hu-rah! 'Rah! for the man—who—made the window where one man threw the other out! Hurrah!"

And here a wave of arms—and short "Hip! Hip!" and then all shouted with a will:

"Hurrah! Hurrah! for Father Lindsay!"

"And hu-hu-rah! rah! for the schoolhouse

which had such a man—and such a window in it—hip—hurrah!"

Then the shouts and flourishes renewed:

"Hurrah for Father Lindsay!"

"And hu-rah! rah! rah! for every man—who stands by every other man—who—in the school-house—throws a man or any other man—out of that window—or any other window—so he throws him out!"

At this he brought his right fist down and whacked his left, and gave the desk a kick which made it shake again. The crowd all laughed and yelled:

"Hurrah for Father Lindsay!"

"And in conclusion, this is what I say—if there is any man, who is a man, and doesn't throw a man who's not a man, out of all the windows in this old schoolhouse I'll throw him out myself!"

This time, his final kick had broken desk and platform too, but that his laughing friends bore him away in triumph to his seat.

"Hurrah for Father Lindsay!"

No sooner was this orator in his place than Sandy Ramsey rose again and took the floor. To say the truth, he was a little jealous now because the human phonograph had outdone its inventor, and he resolved to talk it down.

"I'm thenkin'," said he, with a caustic grin, "the Lord is vara kind to let such humble een-struments be heard at sic a time—and it was mercy to withhold the same the other night; but when ye want yer talkin' done ye'll call on me. I've had the etch for that these mony years. I learned the treck o' it when I was travelin' in the West. I'll tell ye how it was— ye see—once on a time——"

"Order! Order!" cried the crowd, who knew the genial Sandy's "etch" was *cacœthes loquendi* of the chronic type; but Sandy never took a hint.

"Of course," he said, "if ye go makin' noise I can't talk half so fast or long. Once on a time——"

"Order! Order!"

"Ye mind the time McShaw and I ran off from home—well—then—once on a time——"

"Order! Order!" "The gentleman will take his seat."

"Of course—I didn't thenk o' that. When I am sittin' down I'll talk just twice as fast altho', in either way, I'm just a pump, an' when ye work me up an' down, the suction brings the words, just like the water flowin' in a stream! But that's no matter now. When was travelin' in the West——"

"Order! The meeting must proceed."

"Well, open up!" said Sandy; "ye won't bother me. Weel, travelin' takes siller all the time and so McShaw an' I got poor, and poverty sticks like a woodtick in the Eendean terreetory. Have ony of ye ever been oot there? Weel, one day when we were roound in that veeceenity——"

A low groan issuing from a corner of the room brought Sandy to a halt. He glared around, his swiveled eye on fire.

"Look here," he said; "if ye're so near the dyin' as a' that, I'll just wait till ye're gone an' then I'll come an' murn for ye."

He paused and then somebody prayed before he could resume and asked, with other favors, that if the life of Sandy Ramsey was to be prolonged his speech at least might be cut short. A general "Amen!" resounded through the room and Sandy sat down in disgust.

"Of course," he said to those around him, "if I'd a' known this was to be a funeral or a tellin' o' expeereance I would a' started on that tack mysel'," and here he rose again and recommenced on a religious key.

"Brethern!" he shouted in a nasal twang, "I'll gie ye my expeereance wi' a pair o' mules. I bought 'em frae a deacon in the church just

after I had joined an' when I couldn't swear.
Well, then, he guaranteed they'd pull a two
horse load thro' ony mudhole that I ever
saw. Weel—one day, down by Drinker's mill,
they both stuck fast an' wouldn't pull a pound.
I argued an' I coaxed an' used the whip, an'
tied the halter strap to their forelegs, an' tried
to pull 'em forward, but the place suited 'em
too weel, an' so they settled down to stay.
Then Drinker's boy kem out an' says he,
'Sandy, them is Deacon Drawback's mules an'
ye must give 'em jest the kind o' exhortin' that
he used to gie—I'll show ye how.' An' then
he straddled the nigh mule, an' kicked his
heels, an' cracked the whip, and yelled out
forty rods of D's—with 'gee—ejo—long, therr—
you infernal double d—d fools'—an' such a
scatterin' ye never saw. The boy an' load were
drapped off as they went. I couldn't see 'em
for the dust, and never cotched 'em till they
whizzed around the corner to the barn, just five
miles from the start! Say—if there's to be
more prayin' here to-night—jest eenterject a
few spare words for me an' ask forgiveness for
the way I swore."

"Amen!" and laughter followed this—and
then a silence as the master rose and greeted
an old man who came in quietly and stood un-

covered near the door. His hair, snow white, set off a face of marked intelligence in which was mingled kindness and command. His manner spoke of gentleness and dignity, and as his kindly eye surveyed the room, he smiled and started down the aisle.

At sight of him a reverential hush fell on the throng. The men stood up, the women offered him a seat; Sandy stared as if he saw a ghost, and hoped he didn't hear; the master grasped his hand and spoke:

"Welcome," he said. "This is an honor we did not expect. My friends, our worthy minister."

These words were useless and were scarcely heard. The sight of this good man they loved was like an inspiration. Involuntary shouts burst forth. Men cheered. This was a welcome from the very heart—affecting all alike—the ones who gave it and the one who heard.

There was a moment's pause. The pastor's face turned pale, and then, without a word of thanks or sentence of reply, he raised his hands to Heaven!

"O, God, in mercy bless thy people here, and guide them in the right. And this thy servant, standing in their midst, in sight of Thee, O give him grace and strength and love, forgiveness, kindness, charity, and let his feeble hands and voice aid them in every trial of their lives—in fortunes good or bad—sickness or health—or danger—or that dread hour when death shall come and end all brotherhood and friendship in this world. Amen."

A silence followed this appeal. So solemn and so feeling its effect, no human voice essayed to break the spell. It would have seemed irreverent. Here were no ordinary, worn out forms. No cold words uttered in constraint of sin. No virtuous eyes to look the world to scorn. Here was a man with heart and soul of man—meeting the sinner upon equal ground, with love his only weapon, and with God his only guide.

"Let me preside," he said, "if you will kindly give mo leave. I know your purpose and respect your cause—and such poor help as may be mine to give, I'll freely render you."

"Thanks! Thanks!" all cried. "Speak! Speak!"

For now they longed to see his face and hear his voice who came to them a friend; besides the kindness touched them home, and no one cared to interrupt it by a word—not even Sandy Ramsey with his tireless tongue.

The minister was master now, and standing

in his place he spoke as calmly and as kindly
as a father might to those he dearly loved.

"My friends, the indignities which you have
borne have not been yours alone. The church
has suffered more from men who misrepresent
her cause than from the greatest sinners in the
world. In your case, you can turn the evil into
good; but where we toil the laborers are few,
and one unworthy worker brings contempt on
all the rest. Against such men, with you, I
have a common cause, and for the right against
them I will stand your friend.

"But first a word. Our hospitality must not
be set aside because some stranger has abused
it. Kindness is duty, as our labor is. As
Nature blesses us, so must we others bless!

"Keep then the fire upon a friendly hearth;
the loosened latch upon the outer door. Some
day an angel may come in and say:

" 'God bless this house, for it hath sheltered
those in need and brought them peace and
rest.' "

XI.

CONTINUING, the pastor said:

"Now, good people, no formalities. I call upon the worthy master here and my friend, Donald Stuart, to come and sit with me a little while that we may formulate a plan to turn mischance into the common good."

Donald's name—at all times dear—now uttered in respect by such a man, roused all the slumbering feeling of his friends and seemed a battle cry to conjure up the spirit of the hour.

His lightest word at such a time was as a trumpet tone. His touch a talisman. His honest face—the magnetism of the man—drew every heart and raised emotions strong and deep in every breast.

As the three friends clasped hands—schoolmaster, minister, and tiller of the fields—the people greeted them with heartfelt cheers and felt in them an untold pride; for here were met the virtues and intelligence and strength which make a people great.

Donald bowed till they permitted him to speak.

"My friends," he said, "since last we met
something most strange has chanced to turn
the very current of my life. Two days ago a
package reached me from an unknown source.
In it a book—the counterpart of that same Burns
I lost and prized—the Edinboro and Kilmarnock
bound in one. The same marks and erasures;
the same eliminations, and in every way—excepting that it lacked my father's notes and
name—the same familiar friend. In it a letter
with no signature, and in a hand I never saw
before, with this request: That I would take this
book in place of that I lost, and keep it for my
father's sake and for my father's friend, and
in return the donor asked but this—that I
would seize the inspiration of the hour, and in
some way would use the talents I possessed,
and turn the whole to good. Do this, the letter
said, and be assured that God will bless your
work. My friends, what shall I say? This is
the book"—he held it up—and as the people
gazed, he turned towards the good old minister
and cried: "And here the giver, if my heart
does not deceive, and my dear father's friend.
Generous sir! write here your name and make
this gift forever priceless in my sight, and then
command me as you will."

So sudden this transition that its effect was

startling to all.   Each eye was turned upon the minister, who for a moment bowed his head; but as he looked up, and took the pen and signed his name upon the fly-leaf of the book, he wrote a history of love and kindness every eye could read, though filled with joyful tears. Having signed, he rose and took the book and gave it back as Donald seized his outstretched hand. So they stood—but neither spoke. Words are but feeble, useless things when heart replies to heart.

Used to all scenes of joy or grief, the minister found his composure first, and—spite of the emotion evident in all—he spoke.

"My friends," he said, "this incident and every step that has led up to it reveals the working of that unknown power which governs all our lives. There's something supernatural in all that we call fate. What was—what is— and what is still to be—let man decipher as he will—wise Providence keeps still its way, mysterious and unchanging, often seeming wrong, but in the end, another step in progress and the right.

"How slight a cause has made this an event, and yet how far in undiscovered time, recurring, interchanging causes and effects can reach. Life acts on life—intelligence breeds higher thought—until they stretch beyond the present world and reach to God."

"Let him who now complains of this be sure —that, certain as he lives, the time will come when he'll look back and bless this hour—and for myself, I thank my God for that which made this bond of brotherhood and joined our hearts in confidence and love.

"Already we're ten thousand times repaid for everything we've lost. You, in the knowledge of your better selves—I, in the grand discovery I've made, that he whose hands are worn by toil, whose face is furrowed by the trace of care, whose outward garb is but the honest homespun suit, bears in his breast a heart as open as a sunny day, in which the sweetest virtues lodge, and where, through sun and storm, love, peace, and honor all abide!

"Friend Donald, keep my gift, and read it with the greater one your dying father gave to you and Barbara, your honest wife. For her sake and for yours and all the world I would the blemishes were gone from that, as they're erased from this; for as your father often said: 'No error ever was inspired or ever will be. Nothing is sacred that is wrong.' All evil, all mistakes, wherever found, should be removed or remedied. Revision should revise. And good men should be honest and declare that unknown error, which man voted in, is not so reverend but man, who sees the wrong, may vote it out again. What value has a vulgar word—except to breed a thousand more? What is misstatement but a text for every skeptic and agnostic in the world to build his arguments upon? What wall can stand when an imperfect stone supports the base, or crumbles in the center of the arch? A good book is the best of friends—an evil one an enemy. Let us beware which kind we choose. Facts do not make a bad one good. Poems and fictions make no good one bad. The only right which either has to be, lies in the ennobling, elevating thoughts which they inspire within the human heart!

"On this a final word. To Donald Stuart I reiterate the one request I made, that he would make his love and friendship for the plowman bard the inspiring theme for some commemorating work in honor of his name, and reaffirm what is my fixed belief, that these words, coming from his heart, at such a time, will meet a due reward. What need say more? The time, the will, the cause is his, and doubly now, since both in Scotland and at home, the over-saintly coward hands reach out to tear the laurel from the poet's brow and cast it on the ground.

"Donald, you are the knight to stand in this defence. I name you here protagonist. Who joins in my request, let him say 'aye.' "

There was a thundering shout—unanimously "aye!" Not even Father Lindsay's little voice could utter "no," and Sandy shouted "I" four times, and followed it with all the letters of the alphabet until he reached the "Z."

Donald spoke. "Dear friends, the honor you confer, with grateful heart I here accept. The task you set is worthy those great men our country boasts, who honor all they touch. My hands are all unfitted for the work; but I'll do what I can. I'll think it over in the day, when working in the fields, and when the night has come, my heart shall speak and Barbara set down the words—fictions and dreams and imperfections as they come; but they shall tell a story of the heart—a drama of Lang Syne."

"'Tis well," said the schoolmaster, rising as he spoke, "and I propose that, as each part is finished, Donald read it here, and we'll approve it as we go along."

"Agreed," said Donald, "only this—that our good friend and minister shall first revise the work."

"With pleasure, if you wish," replied the good old man. "But when you pass through

Barbara's hands my task will be a light one. If I could rule, the censors of the press, the pulpit, and the stage should be, at least in part, composed of women. There may be matters where they show inferior to men, but in refinement—never."

And the good ladies present, with one voice "Agreed."

"Good," said the schoolmaster, with a merry laugh. "Then to the refinement and good taste of Barbara Stuart, Jean Cunningham and Ida Deans, we will commit the decorations of this room for the proposed event. It's now the end of the first week in May, and by the final Saturday of the month—if Donald's ready with his first installment then—we'll have an entertainment here—first of a series which we will continue every three months through the year. Are all agreed to this?"

"Aye! aye! aye! aye!"

"Listen, then. Each one must help the cause. Let those who sing, meet and decide what is appropriate, and practice it. Let those who write contribute prose or verse. Some read and some recite; some tell a story——"

This was Sandy's cue.

"Story," he said excitedly, as he walked boldly out into the center of the room. "Story.

Look ye here. I'm not much on stories, as ye ken, but when ye come to octual facts I'll never turn me back on ony mon. When I was travelin' in the West——"

"Yes—yes," the master said, "we understand."

"Ye do?" said Sandy, "weel, ye're queck at comprehenden'. Oot there I met a mon keepin' a barroom full o' dreenks, an' twenty boozin' bummers sittin' round. Says I, 'Have ye ony dreenks in here?' 'I have'—says he—'all kinds.' 'Ye're wrong,' I says—'ye have no scruples here!' Then he looked puzzled like; but after lookin' over me an' all the soakers sittin' round —he said he had. 'All right'—I says—'then I want three.' 'Three scruples, why?' says he. 'Because,' I says, 'three scruples make one drachm.' Aye, ye may laugh, but liquor flowed like water after that, an' just as free!"

"Sandy Ramsey," said the minister with a sober face, "three weeks from now yourself and Father Lindsay there, shall meet in a debate."

"Look here," said Sandy, "I never yet hired out to talk to phonegraphs an' hope I never will. I'll just debate mysel'."

"No. That's impossible; besides, each one must do his part."

"Then I'll debate for both! For ye can juist rely ye'll want another ceelender for him before he's thro'."

"And Sandy," asked the minister, in his good-natured way, "what task will you set me?"

"Ah, weel," said Sandy, "I'm not jest perteekeler so long's ye pray I won't backslide until I've sold old Deacon Drawback's mules. They'd make ye swear yersel'."

"Might I suggest," said Donald, "as the time is short—let each do what he can. The master here allotting each his part, on Monday next. I shall be ready on the night of the last Saturday in May, and this the place. What we take in shall all be given to such people in our midst as may be in distress. Is this agreed and understood?"

"Yes—yes—right! right!"

"And to our worthy master let me say—there are four times a year when those who farm have holiday. First is the time we've chosen, at the end of May—when all the plowing and the planting's done, and when it's yet too early to go through the corn. Next comes on after hay and harvest and midsummer work—say August, then, for our next meeting here; and the one after that, when all the fall work's out of the way and the November nights freeze up the ground. And then midwinter, if you will, shall round our pleasant year. What say ye all to this?"

"Good! Good!"

"Friends," said the minister, "I had forgot. You'll not refuse the organ from the church, the singing-master and the young girls of our little choir? They're at your service any time. And now—good-night."

"Not yet," said Donald, as he stayed their guest. "The honor you have done us we can never pay; but we can go to-morrow to your friendly church and give you our attention and encouragement, and every Sunday—every day —and each returning year—we promise here to greet you and uphold your hands, our honored and our best of friends, while life shall last!"

So heart met heart and hand grasped hand. Tears filled the good man's eyes and deep emotion choked his voice as he dismissed them for the night.

He raised his hands. All stood and bowed— and then his feeling words:

"May God in mercy keep you all! Good-night to every one, and take my blessing home."

L. • C.

XII.

If ever Nature holds sweet converse with mankind, 'tis when she wakes and throws the white robe of the winter off to don the dress of showery spring. Then is her soft voice full of sad regrets that mortals should have waited her so long. Tears in her eyes; love in her soft embrace; and promises of joys to be renewed and happiness assured in days to come.

Into the fields she goes and, where she treads, the scented grass springs up, and where her lips have pressed, the perfumed flowers. She calls unto the south wind "come," and then she hangs the tassels on the trees and covers all the woods with hues of green. There, under the dead leaves, the arbutus and anemones shall flower, and where the hedges blossom birds shall sing, and over all the hills, on field and tree, a wilderness of bloom—and then in sweetest words she speaks: "O mortals, chide me not for the delay. I know you have been faithful and the winter long. Come take my hand and let us not forget. Here let us work together all the sunny days, and I will bring you

THE VALLEY AT MONTMOOR.

blessings manifold and aid you willingly and constantly, your faithful mistress and your loving friend!''

O man, ungrateful and unloving and unkind —what answer have you made to this appeal? Year after year, as Isis did of old, this sainted spirit comes and wooes you for your good; but indolence has caught your ear, and all the yearning of her loving heart is wasted in despair.

Say not you never hear this voice—say rather that you never heed. Nature has few interpreters. None understands the deep affections which are not revealed by human hearts and acts and words. None credits the unseen. Familiarity with things unknown—the visible invisible—has made all earth's great mysteries so common that men heed them not, nor see, nor hear, save as they're things of course. Who thinks on the unknown? Who translates words unspoken? Yet in the darkened chambers of the brain there is a mirror which reveals the shadow of a thought! On pathless seas the mariner beholds, within the glass, the coming storm, and in the binnacle a strip of steel which tells him his true course! In the deep woods and on the open wastes the Indian reads the signs which the Great Spirit sends! Dumb animals are moved by unseen powers and know instinctively which hand is kind and which will do them harm!

Who wonders at these wondrous things or hears their voice?

There is a language none has ever learned. It is the language of another world, which here we know by signs alone; but which, to him who thinks and feels, is more intelligent than all of Babel's tongues.

The omens of disaster may be understood by him who wills to know. The thunder's dreaded tone we can translate. The frightful earthquake, trembling in its rage, and like a giant Samson, seizing on the pillars of the world to cast them down, says why it comes. The so-called messages from Heaven are never miracles, but simple facts, and as an open book for all wise men to read; and Nature's gentle voice is plain as is a mother's calling in the night to loved ones she has lost.

   .   .   .   .

The Sunday morning found fair Barbara communing with herself, and musing over Nature which reflected happiness and vied with her in beauty and in smiles. Branches of bloom and knots of variegated flowers lay in the fragrant shade and yet she gathered more.

"I hate to rob you, my sweet friends," she

said, "but you shall be the incense on the altar at the church to-day, and there the best of men shall tell the worst of women she is wrong to offer you a sacrifice for his dear sake.

> Good Mr. Olds, who cares for souls,
> Each lovely flower that here unfolds
> Bears love for you, good Mr. Olds.

"There, Joan, pray take them carefully and put them in the vases there, and keep them damp and in the shade. Yonder is Diccon in the wagon, now, and Donald helping mother. So run along and mind you three drive around by the north road and take the lame girl and her mother in, and give them what I gave you. Then hurry to the church and give these to the deacon to put on the pulpit, as I said, before the people come. Remember now. Donald and I will go across the hill. Here, Luath, here! Come back here, sir! He never sees a wagon but he wants to go, just like poor Sandy Ramsey's tongue. So you have come alone. Go bring your master, if you please, then we three sinners will be off to church.

> "'Welcome sweet day of rest
> That saw the Lord arise;
> Welcome to this reviving breast
> And these rejoicing eyes—
> And these rejoicing eyes!'"

"Thanks, Barbara," said Donald, coming up, "these good old words and tunes have my respect. They soothe some sorrowing heart—and fiction, fact, poem or sorriest prose that mortal ever penned, if it but do some good—is Heaven-inspired."

The path they took across the fields led to a lane and this into a road that ran along the woods beneath the overhanging branches of the trees. Nothing was said, but thought was busy in the brain of both, and even Luath sometimes paused with a great look of wisdom in his eyes, but he was silent too. So they went on without a word until they reached a gate which was kept closed. As Donald opened it for Barbara, his eyes met hers. She seemed to read his thought.

"Donald," she said, "you have been walking in a dream, and feel about you the same spell that's haunted me all day."

"What makes you think so, Barbara?"

"Your thoughtful face; your attitude of listening when you've paused; the intelligence which has lighted up your eye, when you have something heard."

"What could I hear, dear Barbara?"

"Are there no voices then, besides our own, within these woods and fields?"

"Why ask?   We are alone."

"Donald, we never are alone! I read it in your face.   Your thought is as my own.   Tell me—why were you silent?"

"Because I felt it would be sacrilege to speak when Nature's loving voice was sounding in our ears.   You are right, dear Barbara, we are not alone.   In woods or fields; in cot or palace; on ships at sea there is a friendly spirit comes by night and day and takes us by the hand and counsels us for good.   Happy the man to whom that 'still small voice' shall not appeal in vain, and blessed be all who take into their homes and treasure in their hearts these messages of love!"

"There, Donald, is the bell," said Barbara, as she paused and listened to its sound.   "How harsh the note compared with what we've heard, and yet it chimes in unison or makes so sweet a discord that the angels love to listen to the sound."

"Another proof, good wife, that things inanimate can speak, each in its way—and some are heard in Heaven!   There is a grand cathedral somewhere in the world, which people call 'a prayer in stone.'   Mute lips are often eloquent. Orisons devout are carved on Buddhists' images, or on the Indian rain-God's lips by penitential

hands; and, trust me, Barbara, these are understood and answered in good time. But, come.
The sermon for to-day was not to be within this
wood, but in the church hard by. Yonder's
the humble spire and weather-vane that points
the way—the bell invites—and here the sinners
come."

    .   .   .   .   .   .

"Love one another."

Such the blessed theme on which good Mr.
Olds discoursed in presence of the greatest gathering his church had ever seen. From all the
hills, the country folks had come in honor of
the day, the work, the man. The minister was
at his best. The poverty of his surroundings
could not take away the grandeur of that noble
face; nor dim his intellect; nor change his simple eloquence, nor its sublime effect.

"Love one another." As he uttered these
three words he seemed inspired. He did not
shout them forth as a command, nor utter them
with cold indifference; nor in perfunctory style
speak that which must be spoken; nor give the
subject as dead words to be discussed, then, one
by one, to be dissected and laid bare; but, as a
father might, he took the theme—"Love one
another"—from his own o'erflowing heart and

gave it as a blessing, Heaven sent, to those he knew and loved.

"Love one another"—in the church, the school, the workshop, place of business, in the home by ties made sacred, for a common cause, for happiness, for good, for love itself, and all that love implies—"Love one another."

"Be kind to youth and helplessness. Teach the young boy and girl an honest life—him to be just and her to never stray. Encircle them with all the loving ties your home can give, and when they leave you, let it be in tears and deep regret and the assurance that your love won't change, but they'll be welcome when they come back home. In middle life, or when old age steals on, O love, do not desert, but hold them faithful still—brother and sister; man and wife; father and son; the mother and her child; lover and maid beloved; stranger and friend—where'er on earth you meet, or wheresoever you may make your home—by all the things worth living for in life, love one another and your God will love and honor you!"

Words cannot tell the effect of words. They are the signs and symbols which, when given voice, can readily repeat the very shade of sense and sound of something heard before, but which, although reiterated till eternity, would ever lack the spirit which they first possessed.

The time, the man, the cause which animates his soul; the vital spark which makes his words electrical, all pass, or in imagination only leave their trace.

Thank God, the voice which spoke that day is not yet hushed, and those who heard are living still; and love, grown cold before, is warm in many hearts whose home is there. The flowers Barbara gave are scentless, dead; but others bloom eternal in their place in memory of that happy day. And blessed be Providence which watches all our lives! no flower has yet been brought by loving hands to deck a new-made grave on Scotland Hill.

The service over and the last word said did not dismiss the gathered friends. Some stayed behind to take the good man's hand and give him thanks—Donald and Barbara to ask him to their house. Women and men and boys and girls for just a friendly word, and Sandy Ramsey, when the preacher said "God bless you all," cried "Second the motion!" and "Amen!" to show the working of the leaven in his heart, then went and took the hand of Father Lindsay, his great rival in debate, and called on all to "wetness" he had no ill-will and would be easy on him when they came to talk—or, if Lindsay would tell him now what he was going to say, he'd make his argument against it light, to correspond, and anyhow he'd make defeat as easy as he could, for he had traveled and he knew the allowance should be made for country "egnerence," and if they wanted proof he'd tell them now a story that was just as true as any gospel Reverend Mr. Olds had ever preached. "Once on a time——"

But this was all he said-inside. The schoolmaster and Father Lindsay led him out, in spite of all his gestures and protests, and calmed him down by promising that he should have an easy victory in the debate.

"Here—whisper," said the master in his ear. "I'll not give out the subject till the night has come, so Father Lindsay can't avail of outside help, and falls an easy victim to your ready wit."

"All right," said Sandy, with a knowing wink, "but ef yer lookin' oot for somethin' gude ye'd better let me do the whole debate alone! I've traveled in the West, an' know a lot o' trecks. Ye mind McShaw? Weel, Mac was just a baby in me hands an' he is oot there yet a practicin' my style."

"Of course—of course," his two companions

said, and hurried him along the road—his legs, arms, tongue all running at one time and keeping him engaged till they were out of sight.

"I hear as how he's been complainin' 'bout them mules," said Deacon Drawback, as he rolled some plug tobacco for his pipe, "but what does he axpect? He's talked their ears off. Talk'd 'em deaf an' dumb an' blind, an' they don't understand a cussed word he says. Well —never mind. I'll buy 'em back—half price."

Having decided this, he started up the road, and all the listeners laughed and talked and took their several ways across the hills, and quiet reigned again about the empty church.

XIII.

THE Stuarts lingered when the other folks had gone, and went with Mr. Olds into the humble burial-ground which slopes towards the west, and stopped where one word,—"Father"—marked a grave. On this, as each bent down, they placed the flowers they had brought—the poor old widowed mother taking those which she had pinned upon her breast and placing them with trembling hands, said: "Duncan, these are mine," and bowed her head to hide her tears. "Love one another." After death—beyond the grave—there is no limit where affection stops and says this is the end.

From Barbara's loving gift the minister took but the poorer part, and all the richer ones he gave to his dead friend. "Love one another" —parting is but a name, and friendship that is true extends beyond the present life to be renewed in heaven.

They turned away and, as they came into the road again, there underneath the great red oak, which love transformed into a balm of Gilead

tree, Diccon and Joan were practicing the text
—his arm around her waist, his lips to hers.
"Love one another." Happy hallowed words,
and understood by all—blessing the living and
the dead, the highest and the lowliest, intelligence and ignorance alike—the sweetest, kind-
est, holiest law that God e'er gave to man!
Take this alone, and follow it, all others may
be put aside—all mortals would be blessed.

Starting home, Donald and Barbara passed the
cottage where the lame girl lived, and there
they found her, sitting in the shade, surrounded
by a lot of little friends and, as they passed,
they heard these words:

"We always loved you, Mary, didn't we?
Yes, and we always will."

"Love one another." O innocence of youthful days! How warm your words; how sweet
your voice. Your soothing tones can turn misfortune into joy—affliction into patience and
content. Keep still your faith in better things.
The time is long, but love will lead you to them
yet, no matter what your state.

"Barbara," said Donald, as they walked along,
"the world still holds the many like myself
who doubt and disbelieve much that is told and
taught; but there are truths, not registered in
books—words coming straight from what we

say is heaven, and bringing peace and comfort
to the human heart. What message is this,
Barbara?''

"Love, Donald, nothing more. It is the language which all Nature speaks, and blessed is
he who hears and heeds.''

"Kiss me, Barbara. My thought, like yours
and all the rest, tends to that pleasant theme,
and this great truth all know and feel, that
while this love is in our hearts we never can
do wrong.''

"Right, Donald; Nature ever works out good,
and we are but the instruments and agents of
His will who rules in this great world.''

"Yes, Barbara, I know that this is true, and
he does well who day by day uses the gifts
with which he is endowed to help in some good
work—to cause some tree to grow; some grass
to spring; some flower to bloom; some field to
yield; some dumb thing to rejoice; some generous, kindly word to be proclaimed; some
cheering, hopeful message to be written down;
some sorrow to be soothed, some wound relieved; something to be done that's worthy to
be called the work of man and is approved by
Him who placed us here and in whose fields we
toil.''

"Your pardon, Donald," said Barbara, with a

laugh. "It is the gate which stops your speech
—not I. But we have come to our own grounds,
and yonder in the shade we'll sit awhile and
talk—and when the dinner's ready, Joan will
call. See—there is our old rock beneath the
tree where we have sat and talked so many
times, and where you cut the initials of our
names, in our first days of love."

"Yes, Barbara. Dear the spot to me. I
always have respected it, and always shall.
There is the same old tree, with its outstretched
and sheltering arms—only they're longer now
and overhang the road, and bend so lovingly
above the spot, they seem protecting it. And
there's the hawthorn we transplanted that
November day, in blossom now. Bless the old
place and all the memories it conjures up of
Barbara Douglas and her sweet girl's face,
when first she listened here."

"And am I changed then, Donald?"

"No, Barbara, only to be more loving and
more kind. Just as the tree is changed, which
now extends its arms as if to clasp me in a kind
embrace, while still it steadfast stands, immovable as is the rock, and ever constant in this
changing world."

"Bless you, dear Donald. Here is a kiss for
that. And now go on."

"I cannot, Barbara. All my thought has changed. This spot brings back my dreams, and well it does. Do you forget my task? The work is new. The time is short. This very afternoon I must begin to put my fancies into shape and bring my characters upon the scene."

"What characters?"

"Strangers, Barbara. Except the poet Burns, and some he mentions in his letters and his songs, there is no history. A dozen words tell all have ever said or done. The poet's father, brother, friends—the characters of which he speaks—are mostly mentioned in a line, or else are merely names of those who *never* speak, familiar as they seem. Highland Mary—Bonnie Jean—by love and genius made immortal names —have left no records of their words, no messages of love or joy—no fond or fateful history. The memory of their love alone remains."

"Then, Donald, build your tale on that. A simple story of the heart, without one modern defect or device. No murders and no mysteries, intrigues or duels; no unsexed women; no unmanly men; no faithless wives, lords, ladies, servants, wills, fortunes, long-lost heirs; no poor girl in distress, with but a 'beggarly two thousand pounds'; no wonderful escapes; no going 'up to London' and no coming back; no balls or parties—scandals in society—no——"

"'Stop—stop—my gentle, guileless wife—I can't evolve an unknown race. Leave me a man or two, a little landscape and some sheep upon the hills. I'll plan a pastoral of other days; but Nature's hand grasps many things and I must take the gifts she brings and mould them as I may.''

"Your pardon, Donald. What I wished to say was only this—that you'd not follow in the beaten track, but keep to Nature's ways and all the dictates of your generous heart—for therein you are strong. Fame's temple stands upon a hill, and he will reach it first who chooses the right path, then boldly keeps his way. Let not your humble lot make you distrust yourself. You yet may rise. Where shallow wits pose in prosperity, you have a better claim—for well I know that only overwork and poverty and constant cares have so far kept you down and sunk you out of sight.''

"Thanks, Barbara. You are a goodly monitor, and as I keep my faith in many things, I'll keep faith in myself. Without a touch of fear or thought of pride, I'll do for good. Then, as my work shall merit, let it live or die. Perchance it may be blessed—just as my labor has been in the fields, when it has brought forth in its time, despite of cold, dark days, and killing frosts and burning suns, and other sad discouragements.''

''Be sure then, Donald, your good work shall thrive, and by your fruits you shall be known, although it may not be in present time.   In our orchard here the Summer Bough and the Red Astrachan are apples pleasant to the sight and taste, but never last.   Others there are have some corrupting spot, and hurry to decay; but yours shall be the honest Russet, Northern Spy, and Winter-White, which grow the better as the days pass by, and dearer that the others all are gone.''

''Yet, Barbara, ephemeral things are what the people crave.   Something that neither asks nor gives a thought; or rather say, something that comes from nothing and returns to it.   Let me die poor, forsaken and despised—for rather that, than come to this.   But let's go home.   Yonder is Luath bringing Joan, both wondering why we do not come—not knowing in their simple hearts, that we, the man and woman in this Eden here, grown tired of what is given us to do, seek out the tree of knowledge which shall drive us forth.''

XIV.

THE dinner over, Diccon came, all dressed up in his Sunday clothes, with hat in hand, and said he thought—he'd like to know—if—he "could take one of the horses for a little ride."

"Alone?" asked Donald, with a quiet smile.

"Ye—es, sir. Yes—we only want the one."

"We? Who? There are two, then—eh?"

"Well, yes, sir. Just at present, sir, we're two."

"But if you could be, you'd be one—eh, Diccon—eh?"

"Maybe we will be, sir, when we come back."

"Well, Diccon, you're considerate for the horse. When going he is fresh, and draws the two—but coming back, he's tired, and draws but one. The other walks then, Diccon, I suppose?"

"You're good at guessing, sir; but you are wrong."

"Well, then, perhaps you'll leave the other where you go."

"No, sir—you'll have to guess again."

"It may be you will not return, yourself?"

"Oh, yes, sir, yes. I wouldn't leave you for the world—besides, she couldn't drive the horse."

"She? Who?"

"Her, if you please."

"Which her?"

"The one you caught me kissing, sir, to-day."

"What—Joan?"

"My Joan. That is, she's your Joan yet—until we come back home—and then, sir, if you'll kindly keep us on, we'll do you double service all our lives."

"Go call her here, and bring my mother and my wife. Come here, my gentle Joan, and answer for your crimes. So, Diccon kissed you at the church?"

"Ye—yes, sir; but I told him it was wrong."

"How was it, then, you didn't strike him dumb with your indignant glance?"

"He was so close, I couldn't, sir."

"Why didn't you leave him, then, and come away?"

"Why, sir, he never could have kissed me if I had—besides that would not have been according to the text."

"Oh, yes—I see. You take things literally."

"I don't know what that is, sir; but I never took a kiss afore, so please excuse mistakes."

"Ask pardon of the law. Both Diccon and yourself must answer this."

"That's what I told him, sir, along the road. We must be married now."

"You told him that?"

"Yes, sir, somebody had to tell him, for he didn't know, and what my mother says is true:

    'The man who kisses with delight
    Must marry you before the night!
    And, should his kisses e'er grow cold,
    Divorce before the day is old!' "

"Oh, innocent daughter of a knowing mother! You've no time to lose. Diccon, you love this girl, and will be honest, faithful all your life?"

"I promise, sir, with all my heart."

"And you—confiding Joan?"

"Oh, sir, if I am ever anything but faithful to him, or to you, or to your mother, or my mistress here—then drive me from this place; but let us stay and work for you and we'll love one another all our lives."

"Diccon," said Donald, "here's some money —there, a girl who will make you a good wife. Don't waste your time; but get the horse and go. Don't hurry back. I'll do your work to-night; and, while you're hitching up, I'll write a line for you to Mr. Olds."

"God bless you, sir."

"My mistress, too," said Joan.

"And don't forget the text," said Barbara, "and Heaven will bless you two."

Donald went in to write the note, and now his mother had her chance. Some little questions had occurred to her and these she fired relentlessly at Joan, while Barbara, more considerate and less curious, helped the girl to dress.

"Going to be married, eh?—Huh. When is it going to be? And where? Who is going to stand up with you? Did Diccon understand? Does your mother know? Will you know what to say? Were you ever married before? When are you coming back? Or are you going away? Why didn't you say something? Nobody ever said a word *to me*. How do you know you'll be satisfied? How long was your mother married? When were you born? What did you let him kiss you for, if you didn't want to get married? How do you know he loves you now? What is the color of your mother's hair?" And other all important things, appropriate to the time which might have been extended, but the horse appeared, and Donald handed in the prize and Diccon took the note. Then all said:

"Well, good luck!" "Good-bye!" "Take care of youselves!" "Don't run away!" and

"Hurrry up!" and "Hurry back!" and similar original remarks by which the parting guest is cheered upon his way.

The worthy three stood at the gate and watched the couple driving down the road till they were out of sight. Then Donald turned, and with a twinkle in his eye, said:

"Mother, all those questions must have made you tired as they did Joan. Will you go in now and lie down?"

"Well, yes," she said, "I will, a little while; but do you think it's right?"

"What, mother?"

"Why—didn't you say they were going to be married?"

"Oh, yes—yes—mother. That's all right!"

"And you're quite sure the horse won't run away?"

"Yes—yes. He will go slow. Our horses are never in a hurry to go to the same place twice —especially on Sunday."

"Well, then, I'll go, and take my nap. Good-bye!" And so she went inside and talked herself to sleep. Barbara laughed outright.

"Donald," she said, "what sermon ever had so sudden an effect?"

"None that I ever heard of," he answered with delight. "If that old horse can only make

2.40 now, in twenty minutes' time the Rev. Mr. Olds will make 2.01. That's quick dispatch and happiness enough for any man. The seed of the morning is the harvest of the afternoon. His sermon yields him fruit before it's hardly ripe—in fact, while yet it's green. Thanks to our hasty Darby here, and his impatient Joan."

"No wasted time, or wasted words," said Barbara, laughing still. "They jumped at this as if it were their only chance. Oh, it was too ridiculous!"

"Yes, yes," said Donald, "but you understand these two took the one step that led from the sublime. We laugh; but Nature has her way, and where she speaks of love all hearts are moved—the humblest as the best. O love, thy story told, no matter where—inside the pulpit or upon the stage—within the camp or by the cottage fire, is the one theme of which the world ne'er tires! But come—this day's too good to go to waste. Let's go up to the barn and open the big doors and let the wind blow through; and give the horses some green grass; and bring some water from the well; and sit down on the hay, and there resume our talk. To-morrow we'll have much to do, and we shall have no time."

"With all my heart," said Barbara. "Go and

open up the doors, and I will see all's right about the house, and put the things away, and come when I have done."

And Donald did not have to wait. Within five minutes she was standing at his side and both were looking from the great doors to the north, where the blue hills were stretched along the sky.

"A glorious scene.   Eh, Barbara?"

"Yes, Donald. It is beautiful. No wonder you admire it."

"Barbara, it seems to me just like a picture which the border of this opening frames—a mammoth painting hung on heavenly walls. That was the scene my father loved, and here he used to sit on summer afternoons and watch the clouds, and say those hills reminded him of Scotland. Barbara, this landscape and my book of Burns shall furnish me the inspiration for the task I've set."

"But, Donald, would you not love to see the very scenes which you must sketch? Or mingle with the people who could tell you more of those of whom you'd write?"

"I would; but as it stands with me to-day, I think I never shall. Perhaps 'tis best; for in imagination I can see the scenes and faces which I would not have disturbed. How poorly would

the wretched street of Gretna Green repeat to
me the romance of the place; or Ecclefechan's
stony landscape show the greatness and the
grandeur of Carlyle—or Abbotsford portray the
mighty 'Wizard of the North'—and as for Robert
Burns, why need I ask from the surroundings of
his life that which would make him better
known or better loved? His home is in the human heart and Nature tells his history. There's
not a wave that rolls and surges on the Firth of
Clyde but kisses reverently the shores of Ayr
and murmurs in the ear of Scotland a refrain
which tells of days Lang Syne. There's not a
bird that sings within the woods of Doon, but
in its plaintive note recalls the poet's sorrowing
lay. There's not a tree that waves or flower
that blooms but tells some story of the one
whose ways were Nature's own—whose songs
were of the heart. The heather trodden under
foot—the blue-bell broken from its stem—are
emblems of his life o'erthrown while yet 'twas
in its bloom. The modest daisy turned beneath
the sod,

> " 'Like artless maid
> By love's simplicity betrayed
>
> .   .   .   .   .   .
>
> Low in the dust'

bemoans his fate as he lamented hers, and in her

sweet, remembering way, bedecks the narrow bed where now he lies!

"O gentle Nature, thou art ever kind! And he who loves thee well will never need another friend! Within thy generous heart no harsh reproaches bide—no faith in man is lost—no kindness is forgot! Thy love eternal calls thy children home, and when their weary work is done, to thy fond bosom they may come and sleep upon thy breast."

There was a silence after this which Barbara did not break; but as she saw her husband lost in thought, she went and took his hand and sat down by his side. There was a bond of sympathy between the two which had no need of words. Nature was speaking now to both their hearts. The murmuring wind was bringing in the gossip of the outer world. The twittering swallow's call; the pigeon's "coo"; the bluebird's loving cry. The fragrance of the blossoming orchards sweetened all the air—and, yonder in the shimmering light, hung Nature's painting close against the sky. Why should not man, at such an hour, and in a scene like this, hold some communion with his better thought and feel some love and sympathy for man?

What was the value of the text which they had heard to-day, if those were only empty words and had no other use than pleasant sound?

How poorly great Guatama's blameless life appealed to millions of the Buddhists of the world if kindness and forbearance, charity and love had all been lived and lost!

How vain the Savior's sacrifice—matchless example of pure sympathy for man—if all that wondrous wealth of love divine did not inspire a reverence endless and a love as deep!

"Love one another," is the law of laws. "Whatsoever ye would that others should do unto you, that do ye also unto them." This is the heathen's and the Christian's great command, and comes direct from Heaven!

Let no one grow so wise in this our little world that he can sneer at those who keep an open heart where love and charity can enter in.

There comes a day—before or after death—when God's love is the only guard that watches while we sleep.

"Forgive me, Donald," Barbara said at last, "but are you thinking out your story now, and shall I write it down?"

"Not yet, dear Barbara—time enough. Just now I want to think and talk and call these stranger subjects to my aid and hear what they've to say. But after supper, Barbara, to-night, and every night from this time on, this task shall take the place of all the pleasant readings which have passed. I'll come in early from the fields, and after other work is done, then for my own."

"Donald, I wish that I could aid you more. You're sure of everything?"

"Yes, Barbara—of everything except myself."

"Fear nothing, Donald. Everything you say has worth and strength. Your spirit and your sympathy are sure."

"Barbara, you mistake. Good qualities succeed in practiced hands; but, even in the fields, worth, strength and sympathy will not suffice. A giant cannot turn a decent furrow for the corn until he learns to plow; nor can I hope to shine in arts I've never learned."

"Donald, now you mistake. No matter what the book, I love to read the words which come straight from the author's heart, without the aid of useless ornament. These, often coarse and sometimes ungrammatical, have yet the fire which gives them lasting life."

"That's true, sometimes, I will confess, and in the drama more especially; and therefore, that has always seemed to me the grandest field for authorship. The characters walk forth—not visions, but realities. They live and move inspired by love or hate, ambition or their various desires—succeed or fail; do good or evil—as you will—and all the purpose of their coming and their going they relate—as Shakspeare tells, even

> " 'Life's but a walking shadow—
> A poor player
> Who struts and frets his hour
> Upon the stage,
> And then is heard no more!'

Eureka!—Barbara, see how a little thought or talk may end. Five minutes since I did not know how I could use the men and women who came knocking at my heart and brain to do me service. Now I'll have them come into our little room and tell their story. I will interpret—you shall write it down—and it shall be a drama of departed days, with many characters—Burns and his father, brother, many friends. Highland Mary—Bonnie Jean—drawn and arrayed as best I may. Holy Willie—Tam O'Shanter—the good Earl of Glencairn shall be the heroes of their histories in which their author shall himself appear—and all the rest shall come from the invisible air—as Ariel came to Prospero—to do a willing task."

XV.

THE afternoon was passing by. The sun was on the western slope; the noiseless footsteps of retreating hours unchallenged passed the silent guards. Nothing spoke of change; but quietly ten thousand ambushed figures came and crept towards the east. Then at a sign, these shadows rose and pointed to the dial which proclaimed their reign was close at hand.

Donald Stuart slept.

Stretched on his rustic bed of fragrant hay, with Luath guarding at the door, he passed an hour in peaceful dreams. The work and worry of the week just passed were all forgotten now, and in their place came visions of Arcadian days on Caledonian hills. Sometimes he smiled and sometimes sorrow stole across his face, and Barbara knew that sympathetic look was for the people of his brain who told their mournful story to their best of friends.

"Sleep on, dear Donald, dream," she said. "Forever must his waking or his sleeping hours be blessed, who so forgets himself for other's good—sleep on."

And saying this, she'd sit and watch, then go and come again, till her returning footfall told him she was near, and then he waked and smiled.

"Ha! ha!" he said. "How gallant husbands are! A lover, now, would sit and watch a whole night through and swear that he was never tired."

"Well, yes," said Barbara, "and just to prove he'd lived and lied for love he'd sleep the whole day long the moment he was once alone. Rouse up, good Mr. Lotus-eater, if you please. Though you are in the land of dreams it is not 'always afternoon' in this meridian and night will soon be here."

"Well, Barbara, let it come. We'll be prepared. The lovers won't be back till after dark, and as the song says

> " 'Work is to be done
> Before the setting of the sun.'

Luath, go bring the cows up from the lower lane. I'll get the pails and put clean straw beneath the sheds and bedding in the horses' stalls, and feed in mangers, hay in racks, and water in the drinking-pails. There's nothing else but fun upon a farm—excepting work. And that, on Sundays, turns to cheerful play.

" 'Welcome sweet day of rest' "

But come to think, I will not sing the 'rest,'
but work it out in quite another tune.   O, sweet
is milk, and sweet the way we coax it in the
pail—especially in the fly-switching time of
night when milkmaids moan, and dairymen deal
out 'contagion to this world'!"

"Right, Donald—laugh," said Barbara.   "A
light heart makes an easy task, and while I'm
in the humor, I'll go put the supper on and fix
the south room for the newly married pair.

" 'Let the world slip; we'll ne'er be younger,'
Man nor wife, nor maid nor man.   Be jovial then.
'Before the setting of the sun,'
I'll finish up your song, and then we'll tune an-
other to a merrier note to end this happy day."

"Great happiness comes slow," Donald said
at supper-time, "and so will come our happy
pair.   They can't forbear to drive around and
see their folks and tell their friends.   Then,
more to spare their blushes than the horse,
they'll drive home slowly so they can't be seen
till after dark."

"How well you know," said Barbara, with a
laugh in which old Mrs. Stuart joined.

"Why not," said Donald.   "When I first loved
you, I never dared to look you in the face; and

if I met you on the road I'd tumble over the
first fence and hide in the long grass or in the
rye, until you passed; and when I saw you
coming to the house, my refuge was the fields,
or woods, or barn, where I would stay all day
or till they came and told me you had gone."

"Yes, I remember that," the old lady said,
with many a laugh; "but Donald always was
the biggest fool——"

"Of course," said Donald; "but the horse is
at the gate. I'll go and put him up, and you
two must receive the two unfortunates just as
you would two high-born guests who honored
us by coming to our house."

So they were ushered in with all the honors
due a king and queen. "Welcome!" "Come
in!" "Take off your things." "Now make
yourselves at home." "Your room is ready—
if you'd like to retire." "Well, then, all right—
come in to supper first!"

These were the greetings which upset them
quite, and stopped their speech, and made them
sit and blush and stare and smile a "sickly
smile." The climax came when Donald entered playfully and kissed the bride, and slap-
ping Diccon on the back, said: "Lucky dog, to
win the prize!" Then asked fair Joan for the
certificate which made her his. And Diccon

stood up like a man and said: "My wife!" with that possessive air which men assume when talking of their chattels and their goods—then, starting in to supper, stumbled over something on the floor, and tore her skirt, and grasped two chairs and then sat down in both, and proved that love is something after all—because it makes a man a fool and shows that

> "Joy shall be in Heaven over one"

sinner that is caught, more than ninety and nine others who escape.

But there they sat as in a dream—their wedding supper served by the good people of the house to just their humble selves. However, they partook, and mumbled thanks, and stumbled out, and wandered aimlessly about the south end of the house, and leaned upon the gate, and whispered what no one will ever know or tell, and after all was quiet, stole inside and sat down in the dark.

> "Two souls with but a single thought"

made happy by a text.

"Were you in earnest, Donald?" asked his mother with a knowing smile, when once more they were left alone.

"Yes, mother—Barbara, yes—and never more

in all my life. The room which Barbara prepared we thought scarce good enough for him
who tried to do us harm. Thank Heaven, it's
none too fine for those who do us good.

"As for the other service we have rendered
them—that is a duty we should gladly pay.
We owe it to ourselves as well as to the helpers
in our house and one besides I need not name.
Love is the master here to-night and we are
only servants in his lordly halls."

XVI.

Close now, O glorious day, thy record is secure. The white stone is set up—the mark is made in all the calendars of time. Each heart beneath this humble roof shall call thee blest while life shall last.

Good mother, go now to your peaceful sleep—joy in your heart and laughter on your lips; dumb animals without, lie still, protected by the hand of care; dog at the door, take these, the remnants of the feast—not seven baskets' full, but what is more a miracle, it is enough—and as most suppers go, to the poor dogs of this bone-giving age, it is a feast indeed. As you have watched, good Luath, those who call thee friend repay. All rest secure. All be at peace. And open now that little room—the hallowed home of man and wife—where during all the past and happy years, the master and the mistress of the house have held their sweet discourses, and have read the histories of lives as peaceful and as happy as their own.

The palace of an empire, with its lofty halls

and endless colonnades may never shelter true content—but here four humble walls, adorned by loving hands, and sacred to a simple honest life, make still the happy home, where man and woman, love and peace, may dwell in happiness while life shall last!

"Donald," said Barbara, "how sweet the air that enters in these open windows, is it not?"

"It should be," said he, "for it comes across the miles of orchards lying to the north. See, the white trees show yet. There is no moon; but there the Dipper and the Pole-star shine— and there's the very scene we saw this afternoon, which father always called the Scottish hills."

"Yes, Donald, lovely as before, but altered by the darkness, as once we saw it in a theatre, when the same scene was shifted quietly and changed from day to night."

"Thanks, Barbara, for the thought. That scene no longer seems the picture of the afternoon, but is the curtain which shuts out the distant shores of Scotland from my view—the act-drop which shall rise and show the very scene of which I've dreamed—the honest people I have met—the loving faces that have looked in mine—who come to visit me in house and barn and field. Behind that scene they're gathered now and I can see them plainly, as I hear and see them in my dreams."

"They come to see you, Donald—how?"

"As strangers come along the road, who stop a moment at the gate, and then walk boldly in. Some do not even knock, nor heed the sign: 'this is my busy day'—but there they sit and will not be denied till I have heard them."

"Indeed; that's strange."

"It is. So strange it sometimes startles me; for most are those I never saw before, and some I never care to see again."

"And they are your familiars?"

"Yes, and seem to know that I will need their services, and put them all to work—the honest at some good, the bad at evil things—and that I'll make myself responsible for all they say or do!"

"Then you'll have much to answer for, I fear, and should demand their characters."

"These I may give, but not receive, dear Barbara. The painter sketches from a scene; the builder works from a design; artists and sculptors have their models set before them; but those who work out dreams must use the agents Nature sends, and take them as they come."

"Which Nature sends! Then men do *not* create?"

"It is their claim; but is it true? To my poor mind all things exist—thought simply calls them forth obedient to our wish. Man is the agent of the higher powers; but his intelligence, though like a God's, is not creative nor supreme—for if it were, all mystery would end and man would reign in Heaven."

"Thanks, Donald. I am glad there is one man who doesn't think he knows all things on earth, and in the skies above and in the waters under them."

"Ah, Barbara, in how brief a space of time men could give thanks for what they know; but prayers would be eternal should they ask for what they've never learned. How grand those old philosophers who besought the Unknown Gods and Unseen Spirits of the earth and air to help their wandering thoughts. In present times, how modest and sublime the greatest men of all the world who ask the Ruler of the universe to guide their failing steps. How beautiful the poet's invocation to his muse to inspire his thought and set his words on fire.

"But, Barbara, we must rest. Our pleasant talks are done. Our work begins. The characters are ready on the scene, and what they have to say and do they're eager to impart.

"Listen. I almost hear their voices in the

night—some happy and some sorrowful, and some with scraps of romance and of song—and told so quckly that there's hardly time to set their sayings down. But it must be. In less than three weeks' time the first part of their story must be sketched, rewritten and revised. So let us note it well—a silent record—nameless to all except ourselves until the night it must be told. There is your table and your easy-chair, and there your pens and ink and paper and the light—and there's a kiss for all your love and kindness of these many days!— and yonder, underneath the bordering sky, the curtain rolling slowly upward shows the scene. Is it reality—or but a vision passing in the night? Where are the forms familiar to the place? And will they come unsummoned here —or do they wait my call? O, Muse, who ministers in peaceful haunts, presiding over groves and growing fields, guide me where I shall find the shepherd and his flock—the peasant at his plow—and where the loving swains rest in the shade and listen to the distant pipe. There let me come and pass the afternoon in their good company! Bonnie Scotland, on thy heath-clad hills let me lie down in thoughtful sleep and dream a drama of the bygone days."

"Lulled by the murmurings of Ayr and Doon, bring memories of their poet, Burns!

"Call Mary Campbell in her artless ways, and let the lovers sit beneath the scented shade of yonder hawthorn tree and pass the all too short and happy day!

"Light up the house where peasants gather round the family fire, and cotters read again from the great Bible in the hall the words of comfort and of peace!

.   .   .   .

"Then take me to the town of Ayr. To the auld Inn and Tam O'Shanter, Souter Johnny and their spree—the landlady and all her gracious talk before the going home.

"Let Robert meet his Bonnie Jean, and with the ones he loved revisit Alloway.

"Then Tam O'Shanter and his midnight ride —the kirk by night—and the lone road where carles and witches scare him o'er the Doon!

.   .   .   .

"Shift then the scene to Mossgiel Farm, and all the struggles known on its cold soil. The days of toil and dreary nights—the only light the weird sheen of Coila's vision and the glimmering biggin fire! Bring Highland Mary back —a faded dream—his love again in Heaven!

"And now to Elliesland—the Ingleside—Burns on his birthday, in his brightest hour, when he acknowledged Jean Armour his wife! Glencairn their guest, and all the country met around their fire.

"Bring these to me, and as I welcome them with loving heart, so will I tell the world my dream!"

BOOK II.

A DRAMA OF DAYS LANG SYNE.

BOOK II.

Bonnie Doon.

A DRAMA OF DAYS LANG SYNE.

PART FIRST.

Last Saturday in May—and Decoration Day it chanced this year—hence double holiday on Scotland Hill. A day to bless the living and the dead—a day on which the sun had set in peace.

Up in the western sky fair Venus shone, and the thin crescent of the moon looked down upon the silent burying-ground where slept the dead beneath a coverlid of flowers.

Within the schoolhouse, soon as darkness came the lights were lit, revealing pictures hung about the walls, and bordered with fresh blossoms set in evergreens, or circled with great wreaths of laurel, holly, oak and pine.

Shakspeare and Irving and their friends were

there—Scott, Cooper, Longfellow, Tennyson, Hawthorne, Poe, and that long line of literary lights whose glory has encircled all the world—and, in the center where the platform stood, masked in by branches to the opened window-tops, a life-size painting showed the poet Burns—and on either side, a picture from his works completed the effect.

All seats were filled and many stood about the door, or at the windows, which were opened wide that all might see and hear. Diccon and Joan were there, both on one chair it seemed, they sat so close; and Deacon Drawback stayed outside to watch his mules—which he had just bought back for "only half the money Ramsey paid"—and Sandy told his friends inside, it had to be—either the mules must go, or he must learn to swear, and so they went—about the only time they'd done so since they had been his.

On the left the organ and the organist and little choir, and on the right a desk with student's lamp and Barbara's manuscript; and Barbara herself, with Donald and his mother by his side, sat in the corner near, where they would take least room—and on the platform, like a patriarch, chosen to preside, the good old minister, all honored and all loved. From his lips came the words of welcome—announcement of the August meeting, a blessing and a prayer—and then the music by the choir, with other voices joining in the proper and improper place. Then recitations of a humorous kind, followed by girls in white and tartans, giving old-time songs—then the schoolmaster with some curious verses of his own, which no one but himself could understand, but which, as he announced, would win a prize to any scholar of that school who should correctly tell the different languages, abbreviations and quotations, and what each meant—the answers to be handed in at their meeting at this place in August next. After which, as he proclaimed with serious face, the great debate between the well known orators, Father Lindsay and Sandy Ramsey, who would now stand forth and discuss the *Zeu-glou-idio-co-hem-o-fisty-isty-cuss!*

"What cuss?" asked Sandy, with his leery look, and made the schoolmaster repeat amid the snickering of the crowd. Father Lindsay never moved a muscle of his stolid face; but Sandy who had stood forth in his pride, until the subject, now first heard, submerged him, looked as wise as Solomon and twice as wicked as two Hamans rolled in one.

"Look here," he said, "I'm out of politics,

and I ha' done my princeepel travelin' in the West, but if ye thenk a few New England words can fluster me, ye'll mess yer guess. I have the soobject an' I'll do me part; but do ye want our talkin' loud, or soft—or how?"

"Oh, soft will do best in this little hall," the schoolmaster replied, with a long face. "Besides it's in your style."

"It *will* be," Sandy answered, as he pulled Father Lindsay's head aside and whispered in his ear. Lindsay looked relieved. They understood—and then commenced the great Zeu-glou-idio-co-hem-o-fisty-isty-cuss debate which put all duels oratorical aside, and stands unrivaled in these talky times.

Ramsey led off, with outstretched mouth and arms, pounding the air and making points, but softly—softly—not a word above a whisper—something in his "style"—and Father Lindsay's too, for, as Sandy finished, *his* Damascus blade shone forth. The keen satire, the polished wit, the sharp retort, were his. But Sandy beat him off with stroke on stroke, parry and thrust not only, but a great sweep of rhetoric, delivered as a claymore might have given it—strong, forcible, but soft—oh, yes, in whispers as they wanted it. All those who looked in Sandy's face, and caught his swivel eye, knew now that he was in his element and he had found his "style" and carried out his joke.

Roar followed roar, for points were made in comic pantomimic style and all were understood.

"Good! Good!" the people cried. "Hurrah for Lindsay!" "Sandy's right!" "Hurrah! Hurrah!" and thus encouraged each renewed his gestures and his stamping till the building shook, and then the *coup!* The grand climax. A peroration in which both spoke at once! "Liar!" they seemed to say, and "Double slave!" And then they clinched and each one's partisans bore off the double champions, alike triumphant and alike approved—the only time in any argument that both sides won.

Hilarity was at its height. The people and the two participants—schoolmaster, minister and all joined in the cry, "Hurrah!" "Father Ramsey!" "Sandy Lindsay!" "Champions!" "Hurrah!"

In the excitement Sandy went outside to cool, and Deacon Drawback came inside and took his place. So Sandy won applause, and much to his disgust, he lost his seat.

Five minutes passed before good order was restored—then Donald Stuart rose—and as he did so all was still as death—and as he took the writing in his hands, all was attention and respect, each eye was turned toward him and each ear attuned to listen to his friendly words.

Amid a breathless silence he began:

To the poor—my brothers and my sisters in adversity—those who cannot favor, will not flatter me—I devote this strange and true romance of

BONNIE DOON.

The Drama of

The Life and Loves of

Robert Burns.

PART FIRST.

"Where-by the winding Ayr we met
To live one day of parting love."

The time one hundred years ago; the country Scotland, and the scene the road that leads from Doon to Ayr.

Of all who passed upon that road, or wandered up and down the shady paths which bor-ered it—who now shall tell? Who can go back to that far distant time—journeying in memory through the long forgotten years—and sit down by that highway, now so famed, and see the people of the past go by? The little children with dust-covered feet; poor boys and girls unconscious of their sorrows in their play; the lovers happy and forgetful of the world; the careless husband and the anxious wife; the widow and the stranger and their cares; the father and the mother worn and old—who shall behold their faces or their forms again or hear their happy words, or listen to their woes, or catch the distant echo of their songs of love? Not one. No book preserves their history; no record tells their deeds or marks their fate. One matchless book of song—written by him the hero of the scene—recalls their names—but further all is still. Wish as we may, we look and listen, but in vain. All who lived then are silent now. All who live now speak only of a past they never knew.

But there's a Pilgrim who has wandered far and made his journey through the land of dreams. Invited by your welcome, he comes in, and takes his wallet off and hangs it up— and tells a story as a stranger might who sits beside your fire—and, as he speaks, his staff is turned to a magician's wand, and by a single touch all things are changed.

Behold! We are no longer on our well known hills; but this is Scotland and we stand upon her soil.

These blossoms bloom upon the banks of Ayr, and in these branches lint-whites sing—and yonder, coming up the road, appears the wife who all day long has nursed "her wrath to keep it warm"—and so she speaks, and others come and go—revealing all the secrets of their lives and telling us their loves and sorrows in this DRAMA OF DEPARTED DAYS.

———

SCENE 1.

"A weel! A weel!" says Katy O'Shanter, as she stands looking toward the town, "not hame the live lang day—an' yet na sign! O, Tam O'Shanter! Tam O'Shanter. It's weel yer awa'. The gudewife canna haud her tongue forever, an' when ye do come, my words will flow like a stream doun the side o' 'Ben Lomond.'"

She looks again, shading the sun from her eyes.

"What's this comin' doun the road? A bogle or a ghaist? Or Beelzebub in black? Eh! it's

SCENE OF BURNS' MONUMENT, AYR.

Haley Willie—wi' his long legs and longer face and groanin', heepecreetical voice. He's the ane mon in a' Scotland who minds everybody's business but his ain. He'll no learn mine.''

She retires, as Holey Willie appears. He stands and clasps his hands and rolls his eyes and heaves a sigh:

"A-ah! It's ma dooty. These lang Scots miles may mak me tired; but what's a' that to Willie? All the afternoon I've wandered on the Ayr to spy on Robert Burns. This must be near the trysting-place where he meets Mary Campbell. My dooty is to save her frae his arms, an' maybe for ma ain. Let ithers preach; I'll proctice. I'm the schoolmaster to counsel the erring. I'm the shepherd who gathers the stray—(he sees Katy)—Ah! ane o' the lombs o' th' flock. I must encompass her in ma arms and carry her back to the fold. Gude woman, I gie ye good e'en.''

"Ye do?'' says Katy with contempt. "Weel, then, I gie it back to ye, gude man. I accept naething frae strangers.''

"But my counsel is free.''

"It's like yersel'. Good e'en.'' (She starts.)

"Stay,'' cries Willie, "ye're alane?''

"I am, an' I wish to remain alone.''

"Ye're here by yersel'?''

"O yes, be sure o' that or ye'd no be speerin' the question."

"But ye'll be wantin' protection."

"I would na' were it not for ye."

"I'll protect ye. It is ma dooty."

"Forget yer duty, then."

"It's naething but a woman, like yersel', could make me."

"I wonder. Weel-a-well. Ye could forget it then?"

"The deil is in a woman's eyes to drag the best man down."

"Aye—mon—an' what a little thing can make a saint a sinner."

"Nay. What is seenfu' in th' weeked is only natural in the gude. Listen—ye're alane. The husband neglects ye, and a friend would care for ye. What then, is a gudewife's dooty?"

"Ochon! What should a poor woman do?"

"Aye!"

"Tam O'Shanter is my husband an' he neglects me."

"Aye! Aye!"

"I am Katy, his wife, who's forgotten."

"Aye! Aye! Aye!"

"And ye're Willie, the gude friend who would comfort me?"

"Aye! aye! aye! aye! 'Twould be my dooty! What then is yours?"

"This!" (She suddenly seizes and throws him to ground.)

"Nay!" he cries. "Haud! Haud!"

"And this!" (Places her foot on his breast.) "When the husband's awa' the gudewife will na' forget!"

"Mercy! Haud! haud! For gudeness sake!"

"This!" (Stands on him.) "When the gude man's gone, the honest woman takes his part an' her ain"—(kicks him)—" Go!"

"It's ma dooty!" groans Willie as he hurries off.

Katy stands, in tears, and exclaims:

"O, Tam O'Shanter! Tam O'Shanter! Thank yer stars that ye're spared that much o' my strength. What I have wasted on him is that much less for you!" (She sits on bank.)

"O, gudewives! gudewives! Men may try us; but, an' we want to stand, we need na' fall." (Rises.) "But I could murn for the sorrow o' it and sing dool for mysel' an' my 'bletherin, blusterin', drunken Tam! Weel-a-weel! Will-a-wa'! Ochon! Ochon! ochon-a-rie!" (Sits weeping.)

Tam is heard singing on the road:

"Saw ye roarin' Katy, roarin' Katy, roarin' Katy!
Saw ye roarin' Katy, lookin' for O'Shanter?"

(Very loud)

"O, Tam he was a ploughman gude
As ever sprang frae Highland sod;
But to the gudewife by his side,
A loon was Tam O'Shanter!

"Saw ye roarin' Katy, roarin' Katy, roarin' Katy!
Saw ye roarin' Katy, lookin' for O'Shanter?"

(He repeats in drunken style.)
(Katy speaks.)
"It's himself, as fou' as the reever i' th' spring
flood.   I wonder he can sing when he's too fou'
to ride.   He's sae droonk he makes even the
mare stagger."
(Tam shouts.)   "Whoa! whoa! there, Meg!
Whoa!"
(Katy looks.)   "I wonder what's the matter
now?"
(Tam shouts.)   "There' a bogle in the road!
Heh!   Hide yersel'.   Ye scare the mare!"
"Aye, mon!   We'll see."   (She calls.)
"Come, Meg!   Come here! Poor beast!   I war-
rant not a mouthfu' all the day!"   (She pulls
up grass.)   "Here, Meg!"   (Calling and cry-
ing.)   "Come, Meg!   Come, Meg!   Come!"
Meg comes, with Tam drunk on her back—

she runs to Katy and eats out of her hand. Katy speaks to her and fondles her, but does not notice her rider.

"Ah, Meg! ye dear auld friend an' beastie! are ye comin' home the day? I'm lonesome wi'out ye, Meg! Ochon! Sae lonesome!" (Cries.) "But ye'd na' leave me a' alane! It's no yer fault. Ye'd think o' those who cared for ye; I know ye would, poor Meg. Ye're but a beast, but ye ha' heart enough for that; an' sae I love ye, Meg! An' sae I'll do for ye sae long as either live! My arms about yer neck! My hand to smooth yer top and words to soften yer sorrow! Poor Meg, when human cattle are unkind, ye'll na' forget. So—we'll gae hame! I'll get yer supper an' a gude dry bed. Come, Meg, my gude, my only friend, come hame!"

(Takes hold of bridle.)

Tam sings while stupidly drunk:

"Saw ye Tam O'Shanter—Tam O'Shanter?"

Katy—unnoticing—replies:

"I've na' seen him. Ye've na' seen yer master, have ye, Meg? Nay, an' ye had, ye'd nae stand out in rain an' cauld, tied to a post, whiles he sits drinkin' by the bleezin' fire! Come hame!"

Tam sings loudly:

"O, Tam, he was a ploughman gude," etc.

Katy replies to Meg:

"Once on a time he was, Meg; but this is no the master of your better days! That's na' the man was kind to ye! That's na' the gude man swore he lo'ed me, nay—let's gae hame—perhaps he's waitin' for us there—come, Meg."

"Whoa!" cries Tam, "ye lanky loon! How can I haud my seat? I'll fa'." (Sings.)

"Sae fou' was Tam O'Shanter!"

"Aye," says Katy. "Meg, what's that load on yer tired back? E'en drop it off and let it lie awhile an' maybe it can learn to walk. I walked the ways here—*it* can walk it hame." (She drops Tam off.) "Come, Meg, I know ye feel easier now." (Leads her to bank and gets on.) "Gee up, my bonnie Meg, *the gudeman's waitin' for us hame!*" (She rides off on Meg.)

Tam sits on ground in drunken stupor and shouts after her:

"Ye'll wait till I come! A' right! A' right! Put the mare in my bed an' curry me off! Whee! Gie me some oats an' let me sleep i' th' barn! When Katy's hame the house is too fou'!" (Sings)

"An' sae is Tam O'Shanter!"

(Falls over).

Holey Willie returns and looks after Katy and Meg.

"Ah, Heaven be praised! The auld mare's bearin' her awa'. Weel, let her gang. She's a sour grape to Willie. What's this she's drapped? Tam, as I live, an' drunk as usual. My duty is to raise the fa'en; but sin' I could na' conquer the wife, I hate to carry the husband! Ah, weel! It's ma poonishment. I'll bear ma load. Get up, ye sawney!

"What's there?" says Tam. "Eh! What's that? A bogle or a deil?"

"Neither, but ye'll see onything."

"Naething like you! Eh! now I see; ye're my mare, Meg. Whoa! ye auld tail-swetchen deevil, ye—whoa!"

"Ye're a donkey," says Willie, in disgust.

"Hic—" says Tam, "I'm vera near one—whoa!"

"Ye're a mon o' no standin'," says Willie.

"That's reason I ride," says Tam. "Whoa! ye gray grump, ye—whoa!"

"Get up!" says Willie.

"Up where?" says Tam.

"Here on me back."

"Where are yer stirrips? Whoa!"

"Oh, what a load o' sin," groans Willie.

"Well—if I am, ye'll carry me easy! Stand still, ye cloutie!"

"Get up!" says Willie, as he mounts Tam on his back. "It's screepture—bear yer load!"

"Ye're right!" says Tam, "I'm Baalam! Gee! Gae lang!"

He rides off on Willie's back.

As they disappear, William and Gilbert Burns come up the path. Gilbert—assisting his father—speaks, as he advances.

"Do you feel better, father?"

"Ah, Gilbert, I don't know. Sometimes I think I do and then——"

"Well, father?"

"Gilbert, it's no the Eastlin wind that chills my heart, nor a' the cold that blows frae Highland hills. It is the thought that when misfortune comes to me all my poor bairns must share it."

"Have we not always done so? And think you we should sorrow now, except, dear father, it should be for you?"

"Thanks, Gilbert. Oh, my boys! my boys! your sisters and my wife! How patient and how faithful ye've all been to me."

"No, father, we've never half repaid the love and care you've given us."

"I'll not hear it. Since Robin was a boy in

Ayr—half-clothed, half-fed, as well we know, he's always done the labors of a man. Summers and winters, worked all day to keep us all together! And now he's come to be a man, with naething to reward, and only you to help him; for, God knows, when I die I leave you no inheritance!"

"The best, dear father—a brave example and an honest name."

"Ah, well, I've done the best I might in all our poor surroundings—and having done my all, it may be better I should go—there'll be one care the less—one less to worry you!"

"Father, I will not hear you say it."

"Ah, well, my son, I know that Robin feels restraint. His temper's like to mine—sometimes despairing, sometimes all astray. I see it. Others tell me. Murdock, his friend and tutor, knows his mind. He often says he'll go away from Scotland and from endless toil—from counsels, cares and miseries, and I don't blame him—no! my God! I do not blame him!"

"Father, you do no justice to his heart. He loves you—loves us all, and for our dear auld Scotland, he had rather die a peasant on her hills than live a prince elsewhere."

"Ah! ah! If I could know all this, as you do. Brothers have secrets which no father ever knows. It tears my heart to think it, yet I feel he would be leaving us!"

"Father, look there!" (He points down the path.) "There is your answer—there the man and there the lass that binds him."

"Robert—and Mary Campbell!"

"Does that not tell ye all? Worlds could not tear him from this place while she is here! Come. The man whose heart is hallowed by a woman's love can never harm his kindred."

They disappear. Willie returns and speaks with mock humility:

"I ha' done ma dooty! I've cast down ma load o' sin! An' I feel the relief o' the blessed! Brither O'Shanter is lyin' by the roadside amang the birches he so reechly desarves. A-weel! I'm repaid for the humeeleation, for, on bearin' awa' ane ineequity I came upon anither—Mr. Robert Burns wi' his sinfu' arms around the slender waist o' Mary Campbell! Ah, weel! What we hunt for in vain, we stumble over un-awares. I'll do ma dooty! The sinfu' crea-tures maun be parted! They're standin' on the pracepece of love! It's ma dooty to gae below an' catch the ane who falls!"

A voice is heard down the road and a bonnie lassie—Madge McGowan—appears, with a stick and bundle, and a plaid on her arm. She walks

along singing carelessly until she encounters
Willie:—

> " I'm bonnie McGowan
> Frae Greenock I came
> To the hills an' the dales
> Where the sweet birds are singing——

"O—O!"—(she sees Willie)—"Shade o' ma
mither! Wow! It's a mon! Stan' back! stan'
back! Dinna ye come near *me!* I'm a' the
way frae Greenock an' I ha' na' seen a mon sin'
yesterday!"

"Then ye are ripe for the seckle," says Willie.
"Whither does the fair lambkin wander?"

"Ah—sir—I now see ye're na' sae young nor
sae attractive as I thought, an' I can trust ye!"

"Ye can. I'm the bell-wether o' th' flock!
What I ower-loup the ithers crawl under!"

"Then, sin' ye give me leave to speak to a
mon by the wayside——"

"A-weel! If ye thenk it's too public we
can just gae further in the wood."

"Oh, weel! ye can gae as far in the wood as
ye will; but Madge McGowan sees mair attrac-
tion in the dirt in the road!"

"Ah—weel! Weel, if ye prefer the broad road
that leads to destruction to the narrow ane that
leads elsewhere wi' me—I'll not stay ye—as

yer business may be urgent, and Greenock will be lonesome till ye get back!"

"Not at a'! The boys were fighten aboot me when I left, an' they'll keep it up till my return."

"I dinna thenk I'll gae to Greenock," says Willie; "when do ye gae back?"

"The Soonday after Saturday. Is yon the loaning to the Castle o' Montgomery?"

"Ane end o' th' path gaes that way—the ither awa'. An ye come wi' me ye'll be on the right road."

"Dinna fash yersel'. I dinna care for it."

"But it's ma dooty, an' I must."

"Then tell me, does Mary Campbell o' the West Highlands live there still?"

"Weel, just at present she's engaged elsewhere!"

"An' where then can I see her?"

Willie takes her hand and speaks mysteriously:

"Hush! never disturb a cooin' dove! Let me lead ye into new pastures."

"Ah, bah!" says Madge. "Lang-shanks, I'm no sheep!"

"Na—then," says Willie, putting his arms around her, "yer just a female lamb!"

"But no for you!" (She tears herself away.)

"I'm Madge McGowan, a free girl frae Greenock, and I dinna want any auld bell-wether bleatin' around me! B-a-a-a!"

She goes. Willie looks after her and exclaims:

"Ba-a-a! Ye may be, *ma belle, whether* ye will or noo! Ah! I maun strive to turn her on the right path! An' if I do, I'll tether her! But first I'll turn the flock o' gossips on this fertile field an' let them graze upon one scondal while it's green! This Master Burns has scurrelized me in his sotarical sangs—I'll scondalize him in his stolen love! I'll skaur the kintra round but I'll bring them a' to catch this Master Robin cooin' wi' his mate! Ha! ha! I'll do ma dooty noo!"

He rubs his hands and steals out of sight. After a pause a love tune is heard—and Robert Burns and Mary Campbell appear—coming down the path. They advance slowly, his arm around her as they walk—Mary speaks:

"Robert, it is growing late, and I must leave you now."

"Mary," says Robert as he clasps her to his heart, "I cannot speak the word that parts us even for an hour. Oh, say you will not go. Come, let us talk all night as we have done all day!"

They sit on bank, under blossoming haw tree.

"Tell me again you love me, Mary!"

"I've said it over half an hundred times," says Mary, as she smiles and looks into his face.

"Well, then," says Robert, "let the echoes shout it back a thousand more, and Ayr repeat it, talking as it goes!   I'd never tire to hear it!"

"Then, Robert Burns, I love you!"

"And Mary Campbell, this is all my answer," says Robert, as he presses his lips to hers. "For well ye know my heart is yours beyond the poverty or wealth of words to speak!"

"I know without the asking, Robert! and if you ask me why I love you so, it's only—just —because—I love you!"

"Mary, there is no other reason half so good. *I love you.*   Only that—*those three words turn the world!*

> " Tho' I were doomed to wander on
>   Beyond the sea, beyond the Sun,
> Till my last weary sand was run—
>   Till then—and then I love thee!"

He clasps her passionately. She modestly releases herself, and starts to go.

"Robert, it is growing late."

He stays her—and still holds her hand.

"I know—I know; but still I love to linger

with you here, as in the days when first we met. Ah, Mary, that sweet time when first we thought of love, and when I took a briar or a thistle sting from out your girlish hand and dared not look into your wondering eyes!"

"I'll ne'er forget," she answers, lost in revery.

"Tell me. dear Mary, you'll not go."

"I must," she answers sadly, "for your sake and for my own."

"No—no! Not leave me now, when, maybe, you'll be going far away—to your old Highland home."

"Oh, Robert, don't remind me we must part!"

"Mary!" he says in deep surprise; but she continues in a troubled voice and speaks through many tears.

"It had been easier had I gone before. I should have gone three days ago—for my father and my friends must see me and know all before I am your wife, dear Robin; and then I only go that we may sooner be the happier."

"Mary!"

"But when I'm gone—then, Robert, you'll forget me!"

"No, Mary, no. A man may sometimes in his life forget all else—his first love never! It lingers in his heart till the last throb and ceases only when his eyes are closed in death!"

"Robert," she replies, "I love you very dearly; but never selfishly. It is your happiness more than mine I think of, and if I ever found you could be happier without me, I'd go away forever!"

"Mary, you would not—nay, you could not do so. Go where you will you cannot leave me! And come to me what may—what other love or other sorrows—my Highland Mary ever will be with me!"

"Robert!" she cries, embracing him.

"Yes, Mary, for I feel, let fate do what it may, our fortunes and our lives will be inseparably linked together, and love will be the theme where'er our names are spoken!"

"I've sometimes thought so, too," she says—and then continues, marked and solemnly, as she looks her lover in the face: "I dreamed one night you were a great man, Robert—famous around the world—and yet your heart was then as now—you called me Mary still!"

"Wife of my heart!" he answers, clasping her. "Mary, forever mine! What then?"

"I am afraid to tell—I thought—I thought I never could be yours, but I could help to make

you great! And that alone was happiness to
me."

"Mary, my better angel! All your love is
like an inspiration! I never may be much in
this great world, but of one thing I am certain
—no man is ever poor who has an honest
woman's love!"

"Be sure you have that always," Mary says,
"whether I am here or far awa'. Then rest
content till I return—and should I never
come—"

"Ye'll be my Mary still! Some think a spirit
dwells in every star—and of this hope ye canna'
altogether rob me—*you will be mine in Heaven!*"

"Yes, Robert, yes—and more—I will be faithful until death!"

Both seem greatly impressed, and Robert, who
has removed his cap, speaks with much feeling
and solemnity.

"Dear Mary! As you promise me, I pledge
my word to you, and on this sacred book you
gave me, here we plight our troth; so swear
with me—to live for, to love one another until
death do us part!"

These words they speak together, and this
done, they look into each other's eyes and read
there what no words need tell. They rush into
each other's arms and utter one another's names.

"Robert!"

"Mary!"

In this position Madge encounters them—and starts back in an innocent surprise.

"Oh—ah! yer pardon!" she exclaims, "but ye're sae mexed up, I dinna ken ane frae the ither! Which of ye's Mary Campbell?"

At the sound of Madge's friendly voice Mary starts.

"Why! Madge McGowan!"

"Aye!" says Madge. "A' th' way frae Greenock—who's the Jo?" (Points to Robert.)

"My best friend, Robert Burns," says Mary, introducing him.

"An' *your* friend a' the same!" says Robert, as he takes Madge kindly by the hand.

"How queek he is acquaint!" says knowing Madge, with an arch look. "He ought to live in Greenock. There's business for him there!"

"But, dear Madge, tell me," Mary says, "what brought ye?"

"I brought mysel'. Was goin' to the house; but, lookin' for the gate, looked back and saw ye here. I've come for ye."

"For me?"

"For Mary?" asks Robert, in surprise.

Madge answers Mary in a breath:

"Yer uncle's dead; your brither's sick;

BURNS' COTTAGE, ALLOWAY.

faither's awa' an' mither lonely—want ye to come home!"

"I heard a rumor of it," answers Mary, "near a week ago and should have gone, either to Campbellton or to Dunoon."

"I see," says Madge, as she looks at Robert knowingly, "I see what kept ye back. If I'd a Jo like that I'd be in Greenock eight days every week."

"We'll go to-morrow morning," says Mary sadly. "Robert, you will not blame me now?"

"God speed ye!" Robert answers. "But come back; and now the gloamin's near—I'll see ye to the yett, an' you, her friend, the same."

"Na, na!" says bonnie Madge, "ye'll gang yer waus alane. I dinna thenk yer talk would eenterest me, an' it might enterfere wi' ye! I've been thot way mysel'."

"Then follow us," says Robert, as he and Mary laughing, turn to go—"not our example —follow us! Mary, come!"

And as they go away in lover fashion, arm in arm, Madge stands and looks—a sort of envy in her eyes.

"Aye, I'll come too," she says—"but out o' sight, and out o' hearin', mind. I'm only a poor innocent girl frae Greenock, an' I dinna wish to blush when I'm awa' frae hame. Ah, weel! if Mary should, by ony acceedent, be unable to gae, maybe he could gae in her place. I'm sure I'd take good care o' him an' return him safe after he'd seen the sights o' the town. But what a flock o' bonnie lasses ha' we here? These are some more o' his best friends—nay, but the bell-wether's after them—aha! He sets them on to Mary's lover—oho! this is an ambush! Weel, I'll no' see that young mon harmed if Madge can cercumvent it! Greenock, you've taught me mony trecks, teach me ane noo!" (Saying which she hides among the bushes by the road. No sooner is she concealed than a lot of Scotch lasses come down the path and peer about the place.)

"There's na ane here," says Nannie.

"Na sign o' Robin, let alane a woman," says fair Chloris.

"Naething but tracks in lover's lane."

"Then Willie must ha' fooled us!"

"Nay—nay, it's real," says Clarinda, looking in the road. "Here are the marks o' hob-nailed shoon——"

"An' here a milkmaid's patten," Nannie says—examining the marks.

"Right!" says Clarinda. "It's Rob an' Mary Campbell!"

"Haud!" says Sylvie, "here's anither. The footgear o' a city girl!"

"That's me!" says Madge, as she peeps slyly from her ambush by the road.

"Gude Lord!" says Nannie, highly shocked. "He's after every girl in Scotland!"

"He's written to me!" Clarinda says, producing proof.

"Verses to me!" says Chloris—showing them.

"Love-talk to me!" says Nannie.

"To you! He! Love to you?" Clarinda asks.

"What! my Jo write to you?" cries Chloris.

"Ye see—I ha' the ca' o' you," says Nannie proudly.

"Oh! ha' ye?" Sylvie says. "Weel—take that!"

"An' that! An' that! an' that!" shout all the three—and start to fight—while Nannie, taunting, sings:

> " What's a' the steer, kimmer?
> What's a' the steer?"

and Chloris sings in answer:

> " Robin is fra hame, lass,
> An' still he is na' here!'

To which her rival readily rejoins:

> " Then lace yer bodice blue,
> An' trim yer cap anew;
> But Robin, when ye find him,
> Is na' the ane for you!"

And then, together, tauntingly:

"What's a' the steer, kimmer—what's a' the steer?
Robin is frae hame, lass, an' still he is na' here!

> In vain yer bodice blue;
> You may set your cap anew;
> For Robin, when ye find him,
> Is na' the ane for you!"

Tam O'Shanter, roused by the singing, staggers in among the girls and joins in drunken style, with his own tune and words:

" Saw ye gudewife Katy,
Mother Katy—scoldin' Katy?
Saw ye my wife Katy, ridin' on auld Maggie?"

At sight of him all the girls exclaim:
"It's Tam O'Shanter!"
And as well as drunkenness will allow, he answers:
"Hic! aye! An' Tam O'Shanter weeshes to enform ye—hic! that he canna' sleep in sic a squeelin' noise! Hic! Eh, I thought it was my wife come back, an' it sobered me up a bit —wow!"

"An' were ye here then?" question the girls.

"What then? Where then? Hic! Nay! I was *there* then!" (Points up the road.)

"But have ye seen 'em?" the girls inquire.

"Ha' I *seen* 'em? Yes, an' *had* 'em often. Hic! an' sae has souter Jonny, too. Hic! Don't talk about 'em, or I'll see 'em crawl—hic!"

"Eh," say the girls, "they're hidin' in the bushes then!"

"The deil they are!" says Tam. "Tak' 'em off! Tak' 'em off!"

"Oh, we know," says Nannie, "we saw their tracks in the road."

"Ye did?" says Tam, "then don't ye let 'em come near me! Keep 'em awa'! Keep 'em awa'!" (He hides behind the girls.)

"But let 'em gang their gates," says Chloris. "We wouldn't be in their shoes——"

"Don't!" cries Tam. "Dom but they'll be in my boots!"

"Tell us about 'em," the girls demand as they gather about him.

"An' I do I'm dommed!" says Tam, as he stamps about in the road. "Let's change the soobject! Hic! where's Meg?"

"Your mare? We haven't seen her."

"Well, then," says Tam, "I know a woman

has, an' straddled her, an' rode her off, an' left me here just like a gowk!"

"To walk! eh, Tam? Ha! ha! ha! ha!"

"To walk? Nay, nay, I rode the donkey."

"The donkey!"

"Yes, Haley Willie! till he threw me off!"

"Oh! ho! ha! ha! ha! ha! ha! ha!"

"Aye, ye may laugh, girls; but it was na laughin' matter for him to carry me—nor for me, when he let me fa'. Look here—I paid my siller for a gude drunk, an' now it's a' knocked out o' me! But I'm avenged!"

"How so?"

"Dinna ye see? I was left here for drunk an' I'm sober! I was left here to walk, an' I ride! I was left here, by ane woman, to be alane, an' I'm surrounded by a dizzen o' 'em!" (He sings in great glee:)

> " Oh, Tam he was a ploughman gude
>   As ever sprang frae Highland sod," etc.

As he sings all the girls encircle him, and hand in hand, sing and dance around him:

"Saw ye Tam O'Shanter? Tam O'Shanter!
Saw ye Tam O'Shanter, lookin' for his Maggie?"

"Oh!" says Tam, "but I'm too sober! It's ma poonishment! A-weel! If I maun walk,

I'll dance, too! I maun soofer for ma crimes!
But eh! to be sae lanely!'' (He leers at the
girls.) "It's a dreadfu' contreetion! It makes
me repent o' ever bein' married!''

"Weel, now, Tam,'' says Nannie, "now that
ye can understand——''

"Hic! aye!'' (He tickles her.)

"Tell us what we want to know.''

"Ah!'' says Tam, "it's muckle a woman
wants to know an' it's little she *don't!*''

"But tell us, Tam,'' they all exclaim.

"Eh! what? ye sousie lasses. Were ye ever
married?''

"Never.''

"There's no a married ane amang ye?''

"Nay,'' they answer, "but there should be.''

"Ye're right,'' cries Tam, "come to me arms!
Eh! but it's dreedfu' to be sae lonely! Come
to my arms again!''

"Nay,'' persists Nannie, "but tell us. Did
ye na see Robin an' Mary Campbell here
about?''

"O-o-h! He's the ane ye're speerin' for?
Oh, aye! Tam, ye can tak' a drap!''

"Tell us,'' says Chloris, "where they are.''

"Well, then, they're doon there by the path
awaitin' by yon haw-tree!''

"They are?" exclaim the girls in great delight. "Come on!"

"Stop!" cries Tam, as he stands in the path and waves them back, "ye'll no disturb them!"

"Why?"

"I'll tell ye. There, by the road, where Willie let me fa', 'twas Robin stooped to pick me up, an' Mary Campbell helped him! Now Tam O'Shanter stands their friend 'gainst a' the cry o' Scotland!"

"Gude! gude!" cries Chloris. "Tam, we like ye all the better for it!"

"Aye! aye!" they all exclaim. "Tam's right! We like him for fair play!"

"Ye do? Then, bonnie lasses, I am yours as well!" (Calls down the road:) "Meg, gae on hame, an' tak' the auld woman wi' ye. I'll bear ma poonishment alane!"

"But stay," says Nannie, "there's Haley Willie back again!"

"Aye!" says Tam, "an' as fu' o' the auld deil as I was fou' o' barley corn!"—pointing out Willie. "There's the oreegenal frae the garden o' Eden. Awhile ago I had 'em in me boots, now ane o' them's in me eye. Gee! If I only had me feddle here I'd make him dance! But whist! Let's catch the deil at his ane game." (He whistles and beckons.)

"Hey! Robin—hey! Come here!" (He hides with the girls, among the trees, as Willie re-appears and looks after them.)

"It's Tam! The lasses will lead him a chase. If they don't sober him naething will! I've stirred them up all round!"

(Madge comes out and stands on bank watching.)

"The giglets hae gotten the gillie, an' auld lang-shanks is mutton for me. This is the game the Greenock girl brings doun when she veesets the kintra!"

(She sits on the bank and pretends to cry, "Boo-oo-oo-ooh!")

"Eh!" says Willie, "the lomb! she's back in the fold. They never stray far alane. So, the lambkin's back in the right road again?"

"I om! I om! O, maister shepherd, tell me where'll I find ma mither?"

"Yer mither! Ah, I dinna ken; but would no the auld buck that wears the bell, do juist as weel?"

"Ah—weel!" she sighs, "l thenk ye would. I'm calling to ye—ba—a—h!"

"Come to ma arms!" says Willie in delight, as he sits down beside her. "It' ma first dooty to look after the weaklins o' the flock." (Embraces her.)

"Oh—baah!" cries the lamb.

"Weel—bah!" says Willie, soothingly, "but dinna be afraid. I'll be a mither to ye!"

"An' is that all?"

"A faither an' a mither."

"Naething else?"

"Aye! a' the bell-wethers i' the flock! Ba! Baa! Baah!"

(At this Tam and all of the girls come out of the wood and surround them—all crying:)

"Ba—ah! Ba! baah!" Then all go round them singing:

"Saw ye Haley Willie—Haley Willie—Haley Willie?
  Saw ye shepherd Willie doin' o' his duty?"

(All laugh and point at Willie, who starts up indignantly. Madge laughs.)

"It's a lie!" cries Willie. "It's no me! I'm not myself! I'm anither mon!"

"Aye! yer waur nor ye thenk," says Tam, "but ye're Ill-willie a' th' same!"

"An' ye?"—ask the girls of Madge.

"Me?" replies the innocent Madge, "I'm just a playfu' lettle lomb! I set the trop an' lured him wi' a baah!"

(Girls all laugh and point at Willie, and cry:)

"Baah!!!"

"The artfu' hizzie!" cries Willie furiously. "It was a' her faut. The trap I set for Robert Burns——"

"Ye got yerself, ye deevil ye!" says Tam.

"But he shall pay for a'!" says Willie. "See here's his scondal upon me!" (He gives written paper to Tam and takes others from the girls.)

"An' here—an' here. There's not a lass but has some seenfu' love-sang frae him. *Here, read you!*" He hands them to Father and Gilbert Burns, who now appear.

"His faither! Weel, I'm glad ye ken!"

"Thank God, I do," says the old man proudly. "I ken the guid o' Robert Burns—an' for the ill that's true, I warrant there is naught sae bad his father canna hear it."

"Read for yersel'!" says Willie scornfully.

"I will," says Father Burns, with emphasis, "and his own words shall answer for him to the world."

"Aye, judge him by them, father!" Gilbert says; "if what he's written's to condemn, then what he's written shall uphold him, too."

"That's justice," says his father, "and so it now shall be. But why this stir? Willie, why are you here?"

(Tam explains:)

"We found him kinttlin' wi' this Greenock

lass—billin' an' baain'—heads an' thraws the-gither—bah! ye auld bletherin' Beelzebub!"

"Nay, Maister," says Madge quietly. "I'm but a lamb. The auld bell-wether lured me!"

"Na doubt! Na doubt!" says Father Burns, as he looks over the writings Willie gave him.

(Two little boys lead an old ewe down the path. She is tied by a string and has about her neck a flowery wreath.)

"More eenocence!" says Madge. "Don't blame *me*. Here's anither stray. Aye, callans, it's a braw bet of a sheep."

"She's lookin' for the maister," says the boy.

"Just like the ithers," Tam suggests.

"An' what's it's name?" asks Madge.

"It's Robin's pet yowe, 'Mallie.'"

"Mallie! A female!" Madge exclaims, as she takes her by the string. "Come yer waus, Mallie! I dinna ken muckle aboot ye, Mallie, but, an' ye've ony respect for yer mither, gie the bell-wether a wide berth." (She leads Mallie away, looking back at Willie, as she goes.)

"And now speak *you!*" says Father Burns to the assembled girls. "Why are you lasses here?"

(They are silent.)

"Aha!" says Willie, as he rubs his hands. "They'll na answer; but I will! Sin ye put ane on me, I put a' three on Robert Burns! now let him answer it who can!"

"I'll answer for them all!" says Robert manfully, as he appears in the centre of the group. All exclaim:

"Robert!"

(Madge rushes to his side.)

"Ah, my only frien' amang them!"

"Eh!" cries Willie with delight, "even her! Guid! An' when he onswers for 'em a', let this young hizzie answer too!"

"Stop!" cries Robert interposing, "not a word against this lassie here, or I'll na answer for myself!"

"You would protect her then?" the girls demand.

"Protect her! Aye!" Robert answers, "as I would you, or you, or any other woman!"

"Robert!" his father asks, "who is the lass?"

"Until a half an hour ago I never saw her," Robert answers with respect.

"A stranger here?"

"A friend of Mary Campbell, and that name makes her sacred!"

"But still—alone——"

"Therefore has need of friendship most! When a woman is upright, give her your love! When she's downright, give her your hand!

When she's fallen, your pity and your help!
And when a stranger, homeless and alone, no
matter what she may be, give her protection
and defence!"

"Gude! gude!" is heard on every side.

"Guid!" cries Tam, "dom but it's mair than
guid! Scotland forever! Come oot in the road,
auld Beelzebub, an' I'll wallop th' ground wi'
ye!"

"But stay!" says Father Burns, "what answer
ye to these?"—showing the verses to Robert.

"Nothing, father. What a man speaks he
may deny, but what he puts on paper speaks
against or for him for all time. I stand by what
is written—or by what's written fall!"

"Robert," says his father sadly, "these are
the love songs of an idle boy. They bring you
but discredit and disgrace!"

"Well, then to me let these dishonors come;
but spare you, father, and the ones I love each
word of mortal harm."

(Burns bows; goes up to Mallie, and then retires. Madge follows him.)

"A—ha!" says Willie.

"Ah—baa!" says Tam.

(Gilbert goes to his father and feelingly exclaims:)

"Father, for fifteen long, hard-working years

my brother's never had an idle day, and for the writings which discredit him and bring him but disgrace here's something from his last. It's called 'The Cotter's Saturday Night.' He read it to me Sunday when we took our walk." (Gilbert takes the verses from his pocket and gives them to his father.) "Read *these*, aud if there's idle love in *them*, 'tis of a kind that blesses every home; that graces every man and woman in the land and gathers honors all around the world!"

(Robert appears, leading Mary Campbell forward—followed by Madge with Mallie. He passes Mary to his father and then turns sadly away. All stand in great respect. Father Burns addresses her solemnly:)

"Mary Campbell, tho' you have faith in Robert Burns, trust not to what he says of love, for such things men sometimes deny; *but what he puts on paper proves him.* Read"—(giving her a small page of MS.)

(Mary stands in the center of the group, and taking the paper reads with great feeling:)

" Oh, happy love, where love like this is found;
   Oh, heartfelt rapture—bliss beyond compare;
  I've wandered much this weary mortal round
   And sage experience bids me this declare—

If Heaven a draught of heavenly pleasure share—
    One cordial in this melancholy vale,
'Tis when the youthful, loving, modest pair,
    In other's arms, breathe out the tender tale,
Beneath the milk white thorn that scents the even-
        ing gale.

(She goes to Robert and puts her head on his breast, as they sit on bank under the tree. Father Burns comes forward and reads impressively:)

" Then homeward all take off their several way;
    The youngling cottagers retire to rest;
The parent pair their secret homage pay,
    And proffer up to Heaven the warm request
    That He who stills the ravens' clamorous nest,
And makes the lily fair, in flowery pride,
    Would, in the way His wisdom sees the best,
For them and for their little ones provide;
But chiefly in their hearts with grace divine preside!"

(He goes to Gilbert, turning aside to conceal his emotion. Robert advances and stands uncovered in the center of the throng, and, with great feeling and spirit, recites from memory:)

" Oh, Scotia! My dear, my native soil,
    For whom my warmest wish to Heaven is sent,
Long may thy hardy sons of rustic toil
    Be blessed with health and peace and sweet content.
    And oh, may Heaven their simple lives prevent

From luxury's contagion, weak and vile,
  Then, howe'er crowns or coronets be rent,
A virtuous populace may rise the while
And stand a wall of fire around their much loved isle."

(Then to the air of "Red, red rose," which at this hour sounds like some great inspiring battle hymn, the populace take up the cry:)

For Caledonia and her cause,
Whate'er our fate my be;
We stand thro' life a living guard,
And for her we would die!

(And Robert—kneeling in the centre—sings the second part—followed by Mary's solo in a high, triumphant tone:)

ROBERT.—O, Scotia dear! our native land
The freedom Wallace gave,

MARY.—Each Scottish heart and Scottish hand
Is sworn to shield and save!

(Then, rising, she repeats the last two lines, in which all join in one grand culminating shout— the expression of their loyalty for native land and love for Robert Burns!)

*　　*　　*　　*　　*　　*　　*

As Donald Stuart's voice died out a spirit took its place which would not down. The audience in the schoolhouse rose and cheered and cheered again, as if outrivaling the people in the tale. The strong magnetic touch had done its work. Men shouted—women cried. The minister arose and raised his hands and this alone brought silence.

"No words," he said, "no words. Nothing can add to or can take away from what we feel. Thanks to our pilgrim and his magic wand.

"'One touch of Nature makes the whole world kin!' And this shall be my theme to-morrow in the little church. Till then do not disturb the impression and the inspiration of this hour.

"Good-night to all, and Heaven bless and guard you!"

END PART FIRST.

PART SECOND.

THE August night had come, and not come calmly, as the summer nights so often do; but this advanced in surly mood—complaining, muttering, threatening at times, when hidden lightning showed beneath a cloud or low, protesting voices broke upon the air.

The day had been somewhat tempestuous and summer showers swept down upon the country here and there, with eddying gusts foretelling their approach, and then retired, as if retreating on the northwest hills, where, as the night came on, the gathering tempest showed in force, foreboding a disturbing night, and elemental war. Upon the Highland peaks, at intervals, a signal showed, and in the distant Catskills low, rolling and continued sounds were heard, as if the ghostly crew were out and "lit their pipes and rolled their ten-pin balls" in full defiance of the world. Crash followed crash, resounding through the hills, then came the downpour from the clouds; but nothing in the country stops because it rains—going and growing are compulsions when it's wet—and the undaunted

hearts on Scotland Hill drank in the cool damp
air as a delicious draught, which made them
laugh and turn their faces up to the descending
storm and shout, "Ha! ha! come down!"

Lanterns and wraps and heavy shoes for all
those living near, and covered wagons for the
distant ones—"Come on! Who cares? 'More
rain, more rest,' may do for boys, but Nature
works right on except when it's too dry."

The gathering was equal to the first. The
spirit just the same. The decorations all that
summer and the people could afford—sun-flow-
ers and holly-hocks and wreaths of smiling faces
all around—a happy people for a happy time.
Even the minister showed in his honest, loving
face the joyousness he felt and as for Sandy
Ramsey, Drawback, Lindsay, and the others of
that ilk, their features were an entire show
with side-shows all thrown in.

Music, on this occasion, took the lead. A
fiddle helped the organ out, although they were
not friends and never quite agreed. The organ
would insist on its eternal double hypocritical
drawl, the whining, canting monotone and nasal
twang of over-pious talk—the fiddle meanwhile
scraping out a high pitched squeak, and then
relapsing in a comic snoring sound which made
the wicked laugh and pious smile.

But all the vocal parts were of the best; the Scottish songs were never better sung, save in the dear old land itself, and stories, readings, everything essayed showed that the extra time for preparation had been well employed. When it came Sandy's turn—before his name was called—he'd started in his speech, and talked right on while they announced his name—"*Sandy Ramsey—'Straight Path.'*"

"Of course," he said, "that's what I'm talkin' about; but ef ye'd like to know about the crooked path, I'll tell ye that.

"Where I got the three scruples I also got drunk an' went home where I leeved, after a big fall o' snow; an' staggered so I made a path like a ram's horn a' the way from the road to the house, an' it stayed—the drunkard's path; for I made it worse each time I went over it an every one that kem to the house got drunk goin' over it, too. One day a teetotler kem to give me reefermation, an' as he staggered up, says he: 'Young mon, ye're on the broad road to deestruction. Turn while there's time and take the straight and narrow path.' I cut him short. 'Look here,' says I, 'ye're drunk yersel'. I see it in yer e'e, an' I'll jest bet ye a week's board ye can't walk from here to the gate without staggerin' like a gin bottle rattlin' on a tray.'

He bet an' lost, an' I stayed there a week at his expense, an' in the drunkard's room. The path is oot there yet, a wetness to the crukedness of dreenk. Now, Mr. Feddler, an' you, young mon, who keeps squeezin' yer doleful tunes oot o' that sick music-box—ef eether o' ye can play a tune ye never saw or heard, go on and play it—an' I an' Father Lindsay will sing ye a duet! It just came oot frae the West, an' it's somethin' aboot a watch!"

"Music play up!"

At this command the two musicians smiled and struck a prolonged chord, and the two operatic orators stood up, each with one hand behind his back and one shoved in his breast. In this position they tried to look unconscious, and they did—but their delinquent voices failed to arrive in time to start—and Sandy nodded for another chord. It came with every note in the gamut, but none to suit it seemed, for now there was another pause and this time a demand to "play!" The obliging musicians complied—running all over, up and down the scale, lingering on such notes as they thought would do—but nothing lingered in the singers' ears.

Then Sandy laid it all to Lindsay, and giving him a kick, cried "sing!" which Lindsay did— or tried to do—but which was something like a shriek, and Sandy followed suit—each on a different key—and neither nearer than a hundred miles of the musicians, who were going *forte* and *ad lib-crescendo—ralantando*—everything they could—for both were wild with laughter now, in which the audience joined.

This ended the first verse amid applause so deafening that both the vocalists felt assured they had achieved success. To make sure, however, Sandy scowled at the musicians and beat the time—or what was left of it to beat. Then he determined to show how it should have been, and started the first verse again himself—taking Lindsay's tenor part and leaving him the bass. He opened up on a terrific shriek, and raised his head, and stood on his tiptoes; but what he wanted no one ever heard him reach, for Lindsay's little hoarse touch on the bass "brought down the house" and Sandy to his rescue—as he now essayed both parts—screeching out one line—growling out the next—and beating time—stamping and scolding—motioning how to play—and bawling "Larboard Watch!" in several voices and a dozen keys—with a cadenza in which watches, larboards, musicians, and Lindsays all blended in a mass, the audience meanwhile screaming with delight!

"Bravo! Bravo! Both!" the people cried.

"Encore!" "Encore!" But Sandy only bowed (his modesty forbade,) except to say:

"Me voice was cooltevated, plowed, cross-plowed an' harrowed in the West—an' I can seeng deuetts for one, or two, or three, or any number—*ef I ony have the key!*"

At this all laughed.

"Eh, ye may laugh," said Sandy, "an' as for ye, Deacon Drawback, ye have no more ear for music than yer mules, an' no more voice! But if ye'll come ootside maybe I'll mak' ye seeng a defferent toon frae what yer turnin' now!"

But Drawback only "Ha! ha'd!" as the others did, and Sandy rolled his swivel eye about the room, then went outside. Once there, his other eye fell on his adversary's mules.

"Ha! ha!" he said; "well, maybe then I've found the right key now!" and in five minutes' time, with very knowing looks, he came in quietly and took his seat.

The humor of the scene pervaded everything, and Donald rose, his face all smiles, and read from Barbara's manuscript:

TAM O' SHANTER INN, AYR.

BONNIE DOON.

Part Second.

Time:—*A Market Night in Summer.*

Scenes:—
{ The Auld Town of Ayr.
| The Road to Alloway.
| Kirk Alloway by Night.
| The Half-mile to the Brig.
| The Brig o' Doon.

"Ye banks and braes o' bonnie Doon
How can ye bloom sae fresh and fair?
How can ye chant, ye little birds,
When I sae weary fu' o' care?"

SCENE 1.

THE STREET AND INN AT AYR BY NIGHT.

Inn Sign at the corner:

> Auld Ayr Inn.
> Jon Anderson.

(Entrance door—steps and portico—large window, with bench underneath—lights inside showing through window—lamps burn in the street—people pass and repass.)

(Tam O'Shanter's mare, Meg, is hitched to a post on side of street.

(The sound of a fiddle is heard inside the inn—playing "Duncan Gray," to which, amid loud laughter, clinking glasses keep time to the symphony, then invisible chorus sings:)

> "Robin Burns comes here to woo—
> Rob Burns the ploughman O!
> Ere he goes we'll fill him fou,
> Rob Burns the ploughman O!"

(At the conclusion of this Tam O'Shanter sticks his head out of window and sings in loud, drunken manner:)

> " To every lass on Ayr or Doon
> We'll fill a glass an' drink her doun,
> For we are wakin' the auld toun
> For Rob Burns the ploughman O!"

(The chorus inside is repeated, with click of glasses and shouts as before—Tam's head disappears as auld Elfie comes down the street, leaning on a staff. She goes to the window and peers in.)

"Nae, nae," she says, "he is na there; yet where else can A' gae? They told me Robin was in Ayr the day, an' yet, for a' my wearyin' A' canna find him. A' was na hame when he ca'd at the auld biggin; but A'll see him here

—aye, an' A'll speir him who it was that did my work when A' was gane. Aye, but A' ken 'twas he. Ah, monie simmers past an' gane sin' A' saw my braw lad A' dandled i' my arms. A'll see him ance again. A'll wait him here— aye, tho' he come not a' th' nicht, auld Elfie'll wait." (She sits on seat under the window.)

(The singing is renewed and scraping of fiddle is heard inside. Loud laughter follows and the window-bole opens and Tam puts out his head and shouts:)

"Oh—yez! oh, yez! oh, yes! ony ane who has na gotten a saxpence come ye in an' ha' a stoup wi' me!"

(Laughter inside. They try to pull him in— auld Elfie recognizes Tam:)

"It's Tam O'Shanter at his auld trecks."

"Haud on! haud on!" cries Tam as he leans out. "There's something like a lassie here. Ane kiss for Tam!"

"Tak' it, ye deil ye!" says Elfie, as she kisses him.

(Loud laughing inside, in which Tam joins. Then, seeing the old woman he has kissed, he exclaims:)

"Auld Elfie! By me breeks! Weel, I'll na back oot! Anither! A gude theng is a gude theng even when it's auld. Dom but it's a gude thing it's dark! Haud! Here's your stoup to pay for it!" (He passes out a stoup to Elfie and sings:

"For we are wakin' the auld toun,
    For Rob Burns the ploughman O!"

"Aha, ye deil!" says Elfie as she laughs and drinks. "Ilka night yer fou'; but A' forgive ye; for yer heart's fou' too; auld Elfie ne'er forgets yer gudeness a' the winter days. The oatmeal an' the barley rips for me an' puir auld Crumbie—ah, me! Who's this?—why, Rab?"

(She runs to Gilbert, mistaking him for Robert, as he comes to the inn.)

"Mistaken altogether," Gilbert says. "I'm only Gilbert Burns."

"His brither! Laddie, is it ye? An' yese na ken auld Elfie noo?"

"Elfie McLeod? Aye—aye—my gude auld friend! I ken ye now. Ye minded Rob when he was but a bairn."

"Aye, aye—an' spanked him weel; an' sang him sangs; an' tauld him tales, an' lo'ed him a' my days!"

"Bless ye, Elfie—yes, I mind it all; an' Robin's na forgotten ye!"

"An' never will," says Robin, as he comes and grasps her hand.

"Ah—ah! Rab—dear Rab—an' is it ye?" cries Elfie, through her tears.

"Elfie! my gude auld friend!" (They embrace and shake hands—the old woman dancing for joy.)

"Ah—Rab—A' bin lookin' for ye a' the day."

"I thank ye for it, Elfie, frae my heart. Ye were not hame when we called in. Ye got my word?"

"Aye, aye—an' a' th' wark ye did for me! Oh, Rab—the cattle an' the firein'. Oh! ye're sae gude to me! But here A' am!"

"Gude heart—ye're tired—sit down!"

"Nae, A'd stan' lookin' at ye a' th' nicht!"

"Nay, sit ye down. A stoup o' ale; come ben wi' me!"

"Nae, nae, na ben the Inn. They'd turn me oot."

"They'd be right sorry if they did. A-weel, sit here—ye'll ha' a stoup?"

"A' had it here." (Tam and others sing inside.) "Frae Tam."

"I see. Weel, then, tak' ane wi' me!" (He taps on window. Tam sticks his head out and exclaims:)

"The Lord preserve us! But Rab's got her noo!" (He sings.)

> " Robin Burns came here to woo—
>   For Rob Burns the ploughman O!"

"Tak' a stoup wi' me. Three here! (Mugs are set out.)

"Rab, come ye in!" says Tam.

"Elfie," says Robert, "I'll see ye down by yonder light in half an hour. Gae there an' ask for me an' wait. I'd talk wi' ye of other times."

"Weel—A'll be there. Elfie'll no sleep; but sit an' talk a' nicht o' ye an' auld lang syne!" (She goes down the street—Burns in the Inn. Gilbert reappears in company with Davie.)

"An' sae ye came to market here," says Davie. "I'm glad to see ye all frae auld Lochlea. I'm frae hame mysel'; but what brought ye? No more bad luck, I hope?"

"The worst; but that's not it. It was Robert's wish to see his birthplace once again, and bring poor father wi' us. The auld man's failin' fast an' it may be the last time here for a' o' us! But Robert's here!"

"Ah, Davie Sillar!" says Robert, as he comes to greet him, "is it you?"

"Aye, your true frien' forever!"

"Aye? Weel, Davie, Siller's a frien' to stand by."

"Ha! ha! prove me wi'out it, Rob. Welcome to Ayr!"

"Thanks, Davie; gude it's been for a' o' us.
Twa wagon loads o' boys an' girls, wi' father,
Gilbert an' th' rest!"

"Hey! brawlie! brawlie! Rob."

"Ah!" Robert cries. "But it is gude to feel
the glow within the heart. Ane breath o'
liberty; relief from care; the glory o' the country road, wi' Nature noddin' to ye on the
way!"

"Aye! aye!"

"Think o' a day in Ayr! The biggin where I
first saw light."

"Ye mean the smoke," says Gilbert, laugh-
ingly.

"A-weel—the light we could na see! The
ingle an' the single door. I trembled as I drew
the sneck, an' every one of us took off our caps,
an' father knelt an' prayed!"

"Robin!"

"Davie—he'll never come again until he
comes to Alloway, among the graves he
tended."

"Yonder he is," says Gilbert kindly. "I'll go
an' bring him here!"

(As Gilbert goes, Davie takes Robert aside:)

"Robin, I grieve that poverty has dealt so
hard."

"Ah—weel," says Robert, feelingly, "we'd

walked, but we'd a come. But Mallie's lambs
we sold gave us the siller for it—Davie,

> "It's no in titles nor in rank—
> It's no in wealth like Lunnon bank
> To purchase peace or rest.
>
> .   .   .   .
>
> If happiness hae not her seat
> And center in the breast!"

"Right, brither Scot and Scribbler," Davie
says, "there is my hand. A'm wi' ye thro' it
a'. I hear ye talked o' goin' to the Indies,
Rob?"

"When all else fails, I go. Jamaica, or I care
not where; but twa things stay me now."

"And they?"

"While father lives I'll never leave him; but
help him till the last. For him, for all, no
work's too hard; no fare too poor; no sacrifice
too great."

"And the other?"

"My Highland Mary and her love, which fills
my inmost heart!"

"She's worthy, Rob."

"Aye, but one more, Davie, I forgot——"

"Who?"

"Your love an' mine—the Scottish Muse!
She keeps us poor together!"

(Gilbert leads his father forward—Robert turns and greets him.)

"Father!"

"Mr. Burns," says Davie, bowing, with his cap in hand.

"I thank ye, lads. Wi' a' my heart, I thank ye!"

"Father, sit down," says Robert, as he brings a chair.

"Aye, Robin, I'm sae grateful for this visit to our auld home, an' good Kirk Alloway! It's a welcome, an' my last! My heart turns to it, but it canna keep me—naething can keep me wi' ye!"

"Courage, auld frien'," says Davie with regret. "All will be well. Gude-night. A'll see ye soon again. Robert, come here!" (They step aside.) "Rob, there's my han', an' if ye ever need me, ca'."

"Davie, God sain ye! I shall ne'er forget."

"Care for him, Rob, an' take him in! I go to take some lasses hame. We'll pass this way to see ye."

"Ye'll find me here. I'll lodge dear father in the Inn, an' go our ways th' morrow. Sunday's a day for travel, weel as rest. But come ye back."

"I will."

"If I'm no here—ye'll find me where ye see yon light."

"Aye, I ken the place. A' yer frien's are waitin' there to gie ye welcome for lang syne. There's half the lads an' lasses o' the town."

"Ah! Dear auld Ayr!" Robert exclaims.

> " Auld Ayr which none surpasses
> For honest men and bonnie lasses.

"So come ye back when father is asleep, an' a' is weel—we can't refuse a night o' it!"

(They shake hands and part—Davie going up the street—and Robert to his father. Gilbert goes into the inn and Tam and others shout inside. Haley Willie and Katy O'Shanter come down the street in conversation. Robert, while they talk, gives hay to Meg.)

"Woman!" says Willie, "I do ma dooty! I ha' brought ye here—now do the leestenen' for yersel'."

"I ken it a'," says Katy with a glance. "There's Meg tied there a' day—naething to eat, an' he's a' dreenk inside. Willie, ye're vera mean."

"I thonk ye!" Willie answers with a bow.

"But Tam's a worse!" says Katy.

"A-weel," says Willie, "I thenk ye ken. But that young deevil Robin's worse than a'!"

"I mind him there!" says Katy, pointing Robin out.

"Whist! then," says Willie, "I would na eeratate him. He has a way o' keekin' wi' his fute."

(Tam sticks his head out of window, as if for air—and cries out:)

"Whew! I'm glorious!" (He sees Katy.) "The wife! The deevil!"

(He disappears and shuts the window with a bang—Katy cries:)

"Ah, Tam! Ohone! The men! The men! There's no gude in them a' thegither. Meg, stay ye here—A'll come again an' bring ye!"

"An' me?" says Willie, following.

"You? Baah!" (Katy goes up the street.)

Willie looks after her and says quietly: "I'm a baad mon! Ah, weel, there's ane conseelation—twa—Tam is waur—an' Rob's no gude at a'!"

(Robert comes forward and confronts him:)

"Ah, Willie, if ye're preachin', let us hear. Don't waste your sweetness on the Ayr!"

" Jokin' again!" says Willie, "nae wonder ye're poor aff. Ye'd better wark. Yer sweetness is na wasted on the air on ony ither place I ken."

"Because," says Robin, "there's na gude place where ye're acquaint—but as for work—if ye warked as weel for ither's gude as ye strive for their undoing ye might be something like a man instead of the vile auld deevil that ye are!"

"Oh—ah!   Hoot—toot!   A   deevil am I? Heigh?"

"Yes! Never glower! Has na one ca'ad ye by your name before? Then tak' it home frae me, an' write it down against ye next forget!"

"Oh, ho! I'll na forget! I'll warm ye yet! I'll wark for that!"

"Work! work!" cries Robert. "No—no honest work for you! If you'd do manly work— come out wi' men, at mowin', reapin', in the hot sun or the cold—at the plough, or a' day on the weary threshing floor!   Will ye do aught of this?"

"I wull!   That's—nae—ye ken I canna do it."

"Ah, no—and yet ye're big and tall and strong as ithers are; but ye hae not the spirit nor the heart, an' liein', wi' you, is an easier task!"

"Dom!—Young man, see here. Ye're needin' gude advice!"

"Well, then, I'll tak' it frae a mon who comes by it honestly and one who does not give what he has never earned, nor preach what he has never yet performed."

"Tak' care! I ken your doin's wi' each country lass."

"I know, you've spied and speired and told it all—go on!"

"Well, then, I can. I hae the proofs. This day I saw ye in the widow's house."

"Aye—and in auld Elfie's too—what then?"

"Ah! ye confess! The Lord be praised my conscience is clear. I never wranged a widdy in my life!"

"The deevil doubt. They would na let ye! Let that go. Well, then, these hands, this day, have done the widow's work—tended her cattle —cut wood for her fire—warmed her poor home and let the sunshine in her heart!"

"You?" cries Willie, in astonishment.

"Aye—an' Tam O'Shanter, whom you love to revile, has given her the corn he brought to sell—even the fodder for his auld mare, Meg. Now go an' lie about this wi' th' rest."

"I'll say it'll no be for the widdy's gude. What's given by the weecked will no ease her sorrow, but add to her shame!"

"Silence! Not a word! Call Robert Burns the vilest of the vile, but not a slur upon a Scottish woman here—be she lass or wife, or widow or a witch. I'll not stand by and hear it!"

"Oh—ah! Offender and defender!" Willie sneers.

"Be it so! And be I what I may, to this I stand: *He who will not defend a worthy woman, is himself unworthy of the name of man!*"

(He passes Willie in great scorn, then turns and threatens him:)

"Now go! or there's one thing the wicked gives ye'll feel when ye receive."

"The keeck! the keeck! I understand! I'll no stay to receive it. I tak' the will for the deed! It's ma dooty."   He hurries down the street.

(William Burns rises and advancing to Robert, takes his hand.)

"Robert, your hand. If I have ever doubted you, it was my fault. If I have ever counseled ye, it was a father's love."

"Father!" Robert cries, "that name commands my life!"

"I'm sorry that ye lost your temper, Robert."

"I'm glad it's gone—although I hate to part with what you gave me, father!"

"Robert, if I have ever given you one uncanny gift—God knows I could na help it. 'Tis in nature to be imperfect. Let a' your failings come frae me then, if ye will; but a' your gude is Heaven-born, and has upon it, far above your humble birth, the patent of nobility!"

"Father, the bad that's in me I'll endeavor to subdue—the gude I'll try to honor."

"Then leave your loves behind ye—and go on your road of life in peace."

"The road of life's a dark uncertain course. Without the torch of love, we are lost in night an' a' the way's a-weary! Rather a stony road o'er rugged hills, where wild flowers bloom around ye, than a' the clearer and the better ways without them!"

(Gilbert comes out of the Inn.)

"All's ready, father!"

"Boys, gude night. God bless ye!"

"Good-night—God bless you, father!" both reply.

(They lead him to the open door and stand on either side. As the old man is about to go—he turns and speaks with great feeling:)

"Accept a father's thanks for all your love—for the day and its sights and the night and its rest. It is the last will come to me until I come again to Alloway!"

(He turns, and Gilbert leads him in. Robert is lost in thought.)

"Alas, that ruin drives its shadows over one sae good. Age has no hope; but youth can work its way. Toil is the Cotter's curse; but still a comfort, too, to those who can forget.

Oh, Mary Campbell, parted from me here, perhaps forever gone, why do I dream of thee? Why, in my sleep, hear you repeat that you may ne'er be mine? Why has another sweet face, like a shadow, come between? I must not think of it, nor Jeannie Armour more—nor Mauchline fair—nor Mauchline belles! Welcome, auld Ayr! Welcome auld haunts of happy love; and Bonnie Doon—oh, take me back again, that these dear scenes may mind me of the past and keep me faithful to it."

(Madge McGowan, worn and weary—as if from a long journey—appears before the inn and stops—seeing Robert, she exclaims:)

"Eh!—a mon! stand frae the way! I'm but a timid lass and maunna speak to ony mon—especially when in the street—alone at night!"

"Madge!" cries Robert, as he hears the voice.

"Eh!—is it ye?" she cries in joy. "My frien'! my frien'—I've found ye! oh, I've found ye!"   (Shakes his hand in excess of delight.)

"What is the matter?" Robert questions her. "Is it Mary? Speak!"

"A message frae her only," Madge replies. "I came first to Lochlie—found ye had started here, an hour ahead, an' sae I followed, a' the afternoon, the cart tracks in the road, until I found ye—for I could na rest until I'd kept my word—and given ye Mary's letter!" (She takes it from her breast and gives it to Robert, who opens it with trembling hands and reads:)

"DEAR ROBERT BURNS: How little ken we o' the sorrows and the chances that may come. I send poor Madge wi' this, that she may keep my place at the Castle o' Montgomery, fearing I never may come back. Robin, I know your father's ill, but, dearest, my poor brother's like to die. This, an' the cares that come to me, I must stand by, until the day when I can come again —if come I ever can. O, love, my dream is ever in my mind—that I shall see you nevermore. Pray that I may, as I do. Be good to Madge—she's been a frien' through all, and now, poor lass, she has na hame to shelter her. Be patient till I come, and stay assured I'll be there e'er the summer's over—or be dead! Dinna forget me! Remember a' our parting words. Think of our happy days by Ayr, and take the kiss I send ye.

"Robin, my ain, my only love!

"YOUR MARY."

(Robert kisses the letter and goes and leans upon the window-sill to hide his tears. Madge, seeing his sorrow, rushes to him and kneels and cries:) "O, turn me out i' the night for bringin' it Kill me—if it's brot ye harm."

"You know what she has said?" asks Robert kindly.

"More than she'd ever say. I know she'd die for you!"

"What were her words to you?"

"I canna tell ye all; but this she said: You must be patient, like to her, and take no care or sorrow till ye meet again?"

"My ain beloved Mary. Think ye she'll ever come?"

"Nae, never doubt. If she's alive—before the summer's passed—she'll come!"

"Well, then, let's look with brightness on the worst—but I'm forgetting *you!* Are you not tired?"

"It's naught to me. I was born on the road an' care na for Scots miles. I been o'er them a', an' ilka day gae jinketin' about—frae Gretna to Groat's house—Glasco' to Aberdeen—sae the leetle walk frae Greenock here is naething at a'!"

"Poor lass. Have you had anything to eat?"

"Naething. The haws are na ripe, an' my sillers a' gane."

"Take a' o' mine." (Robert gives money.) "Gae in. The best in Ayr is yours."

"Nay—I came to tak' Mary's place at the Castle o' Montgomery. I'll gae there in the mornin', an' I can wait till then."

"Not while I've a farthing or a friend in Ayr.

I'll order supper for ye.   Sit ye down and rest."
(He puts her in seat.)

"Nae wonder Mary lo'ed ye. I wish I only
lo'ed ye half as well!"

"I'd be proud of it," Robert says.

"Ye would?" says Madge, "ye're giein' me!"

"Nae," exclaims Robert; "I'd be proud of the
love and respect of every woman in the world."

"Eh me, an' I'm only ane o' them a'!" says
bonnie Madge, and then she adds as if the
words came from her heart—"But Mary's love
has been more to me than a' the lovers that I
ever met!"

"Good lass!" says Robert, touched by her innocent words. "I'll gie ye a kiss for that!"

"Ah!" says Madge, "ye rover, wi' yer whilly-
was! Dinna ye come near *me!*" (She runs
away.)

"What!" says Robert playfully—"not even a
kiss?"

"Nae! Nae!" (She archly sings:)

" 'Gin a body kiss a body, somebody maun cry!' "

"But," says Robert, "ane for Mary, an' ye'll
take it back to her!"

"Ah—weel—for her sake—gie me a hundred!"
(Burns kisses her as they sit on seat.)
(Tam puts his head out of window and sings:)

> " 'To every lass on Ayr or Doon
> He'll fill a glass and drink her doun;
> For he is courtin' a' the toun—
> Rab Burns, the ploughman O!' "

(As Tam finishes, he snatches Robert's cap from his head and takes it inside.)

"It's Tam," Robert explains, "and Souter Jonny in their spree. Don't mind him."

"Eh! Drunken Tam! I mind him weel frae the last Vesset. He's a bod gillie's, Tam!"

"Nay, Madge—nay, Tam's a' right. Come in." (He takes her into Inn.)

(Willie reappears, watching them as they go.)

"A-ah! There goes the Prodigal Sin—the young deevil. (Looks in door.) "It's wine an' women noo. He'll shortly want the husks, an' when it comes to the swine—then I'll be there. A-ha! then Willie wilna' ge yie een a husk! Aha!" (He disappears.)

(Robert comes out of the Inn, speaking as he comes.)

"I got the supper for the lass; but couldna' get my cap again. Tam's o'erfull, and Souter Jonny's ready to fa' under the table. I ha' stolen away in time." (Loud yells inside.) Burns turns and meets Davie and ladies—at sight of them he exclaims:

"Davie! Bessie! The deil—an' the stranger lass! Your pardon, but I fear you've found me *out*—I mean you've found me *in*. Will ye go in yourselves—I mean will ye gae hame? Oh, what a damnable introduction!"

"The lasses, Rab," says Davie with a laugh.

"Gude e'en to both—I—I must go." (Burns starts.)

"Are ye not acquainted then?" asks Davie.

"Miss Jeannie, by your leave——"

"Jeannie!" Burns exclaims.

"Miss Jean Armour! My friend, Robert Burns!" (They bow in recognition, and Davie exclaims:) "Why, Robert, I wonder ye're no well acquaint."

"Pardon,' Robert replies. "Many are weel acquaint who never met, Frien' Davie. The belles o' Mauchline hae been in my mind, if not in my eye—these many days."

"Take care then, frien'," says bonnie Jean, "they dinna creep into your heart."

"I fear they'd find poor shelter," Burns replies.

"Why?" she asks archly, "is the place sae full?"

(Tam opens the window—shows his head and shouts:)

"Rab, come in! She's waitin' for ye!"

"You see," says Burns, "it's full!" (All laugh.)

"But," says Davie, "ye forget the saw: 'There s always room for ane more.'"

"For ane," says Bessie. "Nay, for a hundred, by his looks!"

"An' thousands, by his verses," Davie says.

"Keep it a secret then in auld Mauchline," says bonnie Jean, "or Mossgiel farmhouse, which he's soon to take, will never hold his female friends and callers."

"Well," says Robert gallantly, "those who pull the sneck, when it is ours, shall aye be welcome to its humble fare; but Mossgiel's a' too cold to shelter Mauchline's fairer flowers. Naething but haws and gowans thrive there."

"Take care," says Jean. "The man who mourns the daisy's fate will one day tend the rose within his sunny window."

"Heaven grant I may! Your hands," says Robert as he bows.

"Gude night."

"Gude night! Gude night!" say all, and Robert answers:

"Gude night—Davie, come back. Bonnie lasses, both—gude night. I'm sorry I detained ye on the street; but for my peace o' mind I'm glad it's dark!"

"Aye!" Jean replies prophetically—"*But there'll come the day when we'll see more o' ye.*" '

"Perhaps," is Robert's answer.

> "For tho' in Ayr we say good e'en—
> We'll say good day in auld Mauchline!

"So *au revoir.*" (Davie goes with the ladies and Burns retires.)

(Katy returns and stands looking at Meg.)

"Now, Meg, an' ye're there yet. Poor beast, ye're better than the beast inside. Ye stand, an' he can't. Well, Meg, an' ye stay there half the night, I'll nae ride ye hame this time. The last time I did he was free for a gude time. Now he maun look after ye, an' weel I ken, Meg, ye're the only ane can bring him hame!"

(Robert, seeing her trouble, comes forward and speaks.)

"Good e'en, frien'! In trouble yet? I'll do my best for ye and Tam."

"Eh, Rab, is't ye? Ye *have.* He'd be a bet-ter mon if he didna keep company wi' the likes of ye!"

"Thanks, Katy."

"Ye're welcome. He's fou' o' yer sangs; he's fou' o' yer saws. He's fou' o' yer canty company; he's fou' o' barleycorn."

"Well, then, good Katy, will ye listen why?"

"Be plain as I hae been wi' ye."

"Because his house is empty—do ye ken? The ingle's out within the heart that loves him, and care's his only welcome by your chimla lug. Gae hame, gude wife, an' put your ain heart right. One smile is better than a hundred frowns. Relight your love. Do this for Tam's sake an' yer ain, and a' the inns in Scotland canna draw him from your side."

"Thanks, Rab," says Katy in a feeling tone. "I thenk ye are my gude frien' after a'. Forgive what I ha' said an' I'll tak' yer advice."

"And I," says Rab—"I'll help ye follow it."

"I thank ye, Rab, but let me gie him ane gude beatin' first—ane lesson that'll settle him and down John Barleycorn as well!"

"Nae—nae," says Rab. "Begin nae gude work wi' a wrong."

"Well, then," says Katy, "the very deil must follow him to scare it out!"

"*He shall!*" says Rob.

"The deil?"

"The deil himself, of whom alone poor Tam's afraid. Whist! Katy, come here. As Tam rides hame to-night, the deil take me if auld Nick does not frighten a' the barleycorn frae out his thoughts forever!"

"Gude! Gude! But how? I ken there's

carles and bogles on the road. Some say auld Clautie has been seen, an' some ha' heerd the screechin' by the dead man's well—an' where the murdered bairn was found—and ghaists about the graves o' Alloway!"

"We've been there half the day," says Robert, "and in the buryin' ground whose walls we helped to build. I ha' the Kirk key now." (Shows it.) "'Tis an uncanny spot when a' is silent after dark—only the haunt for owls that hoot, an' goblins who at midnight jow the bell!"

"Eh—a-a-h!" says Katy, shuddering. "I wonder Tam can ride it by!"

"He'll stop to-night!" says Robert.

"What do ye mean?" asks Katy in a whisper.

"Whist! Katy, in these sorry hard worked times—it is na often I can come to Ayr. Now I'm here, it's for a day and night." (Takes her aside mysteriously.) "Hush! When father an' the auld folks gae to bed, twenty young deevils like myself, will loose themselves on Ayr—and, as for Tam—we'll send him hame a sober man!"

"Weel, then the deil will work a miracle!"

"He will. Down yonder where ye see the light's the room we meet in. There we've auld clothes—guisards we've used for singin' round on holidays—gipsies an' hags; carlines an' carles; war-locks an' withches—which we'll a' put on—an' faith, to make us deils we'll need but sma' disguise—and so, stealin' down to Alloway, we'll give frien' Tam a rouser!"

"Yer hand!" cries Katy. "A'll gang wi' ye! Aye—an' a' the market lasses not gane hame!"

"Aye," says Robert with delight. "Auld Elfie's there—almost a witch herself—who, in the days lang syne—has filled me full o' goblin stories."

"Gude!" says Katy; "an' the bonnie lassie come to ye frae Greenock."

"Aye—aye!" says Rob, "she's fou' o' fun. She'll dance in clothes or out—a cutty-sark o' a' work."

"Aye," says Katy. "But for auld Nick?"

"We ha' him," Robin cries. "Haley Willie! He'll no need disguisin'—he's auld Nick himself."

"The vera mon!" says Katy. "Talk o' the deil—he comes!

"Whist! whist! No word," says Robin. "Get your frien's; meet us by yonder light! Whist!"

(Katy goes up the street—Robin looks after her.)

> "Ah, gentle dames, it gars me greet
> To think how many counsels sweet—
> How many lengthened sage advices
> The husband frae the wife despises.

"Now I'll send Davie and Gilbert after Willie, while I go find the rest. Poor Tam! You'll get a surprise to-night, to wind up a' your joy.

"But pleasures are like poppies spread—
You grasp the flower its bloom is shed;
Or like the snowfall in the river—
A moment white then melts forever!"

(Robert goes down the street. Willie returns and walks about.)

"I'll do my duty to mysel', this time. This is my market night, too, an' ma mutton's inside waitin' to be sold. Bauld Tam O'Shanter don't gae hame this night wi'out his fairin'!" (Fiddle heard). "He plays his feedle. Let him play. He'll be the ane to dance himself."

(Davie and Gilbert come up, and accost Willie.)

"Hey, Willie, mon. Frien' Willie."

"Gang yer waus—I've beezeness."

"And sae ha' we. Revenge."

"Aye, double dommed!" says Willie.

"On whom?" they ask.

"On him!" (Pointing in.) 'That 'bletherin', blusterin', drunken blellum!' "

"Gude! Tam! We're for the same."

"Aye—an' for Rab," says Willie.

"The same! For Rab!" they both exclaim.

"They need a lesson and we'll give them one."

"A hoondred. How?" asks Willie.

"We'll scare the deil out o' Tam—and duck Rab in the river."

"Gude! Gude!" cries Willie with delight. "A'm wi' ye."

"Come then with us to Alloway—we'll tell ye as we go along."

"We'll be disguised," says Davie. "Willie, ye'll be the deevil."

"I?" says Willie. "Mon, I've no disguise."

"Ye'll no need it," Gilbert answers. "Come!"

"A'll be auld Nick," cries Willie as he rubs his hands. "Gude! Gude! For naething else will do for Tam O'Shanter." (They disappear. Robert returns, with cloaks on arm.)

"All's ready for the carts," he says. "Willie's caught, now then for Madge. Nae time to lose. It's almost closing hour an' Tam maun go." (He calls at door.) "Madge! Madge! come here." (Beckons.) "Quick, come wi' me— we're goin' home!"

(Madge appears at the Inn door.)

"A' right. A'm glad to gae. This is no place for ony lass—not even ane frae Greenock. My cockernony's a' touzled."

(Burns looks in door and laughs.)

"Tam's kissing the landlady. Oh, only wait. Come out."

(All the maskers appear on side of street.)

"Hush!" says Robert—"are ye a' right? Back up the carts."

"There'll be a storm!" says Elfie.

"Naething," says Robert, "to what we're brewing for Tam."

"Thunder and lightning!" exclaims Gilbert.

"The deil's in the elements," says Davie, "as well as wi' us."

"Eh," says Willie, "ye're siccan a bad lot, ye maun ha' a speechal deil o' yer ane."

"Aye—an' he's here," Robin says. "We're glad ye're wi' us, Willie."

"Aye," says Willie—"an' yer a' at hame in ma company."

"Wow! there's rain!" cries Elfie.

"Water won't hurt ye, Willie," Robin says.

"Nae," says Elfie. "Auld Nick's always out in the rain."

"Rain!" cries Robin, "never fear it. If Tam escapes us it will only be a *Scotch mist!*"

(They all huddle in the carts, and drive off laughing down the street. When all are gone, noise of laughing and singing is repeated inside. Tam and Souter Jonny appear at door of Inn, steadying each other, and followed by Jon and Joey Anderson, with a light—Tam sings:)

"To every lass on Ayr or Doon
We'll fill a glass an' then fa' doun.
For, Souter Jonny, ye're a loun,
An' sae is Tam O'Shanter, O!"

(The landlord unties Meg, and brings her to front of Inn, her head facing down the street. Joey shuts the window. Tam tries to mount, in every way, but fails. Jonny helps, and finally gets on his hands and knees. Tam then steps on him—and, assisted by the landlord and land-lady, mounts. Jonny falls flat. Tam starts off. Calls: "Stirrup cup," gets it—starts again. Calls: "Good-night kiss," gets it—and rides off on Meg, very drunk, and singing, down the street. Souter Jonny is laid out on bench for the night. Landlord closes the house, as land-lady holds the light. Both retire and close the door. Meg's departing steps are heard and faint voices singing in the distance.)

SCENE II.

THE ROAD TO ALLOWAY.

(Low thunder rolls—distant lightning, which becomes more vivid during the scene. Bagpipes sound in the distance, and die out. It is very dark. Noise of wind. Tam O'Shanter is heard singing and presently appears, riding Meg; but facing the wrong way, and holding on to saddle tree.)

"Ho—ho! I'm goin' h-o-ome! H-o-m-e! Whadesay?" (Meg stops.) "Are we there, or are we past it? Nay—Katy'll let me know when we get there. Hiep! Hic! Was matter wizz mare? She's lost her head! I've often lost mine. Her turn now. Hic! Turn round, ye auld beast—whoa, who-ho-ah." (Sings:)

> " 'We are na fou'—we're na that fou'—
> But wee bet drappee in our e'e—
> The cock may craw, the day may daw,
> But ah, we'll dreenk our barlee bree.'

"Wh-where's that rooster? Why don't he craw?" (Crows.) "Ook-o-ook-o-ou!"

(An owl hoots and wild laughter answers.)

"Wow! Dom but there's something the matter wi' his craw." (Shuddering.) "Gae on, Meg, before the deevil gets us. An' ye nae gae, A'll be hame before ye. Aha! We're gaein' noo. Look how the trees fly by. Hey—but we're flyin' juist. I'll haud her in. Where—where deil are th' reins? She's got the bit i' her mouth. Wha's that? Why, that's her tail!" (Laughs.) "Ha! ha! ha! ha! haud me, or I'll drap. When I fell off I was so drunk an' it was sae dark, I got on wrong way. Why—what the deil! She's standin' still. Haud on, Meg, longer I ride this way, farther I am frae hame! Whoa, turn ye round!"

(Meg turns round—facing the other way). "Nay, it's a' th' same. What withershins is this? How'll I ever tell which way tae gae. It's sae dark I canna tell which is Meg an' which is mysel'; ane o' us is wrang way—dang! I'll turn mysel'." (Turns.) "Now, hang ye—gang yer gates. Gee—whoa, turn round." (She turns and stops.) "What ails ye noo? What's that ahead? A glow-worm or a bleeze?"

(Bagpipes are heard again.)

"Ah! noise o' pipes—an' auld Nick tunes. Gae by 'em, Meg. It's auld kirk Alloway, where deils an' witches often meet at night

KIRK ALLOWAY AND GRAVE OF BURNS' FATHER.

—a-ah, Meg, ye weeked deevil, ye. The Laird preserve yer soul! Gee-up-there—gee!''

(Thunder and lightning.)

"Wow! what a night!'' (Yells are heard!) "Wow! ow! Gae-lang! The deil is in it noo! O-oh!''

(Meg is urged forward, amid thunder and sharp flashes of lightning—Tam crouching on her back.)

SCENE III.

KIRK ALLOWAY BY NIGHT.

(Lights shine through Gothic windows and through half-opened door on graveyard without. Wild laughter. All the characters as devils, ghosts, carles, and carlines discovered in a dance. Burns and Madge are partners in front. Willie, as auld Nick, raised on table, plays the pipes. Ghosts, right and left, hold lighted torches. Tam rides up to opening, and sits on Meg, looking in with wonder and delight. As the dance grows wilder he becomes excited and joins in the music with his fiddle, which he plays in animated drunken manner. The characters scream with delight in the exhilaration of the scene. They play and swing and circle around, leaving Madge in the centre.

She dances wildly, throwing off her gown and outer clothes. As she kicks, all yell and Tam shouts loudly:)

"Weel done, Cutty Sark!"

(At sound of Tam's voice all the demons groan:)

"W-o-o-o-oh!"

(The lights go out, the music stops. The warlocks rush for Tam at the centre opening.

He escapes on Meg, and a yell of execration is heard, with low thunder and lightning as the scene closes in.)

———

SCENE IV.

THE HALF-MILE TO THE BRIG—NIGHT.

(Loud thunder—lightning—wailing of wind and screams! Tam's voice is heard in great fear:)

"Wheugh! Rin, Meg! Rin!"

(Meg bears him on—then stops as if blinded by a flash—loud thunder.)

"Wow! Auld Nick is after me! Before— behind! Where will I go?" (Loud yells.) "Ough! The deevils are comin', Meg. Get me hame!"

(Loud groans are heard, and Tam exclaims:)
"Ow-o-o-o-w-ow! Haud! I swear!" And

he does so in a marked, impressive voice, which trembles in his fear.

"I promise--no, I swear—I'll no go out an' drink again! Dommed if I do!" (This is answered by demoniac laughter, yells, and peals of thunder.)

"A-a-gh! Rin, Meg! Rin! The brig! The brig- *They dare na cross the centre o' the stream!"*

(Meg bears him off—followed by the carles, carlines and devils. As they brandish their torches and give a series of unearthly yells, Burns, as a warlock, in their midst, stands laughing in the road, and cries:)

"Good! Once again!"

(And all exclaim:)

"Heigh! There they go!"

"His soul is out of his body—skirl!" cries Burns.

"Skirl, like the deevil! Follow me!" cries Willie.

(The witches and the dancers shout:)

"Hi! hi! We're after ye! Quick to the brig!"

"Some on the road and some below!"

"Look out for Willie when he falls!" says Robert.

And Willie—all excitement now—looks like

auld Nick, and waves his torch and wildly shouts:

"Skirl, like auld Cloutie, skirl! Yese get yer farin', Tam O'Shanter, noo!"

"Aye! Aye! and you, too!" Robert calls. "On to the Brig o' Doon!"

(And amid the thunder, lightning and wild cries they all rush down the road.)

———

SCENE V.

THE BRIG O' DOON AND RUNNING RIVER—NIGHT.

(Thunder and lightning continue—blended with demoniac yells and the clattering gallop of Meg. Witches' cries and loud singing heard.)

Air—"McGregor's Gathering."
TENORS—"Follow! follow! follow! follow on!"
BASSES—"Halloo! halloo! hallo-oo-ooh!"

CHORUS.

"Tho' he hie for his hame or he hide in the night,
Like an uncanny spirit he's taken his flight;
But the warlocks and witches shall follow him on,
Singing Dool for his soul when his spirit is gone!"

(Witches, in minor key:)

"For the hameless!
Shameless—drunken one!"
ALL—"Then follow! follow! follow! follow on!"
BASS—"Halloo! halloo! halloo-o-o-o-ou!"

THE BRIG O' DOON.

(Then a high screaming note above the rest:)

'He'll no cross the Brig, for the Demon of Evil
Gives his breath to the winds and his flesh to the deevil.
And this night from his breast must barleycorn sever
Or O'Shanter in spirit shall wander forever!''

(As this prophetic warning cry rings through the night, Meg's gallop is heard—faster and faster—approaching the brig.)

(Tam's voice in alarm, urging her on):

"Heigh! come, ye deevils! Gae it, Meg! Ha! ha! Gee lang! The brig! The brig!''

(Unearthly screams and terrific thunder suddenly break forth, and, amid blinding flashes, Meg—bearing the defiant but awestruck Tam—dashes on the bridge—followed by the devils—half surrounding her.)

"Grab her tail!'' shouts Willie.

"Go find your own!'' the demons cry, as they throw him over into the river.

(Madge seizes Meg by the tail. It comes off in her hands. Fearful yells. Tam laughs and escapes, amid the cries of the devils below and the warlocks in pursuit. Witches and spirits are seen flying through the air, as the lightning illuminates the scene, and shows Burns standing in picture in the centre of the brig.)

*　　　*　　　*　　　*　　　*　　　*　　　*

Donald paused—his second task was done.

His friends within the house took up the sympathetic voice without and thundered their applause. The Pilgrim's story did not seem romance, but all the characters and incidents were real. The cause, the manner and the treatment of the theme were so entirely new that they forgave all other things and hailed with true delight this realistic version of the ride.

"Hurrah for Tam!" they cried, "and Robert Burns! and his good friend and ours!"

The minister returned the Pilgrim's thanks; and then "Good-night! Good-night!" and shaking hands—and wraps against the rain, and parting for their homes.

Outside, the elements accorded with the stormy scenes along the road to Doon—a duplication of the thunder and the lightning's flash —and, suddenly a resounding oath—far worse than Tam O'Shanter swore—when Drawback found his mules were stalled and his old wagon anchored to a tree.

"That's Sandy Ramsey's work," he said —then, as the thunder rolled, he uttered a denouncing d— which, as it echoed back from Indian Hill, reverberated an unending string of d—'s of every sound and style.

From up the road a laugh came answering

him—a sort of smile for smile—which, as the people recognized it Sandy's voice, they all took up, until the Drawback oaths were drowned and all the ghostly visitants of Alloway seemed still on Tam O'Shanter's track.

END PART SECOND.

PART THIRD.

November's night. The earth seems still. The moon looks cold. Who heeds? Blow winds without, and whispers of approaching winter come!

Inside the house the cheery fire. Out in the barn all living things are sheltered from the cold, and in the schoolhouse once again old friends have met, and honest "neighbors neighbors greet." The shutters closed—the lights turned up—schoolmaster, minister, and all the goodly company warm outstretched hands at open grate; but hearts within need only the re-vivifying fire which friendly greetings help to keep alive.

Drawback has walked this time. The mules require a rest and so does he, and Sandy Ramsey knows the reason why. Lindsay too, might tell a tale; but he says more with quiet looks than most men speak.

How pretty the young girls look in their new hoods, and Tam O'Shanter caps and shepherd plaids, while Mrs. Stuart's iron-gray hair is smoothed beneath a modest bonnet trimmed

with jet, and her bent body's wrapped in a good
Paisley shawl.

Upon the walls the decorations now are tinted
autumn leaves, with branches of red-beaded
alders showing bright between; and, underneath Burns's picture, knots of faded flowers—
the last remembrance of the dying year.

After opening music, the schoolmaster leads
off with more of his peculiar poetry—for such
his quaintly worded rhymes might well be
called—with all their grotesque thoughts and
jingling points, alliterations and the like, all
natural to the man, and all delivered with the
purpose that his scholars might dissect the
meaning and decipher the intent.

The ladies followed—then mixed voices in a
madrigal, without accompaniment, but with a
fine effect, and then " 'The Great Dissolving
Views!' Something entirely new—painted by
the oldest masters in the West—and now pre-
sented, for the first time, before the ignorant
people of the East. Professor Ramsey, lecturer
and discoverer; assisted by the celebrated
Father Lindsay, the manipulator of the slides!"

At this announcement, professor and assist-
ant stepped jauntily upon the platform, and
went behind a large white sheet which had been
stretched across the room behind the speaker's

chair. There was a pause, during which something was heard to move—then Sandy reappeared, holding in his hand a billiard cue, and looking so awkward and so angular it was impossible to say which was the stick. But he was the professor now, and acted, in his way, what he professed to be.

"Put out the lights!" he said, "an' *let in all the darkness* that ye can. That's right," he said, when all things visible had vanished. "Now, ye see, I have here a white sheet, but jest ye wait an' ye'll see more. A light, ye see; now jest ye look!"

At this a big round moon of light was projected from the lamp behind.

"Ha! ha!" said the professor, "what ye see is nothing yet—but when ye hear what's comin' yer eyes will stick out as big an' round as what ye see here now. These are the great Areegenal Dissolvin' Views! I got 'em in a trade when travelin' with McShaw. I got away an' brought the pecters wi' me. This is the way o' that. Ye see it is a big lantern an' a lot o' slides, an', workin' it, we used to slide in an' out o' towns. One time we both got stuck an' found ourselves an' all these priceless pecters in a little upstair room, an' a leery landlord watchin' us below. We owed him eight days' board. Well, one would watch while th' other hunted up a friend, or countryman to help us out. One night I had an angel all secured—a canny Scot who'd heered o' th' McShaw's, an' who said 'Yes, he'd help us,' an' he did! I brought him to McShaw, an' we three had a talk. 'Yes, yes,' he said, 'I'll fix ye up, or guarantee to help ye down.' I blessed him, an' McShaw fell upon his knees (the only time he ever did in all his life) an' fairly wept for joy.

"'Yes, yes—depend on me,' the angel said, 'for I've been there mesel', an' I'll jest tell ye what ye'll do.'

"'Yes, yes,' I said, 'yes, yes;' and 'Brither, ye're jest a blessin',' said McShaw.

"Weel—weel."

"'Weel, then,' the brither said, 'now I'll jest tell ye what ye'll do.'

"'Yes—yes—what? what?' we begged, as we both wrung his hands, an' heart, an' leestened for the jinglin' siller he had brought.

"Well—well!"

"'Weel, then,' he said, as slowly an' as quietly as a thenkin' judge, 'ye have some gude things in the trunk?'

"'Paintin's an' pecters,' we both said, 'worth thousands ef we only had 'em out, an' when the saxteen dollars are paid, we'll give a show an' pay ye back again.'

" 'Eh—that's a' right,' he said, 'now I'll jest tell ye what ye'll do—ye'll go down quietly an' buy a piece o' streeng; an' then ye'll come back here; an' then ye'll take the streeng an' tie it to the handle o' your trunk; an' then ye'll take it ower to the windy there; an' then ye'll raise it up—an' let the trunk oot by the streeng—an' then'—McShaw an' I exchanged a glance—an' he was nearly faintin' on the floor—but I bore up as I were overjoyed. 'Yes, hush!' I said, 'don't make a noise! Hush!' an' I went down an' asked the landlord for a rope. 'What for?' says he. 'To let something out o' the windy,' says I, jest eenocent. 'Oh! ah!' says he, jest eenocent himself; 'don't scratch the paint off and don't make a noise.' Then I went back an' raised the windy, an' we took that piece o' streeng an' tied one end o' it to the bed, an' t'other we tied round the angel's waist and let him slide. He yelled out 'Stop!' but that was beezness which the landlord 'tended to, for he nabbed him, an' held him fast, so he couldn't get away, while I got off with the trunk and went on further West. McShaw is oot there yet!

"The first pecter is Nebucoodnazar eatin'

grass! I think that's what McShaw is doin' at the present time. Observe he's on his hands an' knees showin' how true it is to nateer—for that's the vera pasheeshen McShaw had the night he thought the canny Scot would pay the eight days' board!

"Next is Daniel slayin' the lions wi' one o' the jaw-bones o' Deacon Drawback's mules. I don't swear to that; but Drawback, deacon as he is, will swear to onything!

"Here is the head o' Herod ridin' on a charger —no, that's Goliar slayin' David wi' a small gin-sling! That fellow Lindsay's mexen up the slides. Thes is the—what is thes? the"—and now the views began to be obscure. A serious picture would appear, but no sooner was the professor in the midst of his intelligent descrip-tion than it changed to the grotesque. Clowns' heads appeared on Shakspeare's shoulders, and Punch bobbed up and winked his eye—or put his thumb up to his nose—then, as the people laughed, the learned professor grew enraged, and finally cried, "Hold on!" and rushed in-side; and then there was a scuffling noise and something was upset! Then cries of "Help!" and "Fire!" for now there was no lack of light —the sheet was all ablaze, and as it burned away, Sandy and Lindsay were discovered on the floor among the slides, with Sandy's auburn whiskers, like his eyes, all fire! Luckily Drawback seized the water-pail and soused the two professors who, when the lights turned up again, emerged two soaking wrecks, and, like the vanished pecters, they too, were dissolved!

As Sandy dripped and dried out by the fire, he yelled at Drawback: "Look ye here! Next time ye put oot fire in winter time, ye'll *warm your water first!*"

These follies set aside—when order was restored—Donald Stuart rose, continuing his story, in which the interest was intense the moment he began.

BONNIE DOON.

PART THIRD.

TIME:—*Autumn, Hallowe'en.*

"When ripened fields and azure skies
Called forth the reaper's rustling noise,
I saw thee leave their evening joys
And lonely stalk
To vent thy bosom's swelling rise
In pensive walk!"

SCENE I.

THE BARN AT MOSSGIEL.

(The interior threshing floor of a Scotch barn.

"JOLLY BEGGARS' TAVERN," MAUCHLINE.

Hay and rye on bays and mows. Flooring of rye down. Large cocks of straw and hay at back. Large doors of barn, which, when opened show gloomy landscape and ricks and stacks of grain and hay—also sheep lying in shelter near doors. Gilbert and Hughoc are seen threshing. Hughoc whistling "A Highland Lad," to which tune they keep time with their flails. After going over the floor once, they stop to turn the straw, and Gilbert speaks:)

"It's nearly dark and we are not yet done. We've got to hurry now." (They resume their work). "Rob will be late. But hark! I hear the horses coming home." (Noise of approaching team is heard.)

"He is here. Hughoc, run and help him with the plough." (Hughoc puts down straw and goes to door. Gilbert places sheaf at back and goes to Hughoc, helping him to open the great doors of the barn. As they swing back, Robert appears in realistic picture.)

"*Burns at the Plough.*"

"Is a' weel, Rab?" Gilbert asks.

"Aye," Robert answers. "But I'll plough na mair—the frost is in the ground for winter now. Ah, but it's been a tiresome day!"

(Hughoc takes the horses off. Robert comes into the barn. He hangs up his coat and cap—

takes flail from hook and goes to threshing. Gilbert tries to stop him.)

"Nay, brother," Gilbert says.

"Nae," replies Robert, "I'll help ye oot!"

(As Hughoc whistles "Comin' thro' the Rye," they keep time with the strokes of the flails— going over the flooring rapidly and ending with a bang—Robert hangs up the flails.)

"Thank Heaven!" says Gilbert, "it's over."

"Are ye a-weary, Gilbert?" Robert asks.

"I'm tired to death; but we hae gotten a' th' rye."

"Aye," Robert answers, "a' that the rattans ha' left in the straw."

(He shakes some rips and binds sheaves as he talks.   Gilbert helps and answers him:)

"'Tis very poor; but the work is a' the same. It's hardly worth our trouble. There, Rab, sit now and rest—I'll finish it."

(They bind and move the loose straw.)

"Ah!" Robert sighs, "I never feel it. Dinna mind me, brither, my thoughts are far away, and I must work to still the feelings of my heart."

"Robert, ye'll no complain, but weel I know your life is wasted here."

"Nay—nay—'tis naething. I maun do my part."

"Aye, as ye always have—more than all, and more than ever now since father died and left his sorrows wi' us."

"A-weel—it does seem hard. Goodby to dear old father. He may sleep in Alloway Kirkyard, in sight of our old home. The dead alone return where they belong, while we, unhappily, live on, to move from place to place, seeking good fortune which we never find."

"'Tis strange, Robert. From the trials in the auld house where ye were born near Ayr, we found worse in Mount Oliphant. Worse still in Lochlea—where our father died—and here, in Mossgiel, where the sun ne'er seems to shine, misfortune, like a storm, is gathering all around us. 'Tis well we have you with us."

"Nay, I think I am your fate! No place do I set foot, but weeds spring up and clouds shut out each ray of hope."

"Brither, dinna say it! There's not a one o' us but knows your worth. Mother and sister shelter in your loving heart. You're never anything, dear Rob, but just our strong right arm and faithful friend."

"But what good can I do? The more we work the poorer still we get. I'd better go."

"No, Robert, no."

"Maybe I'd earn a little somewhere else and

send it back to you. There'd be one less to feed when I am gone, and maybe times will brighten, or the coming spring be better than the last."

"Robert, we'd have no heart if you should leave us—on seven poor pounds a year you've lived—on eighteen pence a week you've not complained, but worked a' thro' long weary days on oaten meal alone. Robin, we've shared the worst togither all these years—we'll share it still."

"Brither, you will not understand. It is not good or evil that may come to me I fear. It is not that—for if it were I'd never go away; but 'tis the thought of others takes me."

"Of Jeannie?"

"Aye—loving, trusting Jean Armour. Since Mary went away—or since she's dead—for she has not come back to me—Jeannie has come, despite ourselves, a solace in my heart. You know the rest. How we have loved—what she has been to me. To save her and to save myself, there's nothing but to go away!"

"Stay—and marry her."

"I've offered it. Done all an honest man could do. Her father has denied me. We are disgraced togither!"

"I can nae more advise ye, Rab, I know

you've done a' that ye could—a' for the best."

"An' that has brought us ill. Gilbert, I sor-row at the thought o' parting. I'll never find a hame or friends so gude. I love them—love ye all—an' dear auld Ayrshire too!"

"An' we love ye the same."

"I feel it in my heart. There is a bond be-tween us never can be broken. I love my coun-try. It is her poverty that makes her great—our sufferings that make us strong. O Scot-land! Not a peasant on thy hills, who works in humbleness for daily bread, but is a king to thee!"

"Robert, ye know what father said: 'God crowns his head with blessings who works out his destiny with patient heart and willing hands!' "

"*And his fate was to die in misery and want.* No more—I go."

"Well, Robert, I would help ye if I could—God knows it—so do what ye will."

"And what I must, but I'll no go till all the work is done. I'll stay and help ye through a' that, and then, auld home an' all ye hold that's dear to me—farewell!"

"And your share of the farm?"

"Shall all be yours. I have no right to any-thing."

"And your book—the first edition of your verses, Robert?"

"The first and last. The little I've received will pay some things we owe, and if what's left don't pay me out, from Greenock to Jamaica, I'll work my way. One song will haunt me as I go—one face—one heart—forever lost—my Highland Mary!"

"And Jean? In other scenes—under that burning sun—you may forget her."

"Forget her! And if I could forget the one who'd loved and trusted me, I'd be by Heaven forgotten!"

(During this Jean enters and stands listening.)

"Forget! There's not a slave that toils in burning fields, but looks towards wife and home with love! If I could e'er forget, I'd be a coward among men—more lowly than a slave!"

(Jean advances and speaks his name.)

"Robert!"

"Jean! My loved and trusting Jean!"

(Gilbert bows — and goes — leaving them alone.)

"Forgive me, Robert, that I overheard. I love you all the better—if that's possible—ah, but the parting—that I cannot bear!"

"My bonnie lass, don't speak of it."

"I will not if you wish it. I will na speer nor

speak o' anything; but, Robert, dinna leave me!"

"Jeannie, trust me. I will do a' for the best."

"I've trusted you wi' a' but life, and that is yours whenever you may ask it!" (She weeps.)

"No tears, my bonnie Jean, no tears."

"Put on your coat, dear Robert, the night wind blows. Ye'll be cold."

(She gets his coat and puts it on him. They sit. She leans her head on his breast.)

"Where's Mallie, Rab?" she asks.

"Dead in a ditch," he answers bitterly; "as would I were myself."

"An' where's the collie, Luath—where is he?"

"They killed him on the night before poor father died. Harm only seems to come to those who love me."

"Then let harm come to me," Jeannie replies, "if I could do you good. Are you cold now?"

"Ne'er mind. I seldom feel it, love. How came you here?"

"I could not stay away—*women like I am never can.* Naething but death should part the ones who love."

"Not even that! Oh, Jeannie, would I had died before we met, or ever I had wronged ye wi' my love!"

"Nay—say not so—better death wi' you than a' the world without ye! Ye'll nae go?"

"I canna answer. It tears my vera heart!" (He rises.) "Oh, Scotland! home of all I love and all that holds me dear—how can I ever leave ye?"

"Ye will na—nay, ye canna go! It's getting dark. Ye could na go to-night. It's Hallowe'en. Your friends will a' be here, and ere to-morrow, God willgie me ane o' these to help persuade ye!"

"Hush!" says Robert sadly; "if Heaven can forget, I think I am forgotten! No more—go join our frien's. I've not the heart to see them!"

"But ye canna avoid them now. It's Hallowe'en!"

"I know—I know—it's growing dark, the 'curlers quat their play'—the evening sports begin—but I canna be there!"

"Nae—for the night—for a' our frien's!"

"No need for Hallowe'en to tell *my fate*—nor show the one I love. Go in." (He releases her hands and kisses them.)

"Nae, Robin, an' ye will nae come—I'll bring them a' to you."

"One kiss, dear Jeannie—go!" (He kisses her.)

"Twa," she answers, "ane for me."

"Anither," Robert says, "that's for us baith."

"That is for ye," poor Jeannie says, "an' this for me—an' a'!" (She goes out of the great doors—Robert watching her depart—then turns.)

"Now a' the past come haunt me as ye may. I have deserved it a'—deserved to be forgotten! My Jean! I would na wrong ye—but, Mary, come ye now—and whether frae the banks o' Ayr or whether ye look down from Heaven—heap your reproaches on my head—but do not a' forget me!" (He takes his cap and a stick and goes out singing sorrowfully as he goes.)

> " Ye banks an' braes o' Bonnie Doon
> How can ye bloom sae fresh an' fair
> How can ye chant ye little birds,
> And I sae weary fu' o' care?"

(As he disappears a chorus of merry voices is heard—first in the distance—then approaching nearer and nearer.)

WOMEN—"Oh, whistle an' I'll come to ye, my lad!
　　Oh, whistle an' I'll come to ye, my lad!
　　Tho' faither an' mither, an' a' should gae
　　　　mad—
　　Oh, whistle an' I'll come to ye, my lad!"

MEN—"Then warily tent when ye come to court me;
　　And come na unless the back yett be agee.
　　Syne up the back style an' let naebody see!
　　An' look as ye were na lookin' for me!"

WOMEN—"Then whistle, an' I'll come to ye, my lad!"
  (Men all whistle the line to the tune.)
WOMEN—"Tho' faither an' mither an' a' should gae
      mad—"
  (Men all whistle the line.)
  (Chorus—All repeat, girls sing, men whistle.)

(Davie, Tam, Boys, Katy, Bessie, Elfie, Nannie, Chloris, Sylvie, Clarinda, lasses, all in line, hand in hand, at finish of song, look in the barn —pause.)

(Then together they cry:) "Boo-oo! Boo-oo-ou!"

"Naebody answers," says Bess. (Pauses.) "Wha's gaen' roun' my house this time o' night?"

"Auld bluidy Na' un!" says Elfie, in a hollow voice.

"What does he want?" asks Davie.

"A gude fot sheep!" says Katy, ruefully.

"Fat?" says Tam. "Everything's poor around here—like the master. Bring him out! Hulloo!" (A pause.)

"He's gone," says Davie; "yet Jeannie said we'd find him here!"

"A-weel," says Tam, "as it's no man's barn we'll tak' possession!" (They all go in and look about.)

"See," says Davie. "They've been threshing the rye!"

"Rye?" says Tam, "dinna mention it! Tread it down! Tread it down, or it'll rise again! There! There! I'll tread ye out! I'll eat ye up; but dinna' ye say dreenk to me, ye deevil ye!"

"Ha! ha!" (All laugh.) "Ah, Tam's afraid."

"Aye, laugh! but an' ye'd seen Auld Nick, as I have—ye'd a' be sae scorchin' hot naething but water would save ye!"

(All laugh.) "To the kail yard, now—to the kail yard!" (They all cry as they join hands in his.)

"Kail!" says Tam, "I'll pull me stump if maukin's left ane o' them stand!"

Men—"Come into the kail yard, lassie, come!"
Women—"We gae into the kail yard green."
Men—"An' ye'll a' pu' your true love up."
Women—"Our lovers in the kail yard green."

(As they repeat together, they go off singing in line.)

(Jeannie and Gilbert, bearing a lantern, enter the barn. Jean pauses and calls:)

"Robert! Robert! Oh, Robin, come—we're waiting at the house."

"Aye," says Gilbert, "the buttered sowens are ready, Rab, come in."

(Jean looks about, as Gilbert holds the lantern—she is agitated and alarmed.)

"Not here! Not gone! Nae—though he's taken his coat, his plaid is there—Robin!"

(As they stand listening—chorus is heard in the garden.)

Chorus—"An' ye'll a' pull your true love up,
               And wander in the kail yard green."

"Ah," says Gilbert, "he's with the others, trying for their fortunes and their love. Come wi' me, Jeannie—Rab's na' far awa'!"

(As they go, all the others return. Each draws three oat straws, and compares them with others, amid loud laughter—Tam holds up a runt of kail.)

"Look at the runt o' kail I pulled. There's naething on it. It's a stump like auld Meg's tail!" (All laugh.) "If that's the kind o' a wife I'm to get I'll keep the ane I've got; she's better than a runt!"

"Ah, Tam," says Davie, "yer wife's the only ane ye'll get!"

"She's the only ane o' the kind I want!"

"Take that!" says Katy—beating him—"ye ne'er-do-weel!"

(Tam runs out of the door, then looks in again and leers at Katy.)

"Runty Stump, can I come in?"

"A-weel," says Katy, "as ye're sworn to be a sober man, ye may, an' find a welcome too. Come to my arms!"

"We're a' right noo," says Tam; "twa daisies on ane stem!"

"It's sweet seemplecity!" says Katy.

"An' Scotch sarcasm," says Tam.

"Try the sowin," cries auld Elfie.

"Hempseed, hempseed, I saw thee," cry all.

"Hemp—hemp-hi-hemp what?" asks Tam.

"This is it," says Davie, explaining; "ye come into the barn alone!"

"Na," Elfie calls, "outside! outside!" And all repeat, "Outside!   Outside!"

"Alane?" asks Tam, with a queer look.

"Aye, outside—alane!"

"Nae, Auld Nick'll tak' me if I do! I mind the night outside o' Alloway Kirk. Deil tak' the outside! Th' inside's gude enough for me!"

"But that's the way o' it," says Davie.

"Aye, aye," says Tam, with a knowing wink. "I ken the way o' it, ne'er fear me! *The only time A' gae outside alane to-night is when ye a' gae wi' me!*"

"Weel," says Davie, "hae yer waus. We'll a' gae *out* an' then come *in* an' saw it i' th' barn."

"I saw it on the road," says Tam. "It never left me till the Brig o' Doon!"

"Ye hae nae seen 'em sin' syne, Tam?" asks Katy.

"Nae. They're a' gane where they belang," (pointing down).

"Nor any serpents, Tam?"

"Deil a ane! A'll keep ma boots hereafter, for mysel'." (All laugh.)

"This is the way o' it," says Davie.

CHORUS.

MEN—"Hempseed, hempseed, I saw thee!
    Let him who loves or thinks o' me."
WOMEN—"Come after me an' pu' me!
    Hempseed, hempseed, I saw thee."
MEN—"Let any lass who thinks o' me,"
WOMEN—"Come to thy arms an' love thee!"

"And now," says Davie, "all outside, an' then a lassie first."

"An' I'll come wi' her," says Tam.

"Nay, ye'll not," says Katy.

(And then all cry:) "Alone!" "Alone!"

"It'll na be alone wi' me!" says Tam. "*A'll come when yer alane thegither!*"

(All go outside, and after a pause, Bessie enters and advances to the centre of the threshing-floor, and imitates the sowing of the hemp—then says in marked manner:)

"Hempseed, hempseed, I saw thee!
Let him who loves or thinks o' me
Come after me an' pu' me!"

(At third time, Gilbert enters at the back, takes her in his arms, kisses her and goes off. Davie is next, repeating the same words, and is met by a lassie, and when he retires, Sylvie, the second girl—of a country sort—advances, tremblingly, and speaks in a low voice.)

(Tam advances to kiss her, but is met by Katy, who drives him off. Sylvie repeats, but no one responds, and she goes off crying very loudly.)

(Tam enters—shaking and looking about.)

"Dom but I wonder is auld Cloutie under the straw! Weel—here goes! I wish auld Meg was here to ride me hame! Hemp—Hi, but I feel it around ma neck! There's na breedge to cross this time. A-weel! Hem—hemp! Hempseed! hempseed! I saw thee!—Dom but I hear a croonin' round the corner o' the barn. The deil is in it sure!—Hempseed! hempseed, I saw thee!"

(Low groans are heard outside.) "Ah! ah! Haud on! haud on! Haud! haud! *I'll swear I never! I hae nae tasted a drop sin' I rode over the Doon! Haud, Mr. Deevil—haud!*" (Looking out.) "I want the ane that loves me—or thinks ony thing aboot me to come in here queeck—an' pu' me oot o' this! An' Auld Nick can pu' me after!"   (Loud groans.)

(Continued while Katy steals in behind him and raises a white sheet above him on a stick. He groans and falls and yells. She raises him and he runs out of the barn with his coat tails over his head.)

(The voices of the others are heard going away, singing:)

> "In their haunts on Hallowe'en,
>   Spirits all from sleep awaken,
> And, where love has faithless been,
>   Love itself is all forsaken!"

(As the voices die out, distant strains of "Auld Lang Syne"—played by the people in the house —during which no other sounds are heard. Mary Campbell—leaning on the arm of Madge —pale and weary, looks in the open door of the barn. After a pause, as if in great disappointment, she speaks:)

"And na one here?"

"Nae, not a living soul," answers poor Madge.

"And not within the house?" asks Mary, with a troubled look.

"Nae, I glinted through ilk window; but he was nae there. Yet a' the crowd o' kintra

HOUSE OF HAMILTON AND GRAVE OF "MARY MORRISON."

folks were sittin', talkin' by the ingle-side an'
showed plain as the light."

"Hark!" says Mary, as she stands and listens, with a look of deepest sorrow on her pale,
worn face. "Do you hear no one?"

(Distant sounds of laughing are heard in the
house.)

"There's nane sae happy as the careless
poor," says Madge, as she listens.

"It's weel for us," says Mary, "they are there.
I'd only see my ain dear Robert by himself!"

"Ah, gude frien', ye are tired!" says bonnie
Madge.

"And ye, gude girl," Mary answers her.
"We've walked all day!"

"Weel, then, come to the house," poor Madge
replies. "I'll knock an' ask for shelter an' a
place to rest, an' weel ye ken the string is out
in every Scottish home!"

"I know, I know, dear Madge; but not till I
see him. It's growing darker. Let's go in."

"I'm no afraid," says Madge. "There's na
tyke, or he'd bark. Haud! Somethin' breath-
in'!" (Gropes about.) "It's the sheep—nae
harm. Come in here. There's hay an' straw—
sit down." (They enter the barn.)

"Ah!" Mary says; "I'm rested by the place
where he has been. How peaceful and how

sweet. I smell the breath o' gowans an' the grass—the sweeter that they're dead. Here is the straw he's threshed, and here his plaid!"

(Mary presses it to her lips and kisses it.)

"Oh, Robert darling, though my heart is full o' sad forebodings and I'm weary unto death —when ye'll come a' is weel! Your love will be the same, and mine is yours forever!"

(The first gleams of the rising moon are seen. Jeannie returns and enters the open doors at the back, as if waiting for Robert. She looks about.)

"Robert—no come back yet," she says. "Who's there?" (She sees Mary and Madge.) "Strange women! and in such a place!"

(Mary stands gazing at Jean, but Madge replies:)

"Are ye no strange to us—an' ye are here?"

"But *you*—at such an hour alone!" says Jean.

"She's not alone!" says Madge. "Ye're a' agley! Dinna ye see *me* here?"

"And who are you?" asks Jean.

"I'm only just her frien'," Madge answers, "but I'll steck like a thestle to a sheepit's back!"

"I'll call," says Jeannie, as she starts to go.

"Stay!" Mary cries, and interposes herself between her rival and the door. "Stay!" she echoes—and then continues with marked emphasis:

"Though we have never met, I've seen your face before. Your name?"

"Why should I fear to tell it. I am Jean Armour!"

(Mary stands as if transfixed and gazes in her face—and then says slowly:)

"Aye, 'Bonnie Jean!' Your name is written oft by him—but you come in a dream! A woman with a bonnie face and dark brown hair—I've seen them a' these sorry days!"

"What do ye mean?"

"I see ye now," says Mary, in the same marked tone, her eyes still fixed upon her. "You're Jean Armour! An' you have come between us!"

"What words are these?" cries Jean. "Woman, who are you?"

"My name is Mary Campbell!"

"Nae—nae—it canna be! He thinks ye dead! Your name he murmurs in his sleep. He loves ye still! But ye will ne'er come back to him!"

"I come to seek him here!"

"You come to see my Robert!"

"Aye," says Mary, defiantly and solemnly. "I come to see my honored, faithful lover, Robert Burns! Don't question me or stay me

—the hour is late—my time is short. Say, is he here?"

"He's not," replies the now bewildered Jean. "An' if he were——"

"No matter," Mary says, "I'll seek him out! and look once more upon his face, though that look be my last!"

"Nae, nae," cries Jean; "for Heaven's love——"

"Nae," Mary answers, "none shall part me frae the man I love! Woman, whoe'er you may be—or whate'er ye are—stand back!"

(Jean suddenly passes her and rushes to the door:)

"Nae, then," she cries, "stand ye! Ye shall nae pass to him who's a' to me!"

"To you, woman!"

' Aye! Oh, forgive me!" cries poor Jean. 'Strike me! Humble me—or kill me! I will na' murmur nor complain—but leave me Robert's love! Here, on my knees, I beg and ask it of ye!"

"I dinna understand ye!" cries Mary in amaze.

"Oh, gude heart," Jean replies, "feel for me, an' spare him too! *You've come too late to part us now. You've come too late!*"

"What do you mean?" asks Mary, in a pity-ing tone.

"Bend down your ear to listen," Jean replies.

(Both look at Madge who, during this has stood in sorrowing wonder looking on. Jean points to her and speaks:)

"Let her gae awa'—I canna' look ye either in the face—soft—let me whisper."

(She whispers in Mary's ear, who bends down to her- and then hides her face in her hands.)

(Mary starts with a groan of anguish.)

"O-oh! My God! Robert! Have I lost ye? Have I come too late? Oh, have I come too late?"

"Nay," says poor Jean; "tread upon me that I've come between, and kill me that I've made ye suffer!"

"Oh, Robert! Robert! Robert!" bursts from Mary's heart.

(Jean, now touched by her grief, approaches her.)

"Nay now, 'tis I must pity ye! Ye're sad an' pale. Ye've suffered more than I ha' done, an' now I am the cause o' more."

"Oh!" Mary cries in bitterest grief. "My dream! My dream! My dream!"

"Nae, gude heart, dinna sorrow," Jean says soothingly. Blame me for a', but, oh, I could na' help the love I bore him!"

(Mary bursts into a flood of tears, crying:)

"Oh, Heaven help me now!"

"Nae—nae—ye are ill," says Jeannie, tenderly. "Come in, wi' me—ye're cauld an tremblin'." (She puts Robert's plaid about her. Mary kisses it again and again. Madge tries to comfort her.)

"Nay," Mary says with resolution, "it is naething. I'm nae very well—but I'll no trouble you—I'll go—I'll go!"

(Madge leads her a few steps—she falters and cries out:)

"But oh, my broken heart!"

"Mary, my sister! Forgive me!" Jeannie cries.

"For his sake, aye!" Mary faintly answers. "And tell him I forgive him, too!" (She turns and falls prostrate on the straw.)

"Great Heaven! She's ill!" cries Jeannie, rushing to her aid.

"Aye!" Madge exclaims, as she caresses her. "She's a' fey an' like to die!"

"Don't raise her head," cries Jean. "There's water here!" (She gets it from stoup by well.)

"Mary—gude heart—speak to me!"

"Oh! She would come in spite o' me!" cries poor Madge, as she wrings her hands.

"Let's take her in," says Jean. "The warmth will comfort her."

"Nae," Mary says, recovering, "don't let him know. I'll bear it all!"

"Dear Mary, come into the house," pleads Jean.

"Aye, darling, come," says Madge, supporting her.

"Nae—nae, I will na' take the place he's given to another! Come, Madge, we'll go!" (She tries to rise.)

"But ye're na weel enough to walk."

"Ye'll help me, Madge." (Takes her hand.) "An', if ye've ever been my frien', come wi' me now." (Tries to go.)

(Jean tries to stop her.)

"Nae," she says; "come in an' let me tend ye. Let me gae wi' ye. I'll work and strive and die to aid ye!"

"Nae," Mary answers sadly, "bonnie Jean, your place is here. 'Tis you must stay by him when I am gone! Promise ye will, my sister!"

"Yes. Oh, Mary, can ye e'er forgive me?"

(Mary kisses her and then replies:)

"No more. You know my heart. Here." (She takes bundle from Madge—opens it, and takes out things as they kneel on the floor.)

"Here is his first book, wi' his songs, and your name wi' the rest. I thought to give it him myself, but now——" (She gives the book to Jean.) "This letter is frae Dr. Blackie wi' the ane that Dr. Blacklock wrote to him. It is for Robert. He will go to Edinboro."

"Go!" cries Jean.

"Aye! an' he walk he'll go," Mary replies; "for fame and honor wait him!"

"Robert!"

"Tell him a' this. *'Twas the gude news I came to tell*, but now ye'll do it for me. Show him the page I marked. Be faithful to him to the last—gentle an' kind I know ye will be— but promise me, upon your word, *ye will nae tell him that ye saw me here!*"

"I must. I couldna' haud ma peace!"

"For my sake—by his love—no word. This wreath is frae the holly trees that grow by Ayr. Dear Robin knows the place. *I made it as we came along, when resting by the wayside. I* thought to be the first to honor him and crown him wi' th' bays, but now——" (She suddenly starts up, exclaiming passionately:) "Nae, nae, my God! *No other hand than mine must place it on his head! No other arms than mine be clasped about his neck! No other voice than Mary's speak to him of love!*"

"Mary, stay here!" cries Jean. "And you, Madge, tend her till I come! Forgive me that I could forget.   Love struggled in my breast—but now my duty's plain!"   (She starts to go.)

"Ye shall nae stir!" Mary cries.   "Madge, help me keep her here.   Where would ye go?"

"To seek for Robert, though he's hid in night and in the farthest field!   For never till he knows your noble heart, shall Jeannie Armour speak of love again!"   (Jeannie hurries out. Mary looks after her, then rushes back to Madge.)

"Let's gae! let's gae before she comes.   Before he—oh! let's gae!"

"Where, Mary, where?"

"Back to the Mauchline Inn, frae there return to Ayr."

"Dear Mary, ye can hardly walk!"

"I must!   I must!   To Ayr!   To Ayr!   For I must take my lang, lang sleep o' th' banks o' that dear stream where, in the days lang syne, we wandered—telling o'er our love!"

"Oh, Mary!   Mary!"   (Madge bursts into tears.)

"*The fatal fever lingers in my veins.   This journey's helped it on.* Oh, could I see him once again, I'd ask no more—but be repaid in this—that he is great at last and happy in an honest love!"

"Oh, Mary!   Dinna greet like this!"

"Nay—all is best. To-morrow I'll gae back, and when I'm dead——"

"Oh, Mary, darling, only friend!"

"When I am gone send word to him and lay me where the gowans spring and heather blooms—where Doon and Ayr will murmur of me, and where he'll sometimes sing one sorrowing song for her, who even when she's dead, will speak o' love for him!"

(Madge listens—then runs to door and looks out.)

"He's comin'! Mistress—yonder see! She has nae found him. He's alone!"

"Alone!"   (A faint tinge of moon-rise shows.)

"Stay—Mary—only speak to him. He's sad wi' thoughts o' thee!"

"Hush! Hush! It may not be!" (Taking Madge and leaving the door.) *Our happiness is past, and only as a wraith, or in a dream, can Mary Campbell ever cross his vision more.*"

(They retire slowly into the dark corner of the barn. In the house, music of "Robin Adair" is played—and is faintly heard. Robert enters, wrapt in thought. He stands leaning by the door, and looking out, his cap in his hand. The moon appears, rising slowly, during scene. Robert speaks:)

"Mary, my ain, why come ye not again?

Where are ye now? I see ye by the braes o'
Ayr, where last we met, there where we passed
one day of parting love, then said farewell forever! Mary, the summer's days are done and
winter's breath has withered all the fields—and
yet, although you pledged your word, you come
not back to me. Nay, then, I know the worst.
The frost that touched the flower's bloom has
laid ye dead before it." (He comes to the
middle of the floor and reclines on the straw.)

> "O, pale, pale now those rosy lips
> I aft hae kissed so fondly
> And closed for aye the sparkling glance
> That dwelt on me sae kindly,
> And mouldering now in silent dust
> The heart that lo'ed me dearly;
> But still within my bosom's core
> Shall live my Highland Mary!"

(He rises and takes a wecht, and filling it with
the threshed rye, advances centre.)

"There's something in my heart that will not
down. Something that speaks of her that's
gone. I feel—wherever she may be—cold in
the earth or in that distant Heaven—that she is
near me still. Oh, spirit of the loved one lost—
come back to me! Come back! If the dead
ever hear or know what passes on the earth—
come back! Nay, I maun call in vain! But

yet I'll try the spell. 'Tis Hallowe'en—and I'll let down the corn against the wind—mortal or spirit, come!'' (He raises the wecht and pours the corn, saying:)

"As the corn fa's sae may I fa'
If I dinna love the one who comes to me."

(At the third time the figure of Mary Campbell, in white dress, and deadly pale, appears in the centre of the barn, and gazing on him with fixed eyes, passes noiselessly away. Robert stands, transfixed, until she vanishes, and then cries out in frenzy:)

"Her wraith! her wraith! her wraith! My God! Mary!"

(He screams and falls senseless on the floor. Mary—returning—rushes to him—kneels by his side and raises his head, which she places in her lap. Madge runs to aid her.)

"Oh, Mary, shall I call for help?"

"No, not for the world. Some water frae the stoup. He'll soon be well."

(Madge rushes for the water—which she brings.)

"Here, darling, here!"

"He is half crazed wi' work an' cold—give me the plaid." (Madge hands it—Mary takes the plaid and also her cloak, which she has removed to appear as apparition, and wraps it

THE MUSE HAILS THE BARD.

about Robert, supporting him by the sheaves of
rye, then says to Madge:)

"I've seen him sae before. He'll be himself
anon and *think it all a dream.*"

"I'll watch that nae one comes!"

"Aye! Aye! *This scene is sacred to ourselves.* 'Tis only for a moment and we're gone
before he wakes. Gone! Gone! My God! forever!" (She kisses him. He partially awakes
and murmurs to himself.)

"*Mary, my muse! My guiding star! The Coila
of my dreams!*"

"Ah!" Mary cries, as she rises, "I understand." (She takes the wreath, and standing
behind him, speaks—as a spirit—these altered
lines of "The Vision," during which music of
"Bonnie Doon" is heard in the distance:)

> "All hail! my own inspired bard!
> In me thy native muse regard!
> Nor longer mourn thy fate is hard—
> Thus poorly low—
> I come to give thee such reward
> As we bestow!
>
> "Then wear thou this"—the prayers I've said
> Rest like a blessing on thy head,
> "The polished leaves and berries red
> All rustling play—"
> Keep green my memory when dead
> And passed away!"

(She places the wreath of holly on his head and slowly retires.)

(The refrain of the Hallowe'en song is faintly heard, sung by the country people in the house. The air of "Bonnie Doon" is continued, blending with it, till the close.)

CHORUS.

In their haunts on Hallowe'en,
  Spirits all from sleep awaken,
And where love has faithless been,
  Love itself is aye forsaken!
Love itself!   Love itself!
Love itself is aye forsaken!

*   *   *   *   *   *   *

The feeling tone in which the Pilgrim spoke—the anguish, sacrifice, the brave despair, which he had shadowed forth, came like a cadence at the close—a lingering note of sorrow seldom heard. It seemed a strain of that old, plaintive song which all the auditors in fancy heard coming from those who reveled in the house. They listened for a moment—breathless—waiting still some sign or sound—another word, a footfall—Jean's return—or Mary to come back, but nothing came. They only saw the minister stand up and raise his hands, and rising, they concealed their tears and the choked sighs that struggled to be free—and bowed before the prayer:

"O God, in mercy keep thy children here and everywhere throughout the world. Console them in afflictions deep and dark—and give them love and constancy—and strength and faith—and peace and plenty now and evermore!"

END OF PART THIRD.

PART FOURTH.

Now Nature sleeps. Wearied with all the varying changes of the passing year, she takes her rest and, though old Winter comes and stands upon the hills and howls all day till he is hoarse, he cannot waken her.

Her flowered silken dress of spring—her summer's gaudy robes of gold and green, and autumn's widow's weeds of sober hues she has put by, and now, disrobed, stripped bare—her jewels and her vesture given for the good of man—she seeks in tears her cheerless bed, beneath whose snowy covering her sorrows may be sacred till the night is passed.

Rest, gentle mother, loving friend, and sleep in peace. From out thy generous bosom springs all that sustains, all that enriches man. Let him who never thought of this, go live a single day without thy aid—then turn again in humbleness to thee!

Welcome, old friends, on this wild winter night! Over unbroken roads and pathless wastes of snow the bond of fellowship and love has brought you to the schoolhouse once again—the last reunion of the year—the birthday of the poet Burns.

Old Age has come—the good old minister and Mrs. Stuart with the rest, in reverence and respect. The boys and girls and younger folks for the romance and the love of all festivities like these. The men and women, as all men and women should, to stand by duty to the living and the dead at any hour, in any place.

Turn up the lights. Stir up the fire. Let music sound a welcome and an inspiration for the scene. See where some loving hands have placed the laurel crown in memory of this day! On every picture wreaths of holly hang, in honor of the great ones gone, and, garlanding the platform and the desk of Mr. Olds, great strings of prince's pine with winter-berries intertwined and glistening in the light.

Come, schoolmaster, a glorious night for revelry inside. The storm without can't wait —nor can the passing hour—go on!

And faith there is a fine array—from tragedy in prose down to "The Living Pictures of the Times! Characters by the only living Sandy Ramsey, and Father Lindsay, the connecting link." Stand forth!

"All right!" says Sandy, as he sticks his head above the sheet, and shows his face devoid of beard, and rolls his leery eye, at which all roar.

"Not yet! go back!" cries the schoolmaster. "You're too soon!"

"Maybe it is for ye, but it ain't for me!" says Sandy, as he shivers in the cold. "I've been undressed in here since half-past four an' got these tight things on me shanks, an' nothing but a Roman shirt without any trousers' legs or arms! I'm shiverin' juist!"

"Hey! Sandy! Lindsay! Bring 'em out!" the people cry, and in response, the sheet is dropped, revealing such a pair of Heavenly Twins as no good Zodiac could do without. Sandy's long legs looked longer still in the thin fleshings which he wore, and his white Roman shirt was much too short, which made him seem a good grandfather graybeard more than half made up of arms and legs. As for his face—deprived of its goat-beard, it looked in keeping with the body it adorned, and by its bareness showed his swivel eye, in a protruding, rolling style which set the schoolhouse in a roar. Lindsay stood still—his body and his face immovable—and his set eyes staring at nothing in particular—his head just reaching up to Sandy's arm.

A shout of laughter greeted both, but this did

not comport with Sandy's Roman dignity, and so he called a halt.

"Look here," he said, "ye wouldn't laugh if ye had on these Grecian panteloons! An', Drawback, as for ye—ef ye had ony sense ye'd jest wait till the laugh comes in, an' not anteecapate the time! ye——"

"The Dying Gladiator!" the schoolmaster called, to head him off.

"Dyin'!" said Sandy with a leer. "Look here! These are the 'leven' pecters, mind ye that. Don't kill the goose that lays yer golden egg, for if ye wreng in onything that's dead, ye'll want some lecters here to drag me off! Call oot yer Ajox an' I'll come!"

"All right," said the obliging schoolmaster, with a smile.

"Ajax Defying the Lightning!"

Sandy struck a pose—and spread himself above the stage in such a style that everybody stared, and even Lindsay gazed, forgetful of his part.

"Breng oot yer lightnin'!" Sandy called, "or do ye want a man to straddle here a' night without a bet o' lightnin' to defy? Here, Lindsay! Ye're the lightnin' calceelater—do yer part. Look here," he said, explaining to the audience, "ye see I've here a ten cup wi' a cover full o' holes, an' candle burnin' in the top, an', inside is a neckel's worth o' leekeepodun, an' I blow through this long tube into the cup—an' now the lightnin' which I here defy!" He blew with all his might, then drew his breath. The powder flew up in a blaze which scorched his eyebrows and his hair, and what remained went down his throat and took away his speech and breath, and set him off in such a fit of sneezing, coughing, sputtering and cries, that all the people thought it part of the "defi" and roared in wild delight!

"The Olympian Wrestlers!" the schoolmaster yelled above the noise—whereat the worthy Lindsay saw his chance, and grasping Sandy— now half doubled up—gave him a swing and dropped him on the floor. The audience howled, and Lindsay coolly bowed and crowed. But Sandy rose and caught him in the act, and raising the back window, seized his partner with both hands and threw him out into a bank of snow. But Lindsay, as he went, took Sandy's raiment with him, leaving the long-legged Roman in his glory all alone.

"The Fall of Rome!" called out the school- master, before the great triumvir had a chance to turn, or even roll his oblique eye, or take in the true meaning and intent of the impending fall.

A moment Sandy stood in classic attitude. The dignity of scorn was on his face—defiance in both eyes—and then he fell—"The noblest Roman of them all!"—whack! The boards and bones in contact gave a thundering crash and Sandy's heels flew up. "Ugh!" came the involuntary cry—then for a moment all was still —Rome was no more. "Great was the fall thereof!"   Io!

As Sandy rose and rubbed himself, and called for "arneeca," there was a general shout, and laughter long and loud, but Sandy simply said:

"I thenk I'll now gae home! Eh! What! See here, ye Drawback, ye'll hand them clothes over ef ye've got them, an' if not, ye'll prove yer eenecence by lendin' me yer hat an' overcoat an' boots until I find my ane!"

And Drawback, just to prove that he was wronged, took off his boots and gave them with his coat and hat, and Sandy graciously received the same and put them on, then groaned, and rubbed himself and disappeared—and he did not come back! The " 'leven pecters and dissolvin' views" were henceforth faded dreams.

What Lindsay did was this. He came in the

front door with Sandy's store clothes on his arm, and of these things he made a seat, and when the time came, took his way—two hats upon his head—two coats upon his back, and his thin legs encased in double pantaloons and boots to warm his homeward walk.

Drawback, in stocking feet, and minus hat and overcoat, went home through the deep snow, running and shivering all the long mile in the cold, but as he went his lips spoke words emphatic and impolitic, and swore at such a rate that everything was blue, and all along the road mutterings of Hades and eternal fire made matters hot beyond belief.

Verily, there are some things for which the sinner does not have to wait. Justice is slow, but in good time, and in her certain way, she comes to all.

．　　．　　．　　．　　．　　．　　．

And now the Pilgrim rose to tell the final part of the absorbing story of the past. At once all changed. The stillness of respect crept o'er the house. The thread of the discourse—broken by these delays and intervals of time—unseen and spirit hands made strong again and sympathy with every word sat still in every heart.

BURNS' FARM, ELLIESLAND.

BONNIE DOON.

Part Fourth.

Time:—*Winter—Burns' Birthday.*

> "To make a happy fireside clime
> To weans and wife
> Is the true pathos and sublime
> Of human life."

SCENE I.

THE INGLESIDE AT ELLIESLAND.

(Interior of Burns' farmhouse backed by a snowy landscape. Large old-fashioned Scotch fireplace with a blazing fire. Window to open and close. Entrance door and hallan piece. Interior door, leading to inner room. Table and chairs and seats for guests. A company of Scotch peasants, in winter holiday attire, also Gilbert, Davie, Bessie, Jon and Joey Anderson sit talking round the fire. The lads and lasses laugh and sing.)

Chorus—"Rab's wife is Jean the bonnie,
She's the darlin' o' th' monie,
An' their welcome to their hame
Shall be as blithe as she is bonnie!"

Solo—"May delight before it dees
    Mak' them fou' o' ane anither;
    An' their bairns upon their knees
    Be monie as their years thegither."

Chorus—"Rab's wife is Jean the bonnie," etc.

(Auld Jon and Joey Anderson advance, centre, and sing.)

Joey—Jon Anderson, my Jo, my Jonny,
Jon—Tho' my days be lang and monie,
Joey—Welcome Rab and Jeannie hame,
Jon—As erst they welcomed us, my hinney!
Joey—I'm the gudewife's lang syne frien'—
Jon—To Robin I'll e'er be a brither,
Joey—Be faither to their weans, Jon—
Jon—Aye, Joey, if ye'll be their mither!

(All laugh).

Chorus—"Rab's wife is Jean the bonnie," etc.

(All dance and hey. Jon and Joey sing with old cracked voices, and dance, with halting steps. All retire to the ingleside, laughing and talking.)

"Hi, Jonny!" Gilbert calls.

"Ho, Jonny!" says Davie.

(Then all call.) "Ha! Jonny! Jonny! Jonny!"

(Jonny mounts a chair and answering, exclaims:)

"Weel, lads and lasses, what'll ye hae wi' Jonny?"

"The orders! The orders! The orders!"

"Crack it oot to 'em, Jon," says Joey. "They'll forget it the sooner!"

"Aye, weel—the orders. Aye, ye see my-sel' an' gudewife came frae Ayr to help Rab out on his birthday an' the welcome o' his brand new wife into their braw new hame."

"Aye! aye!"

"An' it's a' because we seen sae monie berth-days oursel's!" says Joey.

"An' been married sae often," says Jon.

"Sae lang, Jonny."

"Aye, sae lang—an'—an'——"

"An' had na weans i' th' fomily," says Joey.

"Except oursel's," says Jon. "An' saewe're just here to set a gude example."

"Aye! Aye! Aye!"

"We understand, old friends," Gilbert rejoins. "You've come all the way from your little Inn, at Ayr, to honor your old friend."

"Ah," Joey answers, "we'd a come an' it were thrice as far. The road's na long enough to keep his frien's awa' at sic a time!"

"Your friendship honors you and honors Ayr," says Davie.

"We thank ye weel," says Jon. "Whist! Robin's na in hearin'!"

"No," Gilbert answers. "He and the gudewife are dressing in their best to meet their frien's."

"Weel, then," Jon says, with emphasis, "I'll just say this—the man or woman in Ayrshire who does na honor Robert Burns is no honor to his kintra or himsel'."

"Aye! gude! gude!" they all cry out. "But, Jonny, ye forget."

"The orders, aye. Weel, we're a' to assist in the ceremony."

"Aye—an' the ceremony—what'll it be?"

"The ceremony—aye, well—the ceremony'll consist o' ceremony, eatin', drenkin' an' ither sich like eentellectual amusements."

"But, gudeman," Joey says, "they'll no understand."

"Gudewife, I dinna onderstand mysel'; but do ye a' ken what eatin' is?"

"Aye—aye!"

"An' what dreenken is?"

"Aye—aye—aye!"

"An' lovin' is?"

"Aye—aye—aye—aye!"

" An' marryin' is?"

"Aye!—nae—nae—nae!"

"Weel, then the orders are that ye're to follow Rab's example an' find oot!"

"Gude! gude!" all shout.

"Gude? Eh, Jonny?" Joey asks.

"The marryin'? Aye! aye! aye! aye! aye! aye!"

(All laugh.)

"Sae now," says Jon, "the table groans; the bottles are burstin'; the cellar is fou'; the roads are fou'; the river is fou'; the house is fou'; our hearts are fou'; an' if ye're na' a' fou' yersel's it'll na be the fau't o' auld Ayr!"

"Hurra! hurra!" all shout, and lift Jonny from chair.

"An' now lads," Joey explains, "ye're to welcome an' wait on th' leddies."

"And, lasses," Jonny cries, "ye're to wait on an' welcome the lads—if ye ever oxpect 'em to wait upon you!"

(The lasses all come forward singing:)

SOLO—"This is a' th' steer, kimmer,
     This is a' th' steer;
     Robin's frien's to welcome
     And give auld Scotland's cheer!"

SECOND—"For that we're trim an' true,
     In our kirtles neat an' new,
     And each braw lad we welcome
     A lass is welcome to!"

CHORUS—"For that we're trim and true," etc.

(A "halloo!" is heard and music of the "Minstrel Boy." All shout.)

"Wha's comin'?"   "Wha's comin'?"

All run to window and look out.

"A lassie!"

"Aye!" Davie answers. "The flower o' them a'!"   (Auld Elfie enters covered with snow.)

"Auld Elfie?"

"My frien's——"

"Eh, sousie lassie!   A kiss!" cries Gilbert.

"Nae, ane for me," cries Davie.

"Well—ane for a'!" says Elfie.

(As the three hug the others laugh.)

"Hoo's a' i' the house, my frien's?" Elfie asks. "An' Rab an' bonnie Jean?"

"Weel, Elfie, weel, come by the lug," says Joey.

"Nae—nae!" Gilbert and Davie answer her. "Elfie's ours. The lads wait on the lasses! Come!"   (They take her things, and with great ceremony escort her to the fire.)

"Ah!" says Jonny, "Brawlie! The young deevils! I've no had mine!" (He goes to kiss Elfie—Joey comes between.)

"Then there it is!" says Joey. (She gets it.)

"Gude!" says Jon. "It's better than I axpected!"

(The tune of "Duncan Gray" is heard outside. All start.)

"What now! Who now?"

"It's our turn now," cry all the girls.

"It's Tam! Tam O'Shanter—drunken Tam!"

"Nae!" Davie says, "his ride settled that!"

"Aye!" says Jonny. "An' settled his score at the Inn!"

"Whoa, Meg!" shouts Tam outside, then he and Katy enter cheerily.   (All start.)

"Tam! Tam! Tam!"

"Aye, Tam an' Katy!"

"Nae, Katy an' Tam—the wife comes first!"

"An' gaes last. Hoo's a' o' ye here?"

"Weel—weel! Welcome baith!"

(The lasses all surround Tam. The lads around Katy.)

"Come, Tam, we welcome ye!"

"An' Katy, we welcome ye!"

"Weel," says Tam, "here's a' the things. The whip, the cap; the cloak, the plaid. The feddle—dinna ye break it or I'm brucken mysel'. The gudewife—why, where th' deevil's Kate?"

(The lads around Katy are trying to kiss her.)

"Nae, ye young caller clouties, ye! Where's Tam?"

(Tam by this time is surrounded by girls and cries out:)

"Nae matter for Tam—look oot for yersel'!"

"Nae kissin', ye young hizzies, ye!" cries Katy.

"Only ane for his mither!"

"A' right!" cries Tam in delight.

"A' wrong!" cries Katy, as she drives them away.

"We're strangers here," says Tam. "Let get acquaint an' kiss all around!"

(Rogue's March is heard outside.)

"What's that? What's that?" all ask.

"What is it, sure enough?"

"Stan' back," says Tam, "an' let it stagger in; I've been that way mysel'!"

(Holy Willie staggers in, quite drunk, and leans against the door.)

"Haly Willie here!" they all exclaim.

"Hic! It's ma dooty!"

"Nae," says Tam, "nae dooty aboot that. That's barley corn—ye can't fool me!"

"Why are you here?" asks Gilbert.

"To stop the weeked!" Willie answers him.

"Oh!" (All groan.)

"Dom!" says Tam; "but ef ye wanted to stop the weeked ye should ha' fa'en through th' ice when ye crossed th' Nith."

"Nae," Willie answers. "Caud water does na agree wi' me now!"

"How did ye like yer duckin' i' th' Doon?" asks Tam.

"It seckened me o' water; I ha' na used it syne," says Willie.

"Nor I barley corn," says Tam.

"Ah, how did ye like yer ride?" asks Willie.

"Gude! but what I lost, ye found. Ye're advancin' backwards, Willie. I'll have to lend ye Meg."

"Heigh! Hie! Fill me fou', and when I'm glorious let me gang my gates!" (Willie cries, as he imitates Tam riding Meg.)

"We'll na welcome ye!" the girls say in disgust, and then retire.

"I've a *warm one* for *ye*," says Willie.

"Hetch him out in the barn wi Meg," says Katy.

"Nae, have some consideration for the beast," says Davie.

"Which one?" asks Tam. "Weel, we'll no be hard on Willie. I've been a beast mysel'!"

(Music of bagpipes—faintly heard at first—increasing to forte as party appears. Air "Bonnie Dundee!")

"Ah! What's that? The pipes!"

"Aye," says Gilbert, "an' the march o' Bonnie Dundee!"

(All look out and Davie cries:)

"Hunters and horsemen comin' up the hill!"

"The gentlemen o' th' Caledonian Hunt," says Jon.

"And highlandmen!" says Joey with delight.

"Aye," say the girls. "An' see their pladdies an' their braw bare legs!"

"For shame, ye jauds!" cries Katy.

"Pipers, gentlemen and highlanders!" cry all.

"Who's that?" asks Davie, and Gilbert answers:

"Ready to receive him! 'Tis the Earl of Glencairn!"

(Music forte, kept up until all enter. Highlanders and hunters come first and form on either side, preceded by pipers, right and left. These are followed by the Earl of Glencairn, who advances centre, and is surrounded and received with cheers.)

"A welcome all to Robert's friend!" Gilbert calls.

"Hey! hey! Scotland forever! Heigh!"

"I thank you from my heart!" replies Glencairn. "Where is my good friend, Robert?"

"Where would he be," says Davie, "but wi' his ain gude wife, an' comin' here to welcome ye!"

"We are here to welcome *him!*" replies Glencairn. "To give to him those honors which are justly his!"

"Ah, my lord," says Gilbert, with respect, "we never could believe it. When he left our farm to go away, he went so poor he had not even money for the journey, but walked the way to Edinboro—nothing in his pocket and only doubt in his mind and small hope in his heart."

"But in that heart," says Davie feelingly, "the gudeness o' the great, and in his brain——"

"That glorious spark of genius which sets the world on fire!" says Glencairn with enthusiasm. "I care not how he went away, for he returns the prince of Scottish song!"

"He's here wi' bonnie Jean!" says Davie, as he steps aside.

"Then strike for him—and strike for her!" exclaims Glencairn.

(As the music sounds with spirit the air of "Bonnie Jean," Burns, leading his wife, comes from the inner room and advancing to Glencairn, seizes his hand and grasps it warmly. Both Jeannie and himself bow in respect, and then he speaks:)

"My noble Lord! Jeannie, my gude wife—my honored patron from Edinboro—the Earl o' Glencairn!"

"The royal welcome of a grateful heart!" says Jeannie, as she bows before him.

"Your hands," exclaims the earl. "Call me your friend—I ask no more. Friend is the noblest title, Brither Burns!"

"Our friend!" they both exclaim.

"And more than that!" says Burns in gratitude. "For you have made this honor possible!"

"Nay—Blacklock—Mackenzie—Robert Graham—Hamilton."

"Names honored in my heart forever!" Robert answers him.

"True—much merit lies in friendly acts," exclaims the earl, "but the real merit was your own!"

"'Twas nothing," Robert answers. "Went for nothing. For ten years I have been the same. Whatever poor talent I have now, inspired me then—my heart, my mind, the same—and the result more of discredit than respect."

> "I wandered in the ways of men
> Alike unknowing and unknown!

"But come, a cup of welcome—then we'll waste the night till morning shines again! Sit down and let the ingle's warmth assure you such a welcome is your own!"

"'Tis all we poor folks have to give," says Jeannie, with a gracious smile. "But take it from us wi' a love we'd hae ye aye remember!"

"Aye," Robert adds:

"The mother may forget the child
    That smiles so sweetly on her knee,
But I'll remember thee, Glencairn,
    And a' that thou hast done for me!"

"Then come again," exclaims the earl, "to social life and Edinboro!"

"I dare not hope to do so," Robert answers him. "My place is here. Born with the lowly, I shall live with the people and die with the poor!"

"But there your fancy might wing still higher flights——"

"Not so——

In wild-wood grove let wood-lark rove—
For caged larks seldom sing—
The free erne seeks the mountain's top,
For there alone he's king!

"'Tis so with me, and think, these hills I love have been the battle-ground of Wallace and of Bruce, and in their hour of need, gave to the house of Stuart both a shelter and a welcome."

"Stuart!—Robert—you forget!"

"No—I remember—not their rights or wrongs, but that they were unfortunate!

"Oh, never let me live to see the day when Scotsmen standing upon Scottish soil, shall fail to love and reverence their heroic dead, whether their cause were lost or won. Scotia, while in thy borders lies the field of Bannockburn, forever in our hearts, above all other loyalty, abides our love for thee!"

"My friend, your hand. These words do honor to our common country."

"But," answers Robert, "this is not the time to speak them. Forgive me. Come—sit down."

(They retire. Glencairn joins Jeannie by fire. The others group around it. Joey plays with the children on the floor. Willie sleeps in hallan corner. Tam comes forward with all the peasantry and beckons Rob, and speaks:)

"Rab, we're na sae gude, nor sae great as the ithers, but we ken ye as weel, and lo'e ye better than them a'."

"Gude hearts," says Robert, "aye; but na sae gude as I lo'e ye. Brithers an' frien's, I'm wi' ye always, heart and soul!"

(They grasp his hand and cry:)

"Aye! Scotland forever! Heigh!"

"Your hands! Your hands!" says Robert.

"They're yours, Rab—yours! An' no for what ye are, but what ye've ever been—in good or ill—sickness or want—in sorrow an' in toil!"

"God bless ye all!" says Robert feelingly.

"For an' that a' a' that—
A ribbon star an' a' that—
The honest man, tho' e'er sae poor,
Is king o' men for a' that!"

(Katy comes and takes his hand.)

"For a' that—an' a' that
Here take a kiss for a' that!"

(And Bessie, on the other side.)

"Anither ane for a' that!"

(Then all the lasses come forward, singing:)

For a' that an' a' that—
An' this an' that an' a' that—
A bonnie miss is *not amiss*
When she can gie ye a' that!

(All kiss him.)

"Aha!" says Tam; "ye'd better look oot, Rab. Ye've gotten a wife noo. I kend ye'd do it!"

"Sae did I," says Katy, "an' we honor ye for it!"

"Ah, but we poor bodies, Rab?" say all the girls.

"There, there," says Robert, giving them a kiss. "I'll be a brither to ye!"

(Jon, Davie and Gilbert come on with large steaming bowl of punch, which Joey places table to receive.　Willie wakes, smells it and advances with others.)

"Brawlie done, lads—brawlie done," says Jon.

"Weel," says Robert:

> "Let's be merry an' free—
> I'll be sad for naebody;
> If naebody cares for me,
> I'll care for naebody."

"Ah, Rab," says Tam, "as ye did nae gae to Jamaica they've brought Jamaica here to ye!"

(Willie hovers about the bowl and sighs.)

"It's ma dooty!　Said Paul to Timothy—"

"More screpter," says Tam.　"He's search-in' for an excuse."

"Ah, weel," says Rab, "as Shakespeare says, 'the de'il can quote Scripture to suit his purpose.'"

"I have it," says Willie, as he goes up to the bowl.　"I'll suffer in a gude cause.　What I dreenk will be that much spared to them."

"A' gaes in his slot," says Tam; "an' ye've gotten fivepence, Nick'll tak' it."

"Put him out!" the others cry.

"Not yet," says Robert.　"Naebody goes away empty this day.　As I toast, fill him full, 'Soop 'er up!'"

SCOTTISH REEL TO HIGHLAND PIPES

(Robert toasts a dozen different names in quick
succession while Willie drinks, filled up by Tam
with a flourish.)

"To my gudewife, Jeannie Burns!"

"To my noble patron, the Earl o' Glencairn!"

"To my native land!"

"To my dear auld mither!"

"To a' my weans and *their* mither!"

"To a' the women in Scotland!"

"To a' here an' awa'!"

"To a' my friends an' a' my enemies!"

"To the deil—Haley Willie!" (Willie chokes
at this and retires.)

"Open the door," says Tam.

"Fall out!" cry all the others. (Willie drops
out. All laugh as he goes.)

"Nay, lads," says Robert; "that's not our
hospitality!"

"Hoot—toot!" says Tam. "It's ony just to
cool him aff. He'll no go far wi' that load.
Now, Rab, gae on wi' yer whigmaleeries!"

"Aye," says Glencairn laughing, as he comes
forward. "I like to hear your friendly crackin'.
Let's hae a gude talk by the winter's fire!"

"Aye, aye!" they all cry out.

"Yer feddle, Tam, yer feddle!"

(Tam gets it and comes down.)

"What shall it be?"

"All! all! all!"

"Naething alane—a' at once?"

"Aye! A' thegither!"

(Then follows a concerted medley of Scotch airs. Tam accompanies, playing against the pipes. The various singers against each other, without discord. "Jon Anderson," "Bonnie Doon," "Duncan Gray," "Scots wa hae," and martial airs of similar tempi. At the conclusion low cries outside of "Help! help! help!")

(As they listen, Willie's voice is heard:)

"Help! help! for the love o' gudeness, help!"

"Some misfortune!" Robert cries, as he starts up. "Come, lads, come!" (They rush out and return, assisting Willie in door, bearing Madge helpless in his arms. Both are covered with snow. They bring Madge forward.)

"What calamity?" exclaims Glencairn.

"Some woman lost in the storm," Robert answers him.

"The chair!" cries Jean. "Here, here. Not by the fire!" (The chair is placed in centre, the various people run for water, snow, and punch from the bowl.)

"Rub her hands, an' her face!" they cry.

"Give her the liquor," Robert says. "She's exhausted, but not frozen."

(All attend her. The ladies unfasten her

clothes. A wreath falls out. The men take Willie aside and question him.)

"Poor girl," exclaims Glencairn. "She must have fallen in the snow."

"Where did ye stumble on her, Willie?" asks Tam.

"I staggered agin' something i' th' path. I brought it in. The Lord be thankit!"

"Willie," says Burns, as he takes his hand, "ye've done one good thing at last, and we forgive ye a' th' past!"

"Aye, dom it," says Tam. "Gae ye there, an' dreenk every drap i' th' bowl!"

"I done ma dooty!" Willie answers. "I'll do it again." (He drinks.)

"She is recovering!" says the earl.

"Thank Heaven! She is!" cries Jean. "Look up, poor lass, ye're safe!"

"Stand back!" says Robert, "and let me see —some one may know her!"

"Nae! nae!" all answer him.

"She's speakin' now!" says Jean, "bewildered like an' low. Robin, she speaks your name!"

"Robert!" they all exclaim.

"Ah! Let me look!" Robert cries "Why, it is Madge McGowan! The friend of my poor Mary! She's come to seek me!"

"How!"

"Oh, dinna stay to speak or question me. Dinna ye see the mourning that she wears? It is for Mary Campbell—lost to me forever!" (He kneels by her side.)

"Frien's!" cries Jean in great excitement, "pray bear wi' him at such a time and leave us to ourselves. Dear Gilbert, will ye kindly tak' them in, an' come again?"

(All bow in great respect, and Gilbert shows them to the inner rooms.)

"Madge! Madge! My bonnie lass!" cries Robert wildly, as he takes her hands. "My Mary's friend! Speak! Speak and tell me all is well! Dinna ye ken friend Robin any more? Oh, Madge, dear Mary's dead!"

"I hear yer voice!" she answers faintly. "Aye, noo I hear it—'tis Robin!"

"It is! It is!"

"But ah, ye did na answer when I ca'ed, an' sae I ca'ed an' wandered on, until I fell, exhausted on the snaw. But I ha' found ye noo. I found ye noo!"

"Ye're safe!" says Jean. "Poor lass, ye're safe in friendly shelter now!"

"What kind-faced lassie's this?" asks Madge. "Ah, don't ye know me? Don't ye remember i' th' barn, th' night I came wi' her, last Hallowe'en?"

"Aye, now I see. *You were her friend!*"

"Aye, Jean, aye!" Robert sadly answers.

"Then *she'll be mine!*" says Jean.

"Bless ye, dear Jean, an' now o' Mary. Speak!" says Robert importuningly to Madge.

"You remember then, the night you saw her in your dream?"

"Aye!" Robert answers her. "In Mossgiel barn. Her wraith-a vision of the dead! She seemed my guardian muse."

"That week she died!" cries Madge in tears.

"Oh, Mary! Mary! Mary!"

"She said ye'd know of it, for 'she had told ye in a dream an' ye had looked upon her wraith, as even in her death, her face would look on yours!"

"I'll ne'er forget! I'll ne'er forget!" cries Robert in despair.

"Oh, Mary, lost forever!"

"Her dying message was her love to you, an' kiss for your gudewife, on your happiest day. I've waited till the time, an' come to gie them both!" (Madge kisses Jean, who embraces her.)

"My good, my bonnie lass," Robert cries, "what more?"

"Some little keepsakes that I brought, but ah, I've lost 'em i' th' snaw!"

"Poor lass!"

(*Madge sees wreath which was dropped on floor.*)

"Ah, but the wreath is here! It an' the gowans I brot frae Ayr, an' carried i' my breast. Nane could tear them frae that place, nor was there snaw enough in Scotland to stop me on my way!"

"Dear Madge!"

"They're withered now and dead," she cries, "like her who gave them, but they're for ye, and wi' her love!" (*Burns takes them, kisses them and says, with great feeling:*)

"They are scented a' wi' th' blessing o' her touch! 'Twill cling to them until they crumble into dust,! So will her memory ever be with me, till, like them, I shall cease to live!"

"Here is her gift to ye," says Madge to Jean, "these hawthorn buds from Doon. She broke off every thorn."

"But, ah, she left the thorn wi' me!" sighs Robert, in great grief.

"This frae yer trysting place on Ayr. She said ye'd know the very tree!"

(*Burns takes the wreath and bows his head.*)

"The holy under which we used to sit! Why this is like the one I got on Halloween!"

" *'Twas she that gave ye that, an' she that sent ye this!*"

(Burns goes to similar wreath hung on the wall, and as he does so, Jean places Madge by the fire. Robert takes both wreaths and comes forward, saying solemnly:)

"These—Mary—ah, now I see! The *vision's* past! It was not *all* a dream! It was the spirit of a love that outlives life itself, immortal as its maker!"

(Jean comes and puts her arms about him.)

"Oh, Robert, husband, hear me speak. The time for silence now has passed. *She came that night in Mossgiel barn, to see you ere she died.* She knew your sorrow, and she would na give ye more, so charged me not to tell, an' went away. Oh, Robert, she was worthy of your love an' faithful to the last!"

(Burns stands a moment lost in thought, then says:)

"Mary, my ain, look down upon us now, but dinna grieve for those you've left behind. Love does not change with death, and all through life I've my good Jeannie's sympathy!" (He embraces Jean, who cries:)

"Robert, oh, my only love! Her love has hallowed ours!"

"Then," Robert answers, "let it cost your heart no pang. Mary was never mine. I was not worthy of her!"

"You loved her, Robert?"

"I had been less than man, if I had not. Her love but made me better."

"She was your boyhood's sweetheart, Robert."

"You are my manhood's honored wife!"

"And still she'll be forever in your mind——"

"As you are in my heart!" (Gives bouquet.) "Wear these, this day upon your breast, for her sake and for mine!" (Jeannie kisses the flowers and pins them on her bosom. Robert kisses her as he conducts her to her room. He then goes up to the fireplace, and hangs the wreaths upon the wall. Then seeing Madge, he takes her kindly by the hand, and smooths her hair and speaks to her:)

"And are ye warm now, bonnie Madge? And are ye well? What can I do for you, for all your faithfulness to her—your kindness unto me?"

"Oh, sir, but one thing only. She asked that for her sake, ye'd tak' me in your service."

"Ye'll never leave us. As ye were friendly to dear Mary Campbell, be faithful to my dear wife, Jean."

"I'd die for either! An' I'll feed the chuckies, an' tend a' th' lambies, an' nurse a' th' weans, like a mither, a' my lee lang days!"

"BANKS AND BRAES O' BONNIE DOON."

(She goes out crying, at entrance door. Robert, looking after her:)

"Ah, gudeheart, kind as leal, you're queen among the best. No wonder Mary loved her!"

(Madge runs back in excitement of delight.)

"Oh, Maister Robin, here's what I dropped i' th' snaw when a the kind folks brot me in—from her to you alone!" (Exits, L.)

(He takes a chair and sits by fire as he unwraps a book.)

"My God! The book on which we pledged our troth. Oh! Mary, my own, in Heaven! I'll keep my vow. I'll never—more forget ye! Never! Never! Though your death parts us now, my own shall reunite us!"

"Still o'er past scenes my memory wakes,
    And fondly broods wi' miser's care,
Time but the impression stronger makes,
    As streams their channels deeper wear!

.   .   .   .

"My Mary! Dear departed shade,
    Where is thy place of blissful rest?
See'st thou thy lover lowly laid?
    Hearest thou the groans that rend his breast?"

(Jon and Joey Anderson come from the interior door, followed by Tam, with his fiddle. Jon and Joey advance on either side of Robert and place their hands on his head. Tam tunes the violin, by the fire. Joey kisses Robert, and both put their arms about him, as Tam plays "Auld Lang Syne."   Burns starts up and, with great feeling, exclaims:)

"Not now, dear friends! not now! not now. Mind me o' other things. My heart's unstrung!"

"An' dom," says Tam, "sae is me feddle! I can't play now. Here, Rab's, my hand!"

"And, Tam, here's mine forever!"

"An' baith are harder than our hearts!" says Tam. "Let's gae ootside an' fight!"

"Haud!" cries Jonny. "After supper!"

"Aye," Joey says. "Sooper'll soon be ready!"

"Then give the best to *her*," says Robert.

"To whom?"

"The wee bit lass that's just come in frae out the snow."

"Nay," Jonny says, "she would na hold the thousandth part o' it."

(Joey goes to Rob and tries to cheer him.)

"Dinna forget," she says, "the Scotch broth, an' the sowens; the parritch an' th' haggis!"

"An' Scotch whesky!" says Jonny, "an' a' th' ale frae Ayr."

"An' a ' yer frien's an' company," says Tam. "Eh, Rab, I clean forgot! There's ane I left ootside!"

"Ootside?"

"Aye, an' a female, too!"

"A female in the cold and storm?"

"Dom, but I forgot her. Here she is!" (Tam opens the window and his mare, Meg, sticks her head inside.)

"Auld Meg!" they all exclaim.

"Aye! my gude auld naig! My bobtailed frien'!" says Tam. (Burns goes to her and rubs her fore-top).

"You're right to love her, Tam."

"Aye," says Tam. "For she's ne'er ashamed to show her face; as for her tail, that's not on exheebeetion!"

(All laugh, and Robert gives her oatcakes.)

"Here's for ye, Meg. You've done your duty better than us all!"

"Right, Rab," says Tam. "She saved me once, my body and my soul, an' now she makes you laugh an' pass your troubles, as I passed the Doon!"

"Anither cake for that!" says Robert, giving it. "We'll bring her in for supper."

"Eh! but, Rab, see here, I clean forgot."

"What?"

"Why a' the load o' presents that we brought frae yer frien's. The joy inside drove a' else from my stupid head. Ca' a' yer frien's. I'll bring the gimcracks in!" (Tam rushes out, Jon and Joey call in company.)

"Pardon me, friends," says Robert to his guests. "Some foolishness of Tam's."

(Tam sticks his head in window and calls out:)

"Dom, but it's na foolishness—it's real. Here, tak' them in. Lay hold o' that!"

(Gilbert, Davie, Glencairn, Katy, Elfie, girls, Jon and Joey take in the presents, as Tam hands them through window.)

"What's this?" cries Robert. "The auld stone punch-bowl!"

"Aye," says Jean, "I mind it weel. 'Twas father made it."

"And see," says Burns, "it's rimmed with silver now, an' an inscription's on it——

> "'To *Robert Burns, frae the Inns o' Ayr.'*
> With the love an' compliments of
> Jon Anderson and Joey."

(Burns shakes their hands.)

"My dear auld frien's!"

"An' here's anither," says Tam, as he puts in a model.

"Ah," Burns exclaims; 'the auld clay biggin where I first saw light just thirty years ago!"

(Gilbert reads the inscription:)

> "From the workmen of Ayr to their friend,
> *Robert Burns.*"

"An' here's a bonnie pair!" says Tam, as he hands in birds with purses in their beaks.

"A throstle and a lark," says Jean. "Gold in the mouth of one and siller in the other!" (Reads:)

> "*Frae Bobbie Burns* and *Davie Sillar,*
> wi' a wee bit tocher for Bonnie Jean!"

(She kisses them.)

"Look oot for the pecter," cries Tam as he hands it in.   (Davie reads:)

> "*Coila, the Muse, Crowning the Bard!*"

(Burns looks at it in astonishment and exclaims:)

"My dream—reality!"   (He reads:)

> "*From Edinboro and the Earl of Glencairn.*"

(Burns takes his patron's hand and bows in deep feeling. The birds are placed on mantel, the picture hung on the wall. Girls arrange them.)

"An' here," cries Tam, "is ane for Robin's hands alane. Nae ane can do it better nor himself!"

(A decorated plough is handed in. Burns puts it down, and takes position of ploughman.)

"The plough!   Welcome, friend of adversity!
So long as I follow you, I'll never want!"

(Glencairn reads the card.)

*"Frae your brither farmers on the
banks o' the Nith."*

"I thank them," Robert answers; "and shall
remember what the Bible says:

"Who will not plough by reason of the cold,
Shall beg in harvest and have no bread."

"And here!" says Tam, as he enters—"here's
the last!"

(Hands Burns a Masonic square and compass,
made of laurel and heather, with large *G* of red
flowers in centre.   Robert receives it with
honors.)

"An' who sent ye this, Rab?" asks Tam.

"I don't know, Tam, but some one I suppose,
who had the *Scottish right.*"

(Davie reads inscription:)

*"From your brothers o' Tarbolton and
Mauchline."*

"Your brothers?" ask the girls.

"An' how mony brithers hae ye, Rab?" asks
Tam.

"One thousand in Ayrshire, ten thousand in

Scotland, and hundreds o' thousands scattered all over the world."

"Weel," says Tam in astonishment, "accordin' to that, ye've dang near a million brithers!"

"Aye, Tam, it's true!"

"An' yer mither's alive!" cries Tam.

(Madge runs in from outer door.)

"Oh, Maister Robin! Maister Robin!"

"What is it, Madge?"

"A little stray, just like mysel'. I found it strugglin' i' th' snaw, when 1 went out with th' bairns." (She takes a snow covered lamb from under her cloak. Jeannie receives it.

"Oh, the wee hoggie," says Tam.)

"It's ane o' Mallie's breed," says Jean. "The mither's dead, an' this lamb's a' we have to mind us o' Rab's favorite."

"Poor Mallie!" Robert says; "but we'll take good care o' this for her sake. Here, Madge, ye an' the bairns go take it by the shepherd's ingle, an' warm and feed it well. It shall na want, for as they'd say in Ireland, it's the last o' the *yowe Mallies!*"

(Madge takes it to the fire. The children caress, while she feeds it. Willie sees it pass and calls:)

"Oh, bonnie lambie!"

"Baa!!" says Madge, as she holds it up.

"Gae to the deil!" says Willie, who sits and sleeps.

(Glencairn comes forward to Robert.)

"Robert," he says, " I see everything is welcome under this roof, but your house is not large enough to hold your friends!"

"Weel, then," says Robert feelingly, "I hope it's large enough to hold my enemies! For bird and beast and friend and enemy are welcome while it's mine!"

(Bagpipes are heard inside.)

"Aye, friend," exclaims Glencairn, "even the very pipes sound welcome in the hall."

"'Tis well!" says Burns. "They'll teach me to forget."

"What?"

"The happy past!"

"The future, Robert," says Jeannie, as she comes to him.

"Aye, that I must remember! This day 1 turn toward the coming years! This day I mark for duty!"

"An' Jeannie'll aye respect ye for it, Rab; ye'll face it like a man."

(As she retires Glencairn exclaims:)

"Robert, your wife's all goodness, gentleness and love."

"Beyond my poor deserts. No more—for now:

> "To make a happy fireside clime
> To weans and wife
> That's the true pathos and sublime
> Of human life!"

"My friend," exclaims Glencairn, "your hand. If I have ever been your friend before, count on me doubly from this hour."

"I canna speak," says Robert, with great feeling, "my heart's too full! Jean!"

(Jeannie advances to them.)

"Help me to thank our noble patron here, and greet our friends, and Scotland's honored peasantry!

> Now strike for Auld Lang Syne
> And say with me the rhymes
> I canna speak, for something stays my words.

(All the characters advance and surround him. The Highlanders, pipers, ladies and lasses on at the back. The characters in front line.)

BURNS—"My heart's o'er fu' an' fu' my hand."

DAVIE—"Sae fu' o' joy be Elliesland!"

BESSIE—"Where faithful Scots forever stand!"

JEAN—"Then to our ingle welcome a'."

GLEN—"Friends ne'er grow cold, or fa' awa'."

KATY—"As leaves fa' frae th' briken shaw!"

Madge—"Ne'er round ye fa' misfortune's snaw."

Gilbert—"Let friendly feet sound i' th' ha'."

Joey—"An' love-light shine on faces braw."

Jon—"My Joey, will ye staw yer jaw?"

Elfie—"Aye, hens are still when auld cocks craw!"

Tam—"For there's na luck aboot the hoose, this spring, or next summer, or next winter or next fa'——"

Burns—"If your smiles are awa'!"

(All laugh.   The music strikes up and all sing in grand line.)

> "For there's nae luck about the house,
>   There's nae luck at a'—
> There's nae gude fortune in the house
>   When your smiles are awa'!"

(As the others dance to the air Tam is only in the middle of the verse, and finishes the music in same metre in which he spoke the rhyme. Music changes to "Bonnie Breastknots.")

> "Then hi' the bonnie, ho the bonnie,
>   Hey the bonnie housewife!
> To Rab his Jeannie, o' th' monie,
>   Will make a bonnie housewife!"

(D. C., and all dance and hey.)

"Hi the bonnie, ho the bonnie,
　　Hey the bonnie housewife!
To Rab his Jeannie brings the bonnie——

"Auld Lang Syne, my friends—
　　The auld Lang Syne,
Tho' happy yet we'll na forget
　　The frien's o' Auld Lang Syne!"

*　　　*　　　*　　　*　　　*　　　*　　　*

As soon as the last words fell from the speaker's lips the music struck the old familiar note, and men and women, young and old, the minister and Donald's mother with the rest, and all the boys and bonnie girls arose, and clasped each others' hands, and heart to heart and soul to soul with voices blending in the feeling and exulting sound, sang the inspiring song, a tribute to the author dead and to his living friend. Barbara stood clasped in Donald's arms, a smile of joy upon her handsome face, and then she joined the others as they circled round the modern chieftain of the clan.

When the good minister could find his voice, he, in the name of all, essayed to give the Pilgrim thanks; but Donald stayed his words.

"No, no!" he said. "No one deserves a word of thanks for doing what his duty calls on him to do. I am ashamed that I—in all these years —have not done more to help or bless my fellowmen. This work is only words. How poor my deeds compare—for you remember well what Shakspeare says:

" 'If to do were as easy as to say what were good to do, chapels had been churches and poor men's cottages princes' palaces.' "

"My friend," replied the minister, as he took the Pilgrim's hand, "good words are worthy as good deeds. A good book is a constant friend, a sermon seven days in every week, and does far more to advance the interests of the human race than all the standing armies of the world.

"Small as your work may seem, its mission is to bless, and so we hail and prize it!

"See from this spot where now we stand, the light shows in my study window on the hill. Here is a simile which you may keep within your memory, if not within your heart, and know you have recalled it, and since you quote from the immortal bard—in his undying words I answer back:

" 'How far that little candle throws his beams!
    So shines a good deed in a naughty world!' "

FINIS.

NOTES.

I.

A ROMANCE of the life and loves of a celebrity like Robert Burns, which pictures "Highland Mary," "Bonnie Jean," and many notable but unknown characters, naturally excites some question as to the truthfulness of the portraits given and the reality of scenes described.

Regarding the Arcadian country and the people of the first book of the story, a few words may be said:

The pastoral is purely an imaginative work, but those who care to visit the romantic hills of Rockland which overlook the Hudson may find the real scenes as sketched in Donald's narrative —the mountain peaks, hills, valleys, streams, fields, roads and lanes—the very trees, school-house, old church and burial-ground, but of the happy people—save some half-forgotten name upon a gravestone—he will find no trace.

.   .   .   .

As to the Scottish scenes and characters of

the Dramatic Second Part—they are intended
to be faithful pictures of past days—the person-
ages, some real and some—as "Madge"—mere
children of the brain, but the scenes—thanks
to the courtesy of Margary Stuart—are photo-
grahically and historically correct.

II.

AT a meeting of the Scottish Society, held
in Assembly Hall, Fifth Avenue, New York, on
Burns' birthday, 1899, Andrew Carnegie made
an interesting and characteristic address, in
which he stated, among other things, that
"Nothing new could now be said regarding
Robert Burns."

As an answer the author of this romance sent
him the beautiful poem by Robert Reid, of Mon-
treal—which was published in this city on that
day, and which—together with the glowing
tribute of the late Colonel Ingersoll—is given on
another page.

Added to these was promised this work—a
labor of love for all Americans and Scotsmen
everywhere—which, as will be seen, is dedi-
cated to Mr. Carnegie, recalling that occasion.
when "the heather was on fire" and friendly
Scots joined hands for Auld Lang Syne.

III.

THAT the character of the good "old minister" is not entirely imaginary may be gathered from the following letter which relates to Barbara's manuscript of Donald Stuart's story:

"FRIEND AND FELLOW PILGRIM: I thank you for your mark of confidence and trusting in my judgment of your work.

"As promised, I have read and carefully reviewed your so-called 'Sinner's Sermon,' being much struck by the introduction of Robert Burns and his walks and talks with Mary from their first love scene till the triumphal end.

"The quality of the book is of the very best. The spirit of the Eternal drifts through it, and I think you will believe me when I say the true, strong and great writer is back of the work and in it.

"And now, dear brother soldier, may Heaven give you more good thoughts, to weave in helpful stories, making your life useful by service, and keeping you mindful of the thought that He leads ever in the right.

"Sincerely yours,   J. R."

IV.

THE drama of "Bonnie Doon," which comprises the entire Second Book, has been prepared especially for stage production and is protected by copyright in Europe and America.

To those eminent artists, Mr. E. H. Sothern, Mr. and Mrs. Thomas Whiffen, Mr. Joseph Haworth, Mr. F. F. Mackay, Robert Mantell, and Robert McWade, as well as to that successful dramatist and producer, Mr. David Belasco, the author has been obliged for flattering endorsements of this play. The same applies to Mr. and Mrs. Edwin Knowles, of the Fifth Avenue Theatre, and gratefully to Miss Ellen Terry and Sir Henry Irving.

Its production in the near future will be under special supervision and with appropriate scenes and cast.

V.

THE editor of these notes from Barbara's records has discovered—like many others, doubtless—that the human race is a great family of critics. Know-alls are plentiful in all localities; iconoclasts abound. What one, by careful thought and patient toil builds in a year, thousands are ready to demolish in a day.

One of this kind, who seems to have been the "Columbus Cant," and "Holy Willie" of the story, is much in evidence in the following letter, which exhibits a critical spirit quite in contrast to the friendly words of Donald Stuart's other correspondents.

"TWA BRIGS AND AYR," WHERE BURNS LIVED.

This is the brief but caustic epistle, and the equally short and sarcastic reply:

"DONALD STUART:—

"SIR: I hear you have written a book. Even as your worst enemy I could wish you no worse fate.

"*O, that mine adversary had written a book!*"
—JOB.

"Having committed suicide you save me from exterminating you by other means. You call me Pharisee. I call you a fool!

"Now write this title down and your readers will find more truth in it than in your description of people you never knew and scenes you never saw!

"Remember

"*All liars shall have their part in the lake which burneth.*"
—REVELATIONS.

"So good-by, C. C."

"C. C.:—

"SIR: You hear aright. I have written a book whose best recommendation is that characters like yours do not figure largely in its pages.

"With some sorrow I acknowledge that the name you give me is deserved since I waste words on you.

"Your criticism of my descriptions is somewhat correct, but scarcely reciprocal, as I have had more charity for your detailed accounts of Heaven—a country you have never seen, and—sins considered—never will see.

"The 'burning lake' you have such faith in, is probably more in your way, and in good time, no doubt, you will receive your much deserved and proper 'part.'

"A long farewell.   D. S."

VI.

On Sunday, October 15, 1899, an old man, who evidently wished to verify, by visiting localities in this romance, climbed the hill east of Pomona and looked around him on the countless fruit trees in the orchards of Rockland.

Through the blue haze, in every direction, red apples glistened in the sun and, mingling with the tinted foliage, made a fairy scene through which the old man seemed to wander in a dream.

Passing up the hills he turned at the cross-roads and walked towards the English church, from which he saw the country people going home. Following some of these along the eastward road he came to the descent into the great valley which is bounded by Torne peak, the Indian Hill and Highlands bordering on the "river of the North."

Beyond this point, he went down by different

roads towards the south until he came to Scotland Hill and other scenes surrounding what had once been Donald Stuart's home.

Surveying all these places slowly, as if communing with them in affectionate regard, he passed the schoolhouse, then the burying-ground—where a young man and woman strolled about and talked of love—and, finally, he sat down under the great red oak, where "Joan" and "Diccon" sat that summer day, by the Seceders' church, and, as he rested, he soliloquized:

"Again I've seen them all—the old, familiar, friendly scenes—the ones I knew and those my friend described. They are still here. They do not go, like those who peopled them, to the great city yonder. No, Nature's home, love's peaceful haunts and the eternal hills belong to God! Forever, and forever they remain, but of the old-time people there is left but one and his voice never will be heard again in yonder little church!"

ROBERT BURNS ON HIS DEATH-BED.

By Robert Reid, Montreal.

[Prize poem of 1899, to which the Kinnear Silver Wreath was awarded by the North American United Caledonian Association.]

———

Life's day draws near the gloaming,
　　Its heat and burden dune,
And a' its dear delusions
　　I maun relinquish sune;
Sune will auld Mither Scotland
　　The bard that lo'es her tyne,
And hear her loves and praises sung
　　By ither tongues than mine.

Land o' the sturdy thistle,
　　And winsome heather bell,
Thou wants nae quavering minstrel
　　Thy pith and pride to tell;
But strong within his bosom
　　The tide of song should flow
Who dares to voice thy doughty deeds
　　And dreams of long ago!

So well'd in mine the music
　　That broke in waves of fire,
When in the flush of manhood
　　I swept the patriot-lyre;
And though my failing fingers
　　Now feebler echoes wake,
Fain would their hinmaist effort be
　　For dear auld Scotland's sake.

BURNS' HOUSE, DUMFRIES, WHERE THE POET DIED.

O dinna steek that shutter
  And keep the licht awa';
But owre me in its glory
  Let ilka sunbeam fa'!
For in the Vale of Shadows
  Where I sae sune maun be,
The bonnie heartsome Simmer Sun
  Will shine nae mair for me.

Blithe hae I been to see him
  Come owre the hills at morn,
Or in the eenin', gildin'
  Wi' liquid gowd, the corn;
When 'neath his bauld caresses
  Dame Nature beam'd wi' joy,
And ilka thing that breath'd was glad,
  And nane mair glad than I.

Then, rapt in poet-ardor,
  Enchanted ground I trod,
As in my heart, sweet-singin',
  I heard the voice of God;
His warks were a' about me,
  I sang whate'er I saw,
For man and beast, and flow'r and stream,
  I lo'ed them, ane and a'!

Noo, like a wauf o' winter
  That comes afore its time,
The warld's breath has chilled me,
  And kill'd me in my prime;
Dark clouds obscure the visions
  Gar'd a' my being thrill,
And in my cauld and flutterin' breist
  The heavenly voice is still.

O, talents lichtly cared for,
  And noo ayont reca',
How, like a reckless spendthrift
  I've cuist my walth awa'!
What can I gie for answer
  When the dread Voice I hear
That o' my thriftless stewardship
  In thunder-tones 'll spier?

.   .   .   .

Sweet lass,* whase steps like music
  Slips the lown chamber thro',
Whase touch is like an angel's
  Upon my burnin' broo,—
O frae the paths of virtue
  Ne'er let that fitstep stray,
And for a heavenly licht to guide
  This heart will ever pray.

And bairns—my blessings on ye!
  Ye'll sune be left your lane,
Wi' life's sair darg afore ye—
  In God's name—act like Men!
Abune a' fame or fortune
  For this my bosom yearns,
That man for honest worth should prize
  The sons of Robert Burns!

.   .   .   .

Dear Jean, the nicht grows eerie,
  I wat I'll slumber sune;
O lay your loof in mine, luve,
  As ye sae aft hae dune;

* Miss Jessie Lewars.

An' on that faithfu' bosom
  Let this worn cheek recline,
That for a heart-beat I may pree
  The raptures o' lang syne.

O bonnie was the burnside,
  And fair the sylvan scene,
Where, 'neath the budding hawthorn,
  I trysted wi' my Jean;
An' as I fondly clasp'd her—
  A bliss beyond compare—
I trow the munelicht never shone
  On sic a happy pair!

Sinsyne, I've tried her sairly,
  But gude and true she's been;
And for a' that's come and gane yet
  She's still my Bonnie Jean!
There's nane in a' braid Scotland
  That's half sae dear to me,
And ne'er a hand but this dear hand
  Shall close my weary e'e.

Then fare ye weel, my ain Jean,
  My first joe and my last,
Through ilka neuk in Scotland
  Our names entwin'd hae pass'd;
And think na that she slichts us,
  Or sune forgot we'll be—
A hunder year will but increase
  Her pride in you and me!

But now on Life's illusions
  Maun close these ee'n o' mine,
And to the Fount it sprang frae
  My soul I maun resign;

Great Being! in whose presence
    Ere morning I may stand,
Reach from the dark to guide me through,
    Thine everlasting Hand!

BIRTHPLACE OF ROBERT BURNS.

[This poem was written by Robert G. Ingersoll in 1878, while
he was at the birthplace of Robert Burns, in Scotland, whither
he had gone to collect material for a lecture on the ploughman
bard.]

THOUGH Scotland boasts a thousand names
    Of patriot, king and peer,
The noblest, grandest of them all
    Was loved and cradled here;
Here lived the gentle peasant prince,
    The loving cotter king,
Compared with whom the greatest lord
    Is but a titled thing.

'Tis but a cot roofed in with straw,
    A hovel made of clay;
One door shuts out the snow and storm,
    One window greets the day.
And yet I stand within this room
    And hold all thrones in scorn,
For here, beneath this lowly thatch,
    Love's sweetest bard was born.

Within this hallowed hut I feel
    Like one who clasps a shrine,
When the glad lips at last have touched
    The something deemed divine.
And here the world, through all the years,
    As long as day returns,
The tribute of its love and tears
    Will pay to Robert Burns.

BURNS' MAUSOLEUM, DUMFRIES, WHERE THE BARD IS BURIED.

SPIRIT OF THE SCOTS.

THE SCHOOLHOUSE SONG AND CHORUS.

By the Author of this Romance, for Musical and Festival
Occasions.

1.

SOLO. AIR—VAR:
"WATCH ON RHINE."

> The Spirit of the Scots survives,
> It springs from hallowed memories,
> It has ten thousand thousand lives—
> It still survives! It still survives!

Chorus—Air:
"SCOTS WA HAE."

> Hark! the call from Highland brae,
> The pibroch's sound, the bard's wild lay,
> The echoed shouts of "Scots wa hae,"
> For Caledonia Free!

2.

SOLO.

> Triumphant over ages gone,
> Ghost-like and gray, and worn and wan,
> Out of the past it marches on,
> Like sorrows gone—like sorrows gone.

Chorus—Air:
"ANNIE LAURIE."

> While Bruce still leads the way,
> And Wallace' name's the cry,
> As at Bannockburn in glory,
> For auld Scotland we would die.

3.

SOLO.

> Across the present, day by day—
> With dauntless tread and potent sway,
> Toward the future far away,
> On, day by day and day by day!

Chorus—Air:
"BONNIE DOON."

> By Burns' loved Ayr and Bonnie Doon,
> By Scott's fair Tweed and Byron's Dee,
> In romance, song or minstrels' tune,
> Thy Sons, dear Scotia, turn to thee!

4.

SOLO.

> In that unknown and silent land
> Where honored heroes take their stand,
> And peace and love go hand in hand, [mand!
> At Heaven's command! At Heaven's com-

Chorus—Air:
"AULD LANG SYNE."

> For Auld Lang Syne they wait—
>   For Auld Lang Syne!
> "Scotland Forever!" nation great—
>   For Auld Lang Syne!

Call it not vain ; they do not err
Who say, that when the poet dies
Mute Nature mourns her worshipper,
And celebrates his obsequies.
Who say tall cliff and cavern lone
For the departed bard make moan,
That mountains weep in crystal rill,
That flowers in tears of balm distil,
Thro' his loved groves that breezes sigh,
And oaks, in deeper groans, reply ;
And rivers teach their rushing wave
To murmur dirges round his grave.

Sir Walter Scott.

www.ingramcontent.com/pod-product-compliance
Lightning Source LLC
Chambersburg PA
CBHW051111120726
47905CB00005B/1237